swallow me
WHOLE
a friends-to-lovers romance

USA TODAY BESTSELLING AUTHOR
GEMMA JAMES

swallow me
WHOLE

a friends-to-lovers romance

one

SADIE

Moaning. It's the first thing assaulting my ears as I approach my boyfriend's office. My knuckles whiten, fingers tightly gripping the wicker basket I'm carrying. It's late, and this visit is supposed to be a surprise.

Maybe I'm the one in for a surprise.

I stall outside his door, and there's no doubt at what I'm hearing. Releasing a soundless breath, I feel my shoulders sag, same as my spirit. God, I feel like a fucking cliché right now—the clueless girlfriend catching her man cheating at the office late at night. It doesn't help that I have that wholesome girl-next-door appearance bullshit to go along with the overdone trope.

At five feet and three inches tall, with thick red hair that doesn't know the first thing about behaving, I'm not the poster girl for a man's wet dream. And don't get me started on the freckles smattering my nose and cheeks. I've been told my freckles are adorable, sexy even, but I'm sure the people who said it are full of shit. Especially now, considering the groans and grunts coming through the door of Jake's office. I bet whoever she is, *she* doesn't have freckles.

Adorable doesn't get a girl anywhere with someone like Jake Jennings. He's the epitome of mature and successful. Classic good looks, blond hair never out of place, strong jaw and broad shoulders. The man favors expensive suits, and he wears them well.

Being that I'm several years younger than Jake, dating him made me feel mature. My father approved—how could he not, since Jake is on the fast track to becoming a junior partner at his law firm.

Sounds like he's on the fast track to getting laid as well.

Betrayal rises in my chest, coils around my heart, threatens to slice and dice. I should be used to betrayal and rejection by now. Guys have proven they can't be trusted, and as for rejection...

I get enough of that from my father.

But he looks at me differently since Jake and I began dating. I hate the thought of losing that, of disappointing him yet again, but if the sounds on the other side of the door are any indication, I won't have a choice.

Clutching the bodice of my little black dress, as if I can keep my heart from bleeding hurt, I tell myself to close the remaining steps to the door of his office. But I hesitate, grieving the *could've been* of another relationship down the drain.

Another lost opportunity to work past my fear of sex and intimacy, because tonight was supposed to be the night.

It's the slimeball's birthday, and he begged off from celebrating, claiming he had to pull an all-nighter on the case my dad's had him working on. So I decided to surprise him with a homemade dinner I prepared for the occasion, hoping I could coax him into taking a break.

I'd hoped to take our relationship to the next level by giving him what he's wanted for weeks.

A blow job.

A *real* blow job—the kind that involves messy thrusting and sucking, and zero inhibition as his ecstasy spurts down my throat. I'd even convinced myself I had enough courage to give him my fucking V-card.

God, I'm so stupid.

My best friend warned me about him from the get-go.

He's got the douchebag vibe going on.

How can you tell?

It's in the eyes, Sadie. The smug bastard thinks he's better than everyone else.

Guess she was right, but I refused to hear it. A single glance in his direction shattered my brain cells, and I followed his come-hither smile like a cat on the scent of dinner scraps.

"Yes! Oh God, fuck yes, Jake. Your tongue...right *there*."

A warm tingle travels down my spine, which is interesting since I'm angry as hell.

Turn away. You don't want to see this.

I take three steps forward, and my hand stalls halfway to the knob. He left the door ajar—no point in worrying about privacy when everyone in the office has already gone home for the day. One soundless push of

3

that door, and I'll see for myself that Jake Jennings is scum.

No, he's the grime that lines the tiles in my shower, the mud caking the soles of my sneakers from our hike last weekend. Thinking about the time we spent together sucker punches me. I draw in even breaths through my nose, trying to remain silent as tears burn my eyes.

The weather's been mild for fall, even by Pacific Northwest standards, so we took advantage by getting outside for a few hours. Things got heavy up on that deserted hillside, where we'd spread out a blanket to stop for a picnic. His hands explored every inch of me, yet the day ended with a preamble of what was to come.

I should have known.

He'd wanted more, but when it came time to reciprocate, I ended up freezing with uncertainty. And that's how it always goes with me.

Guys want what I'm not ready to give. What I'm not *confident* enough to give.

But Jake said he was different. He said he'd wait until I was ready. He even claimed he wasn't angry last weekend, but the deafening disquiet between us on the long trek back to his car was the first sign that something was wrong. Our weeks of dates, flirty texts, and smoldering looks at the office were about to get complicated. I'd known it, felt it, because that wasn't the first time I'd put the brakes on when he was ready to go full throttle.

For days I chewed over my insecurities before coming to the conclusion that I needed to step up my game. He's a man with needs, and knowing it's beyond time to move past my fear of taking the next step, I wanted to give him the most special birthday gift I could.

Guess he decided to get it from someone else.

"Get on your knees," he groans.

I slap a hand over my mouth to keep from making a sound. Careful not to give away my presence, I set the picnic basket of baked chicken and rice pilaf on the floor then wedge the door open a crack. My heart pounds in my throat as I peer into his office, despite the roaring voice in my head shouting to just walk the fuck away.

Now, Sadie. Walk. The. Fuck. Away.

But I can't. My gaze fastens on the blonde sinking to her knees in front of him. She's his assistant—someone I've never liked—which makes this even worse in the cliché department. Wearing nothing but a pair of heels and a wide grin, she curls her fingers around his jutting hard-on. His slacks puddle around his ankles, and...Jesus, he's huge and ready and already dripping onto her double D's.

I wipe the moisture from my eyes with quick, angry movements. I'm angry at him, and angry at myself for being incapable of looking away as she parts her lips and sucks his length into her mouth. He's fisting her tousled hair as his hips move so fast that I can't help but wonder if he's choking her.

I kind of hope he is.

She purrs around his shaft, making him throw his head back, and a guttural moan escapes his mouth. "You take it like a whore every time." He yanks her head back and seats the tip between her damp lips. "You want to swallow every drop, don't you?"

"Mmm-hmmm," she moans, sliding her lips down his shaft again.

As I watch them, I question the very basis of my being, wading through the conflicting emotions roiling through me. Anger, betrayal, and admittedly, fascination because I want to be the one on my knees.

What would it be like to have a man at my mercy like that, to have the confidence to give head like a whore and enjoy every moment of it? Would our eyes lock on each other the whole time? Would the lustful glint is his stare give me a sense of empowerment?

I should be raging mad at finding my boyfriend with his dick in someone else's mouth. Not to say that I'm not wounded by his betrayal.

But what I really am, at the core of my soul, is curious.

Confused.

Ashamed.

Hurt.

Yeah, definitely hurt. If he'd given me a little more time, not to mention some damn respect, it could have been me on my knees. I would have given him what he wanted. Could have given him what *I* wanted. Eventually, after the red haze of shock and hurt wanes, I know I'll be glad I didn't get on my knees for him.

He doesn't deserve it.

And he sure as hell doesn't deserve my V-card. This asshole doesn't deserve shit from me, least of all another breath wasted on him.

Leaving the picnic basket on the floor outside his office, I whirl with silent footsteps and creep out the way I came. But no matter how hard I try, I can't hold on to the anger long enough to drown out the hurt. Hot drops of humiliation drip down my cheeks as I jab the button for the elevator.

Determined to get my shit together before I arrive on the first floor, I dry my eyes. Holding the tears back isn't easy, but I'm dressed up on a Friday night, and no way am I going to waste it by crying over a loser like Jake.

SADIE

"You better slow down there, Sadie." Ashton Levine, with his caring eyes—the kind of eyes that put puppy dogs to shame—attempts to commandeer my sixth...maybe seventh shot? Before his grabby hands slide it out of reach, I toss it back. My eyeballs water as it burns down my esophagus like the last five rounds of tequila did.

Wait. Is it five or eight? Shit, maybe Ash is right. I've lost count.

"She's messed up over something," Amanda says. Mandy is my best friend. She's also Ashton's twin sister. The two of them cage me in, forcing me into the middle of the cozy circular booth the three of us are sharing. I'm a little annoyed by the furtive glances they keep throwing toward each other. Worried glances.

Probably because I called from Club Hoppin thirty minutes ago, bawling into the phone while camped out in a dirty stall in the women's restroom. That's where Mandy found me.

So much for not crying over losers.

"Ya think?" Ashton arches an incredulous dark brow at his sister. They're always at each other's throats, despite the two of them being closer than most friends. Maybe it's a sibling thing...or a twin thing. I wouldn't know since I'm an only child.

I slam the empty shot glass onto the wooden table and turn to Mandy, blinking several times until her porcelain complexion and sleek brown hair come into focus. "Be a best friend and get me some fries?"

With a sigh, she squeezes my shoulder. "I'm on it." As she rises to her feet, she shoots a warning look at Ashton. "Don't let her out of your sight. She never gets this drunk."

"Got it covered," he says, waving her off.

As soon as Mandy is on the way to the bar, her tall, voluptuous figure lost in the crowd of sweaty bodies grinding on each other, I face Ashton and prop one hand on his chest to keep from swaying into him. Damn, he's built underneath that black T-shirt. Black seems to be his signature color, and it suits him since he could be the definition of dark, dangerous, and handsome.

Especially with those tattoos. His ink flexes with his biceps, and I follow the picturesque mural of a forest in the midst of a full moon traveling down one arm. I've seen him without a shirt, and I know his ink continues its tale on the left side of his chest. I run a palm down his ripped abs, envisioning the masterpiece on his skin.

"Do you live in a gym or something?"

"Jesus." He removes my hand, but instead of letting go,

he twines our fingers together. Holding hands is nothing new for us. We've done it for years.

"You're like a different person when you drink, Sawyer."

Smarting over his chiding tone—and his use of my last name—I give him a drunken glower and try to pull away. His grip tightens.

"Wanna tell me what's going on?" he asks, searching my face with his light blue eyes.

Hell no, I don't want to tell him. He has a tendency of getting under my skin with his questions and opinions on how I should live my life. Now that I think about it, I can see why he and Mandy fight a lot because he's even worse with her.

But one glance at the worry pinching his mouth soothes my ire. Ash has always cared about me, and for some strange reason, tonight his concern sends my heart into a fluttering dance. His fingers, still tangled with mine, cause the strangest, most exciting sensation ever, and a wave of heat breaks out on my skin. I haven't felt this way since I was fourteen and had the biggest crush on him.

Must be the alcohol screwing with my body's chemistry.

"Can we not talk?" I don't want to think about Jake or the betrayal threatening to well in my chest again. Telling Ash what happened is more embarrassment than I can handle right now. I avert my eyes and take in the club, enjoying this floaty feeling from the alcohol. The bass of the music vibrates through me, sending me floating even higher. If not for Ashton's fingers entwined with my own, I could probably just drift away completely.

Not be aware of anything for a while.

"Uh-uh. Tell me what's wrong." He leans closer, and worry pulls at the corners of his mouth. His dark brows narrow over his eyes in two severe lines. "You can always talk to me, you know."

"I know."

Several beats of the pounding music come and go before he shifts at my side. "I promise, I'll keep my asshole tendencies to a minimum," he coaxes, mischief playing on his lips.

God, he smells amazing. His cologne infuses my senses, and I've always loved the way he smells—like pure testosterone mixed with a hint of the woods after it rains. I bet he tastes just as good. Unable to help myself, I lower my gaze to his mouth.

"What if I said I wanted you to kiss me?" The question tumbles off my tongue, completely surprising me. Apparently, I have no filter tonight. For once in my life, I don't give two fucks about what comes out of my mouth.

His eyes widen before lowering to my lips, and as the whirl of music and people and voices around us blast my ears, neither of us move. Maybe my brain is on slow-mo tonight due to the booze because it takes me a few seconds before I realize he isn't going to press his lips against mine. I'm not surprised, but it's still disappointing. He lets go of my hand, and hot flames of humiliation lick my cheeks.

Shit. Letting my hair curtain my face, I begin stacking

the shot glasses on the table, my fingers trembling. "Sorry," I mumble. "I'm buzzed."

Ash slides his arm along the back of the booth behind me, turning his body until his knees graze mine. "It's not that I don't want to kiss you," he says, inching my hair back and tucking it behind my ear.

"What is it, then?"

He slides his fingers under my chin and turns my head toward him. He's much closer than he was a few seconds ago, making my heart pound too fast and hard. The heat of his touch steals the breath from my lungs.

"You're Mandy's best friend." His teeth latch onto his bottom lip, and he watches me as his fingers brush my jaw in a hypnotic way that ignites searing heat between my thighs. I clench them without thinking.

"She wouldn't care." A lie, because I'm pretty sure she'd flip out.

"Okay, you're *my* friend."

"I don't care, Ash." Apparently, I'm full of lies tonight. Losing his friendship is a terrifying thought. He and Mandy are all I have.

"*I* care."

"Oh." I've got no reply to that. Needing some distance, I draw away by a few inches.

"Sadie." He shifts again, and the next thing I know, his fingers are threading through my hair. He hovers at my ear, letting out shallow and uneven breaths. "Jesus. Don't you know how much you matter to me? You have to know."

I exhale a shaky sigh. "You matter to me too."

Seconds tick past before he inches back, dark stubble

grazing my cheek. His lips part as he meets my eyes, and I hate that I have no idea what's running through his head as he searches my face, his sharp blue gaze darting between my eyes and mouth.

"Hell, Sawyer. You couldn't handle me." And just like that, he pulls away. "You're too damn sweet."

My spirit sinks to my toes. I'm the kind of *sweet* that doesn't fall to her knees and suck a guy's dick until he can't think straight. The kind of sweet that inspires a man to cheat because even though I want to do all sorts of dirty things, I'm too inhibited to know how.

I'm almost twenty-three-fucking-years old—the same as Ash and Mandy, who are light-years ahead of me when it comes to sex. But me? I must be the last virgin from our graduating class. How pathetic is that?

Thanks to numerous shots of tequila, the familiar shackles of inhibition are nowhere to be found. I glance around the packed bar and spot Mandy talking to a guy she's been chasing for a couple of months. She works here three nights a week as a KJ, keeping Club Hoppin hopping with karaoke during the bar's slower nights.

But tonight is Friday, and everyone is busy chasing someone, or dancing, or too drunk to notice Ashton and me in the corner booth. Even the barmaid has forgotten us.

Just do it flits through my mind. Before I allow myself the chance to chicken out, I disappear underneath the table and wedge my body between his legs.

His shocked intake of breath spurs me on. "What the fuck are you doing, Sadie?"

"Giving you a taste of how *sweet* I can be." I fumble with the button of his jeans too long, giving away my inexperience and offering him plenty of time to push me away.

But he doesn't.

Licking my lips, I inch down his zipper. God, he's free balling it. His long length springs free of the confines of his jeans, and I had no idea he was hiding such a big cock behind that denim.

An erect cock. The brain above his waist might be putting on the brakes, but the one in his pants is ready to go. It curves upward, the soft tip practically staring me in the face.

"Sadie," he says in a strangled tone, and I think I hear him groan as he sinks his fingers into my hair, holding me still. Holding me back. "You're drunk, and I don't mess with drunk chicks."

"I'm not a *chick*." I fight his grasp, and he loosens his fingers without much effort on my part. Because he wants my mouth wrapped around his cock. His ragged breathing is evidence enough. He combs my hair back as I tilt forward, and I flash back to what I witnessed earlier through the ajar door of my boyfriend's—*ex*-boyfriend's—office. Blondie hadn't just used her mouth; she'd fisted the base as she took him between her lips.

Bringing trembling fingers to Ashton's lap, I curl my hand around the thick root of his shaft and slide my lips over the head.

"Hell," he groans. "You're so much more than just a chick."

My heart is beating out of control as I glide my hand

up and down velvet steel. I roll my tongue over the plump head, and his fingers tighten in my hair.

He lets out another groan as I take in another inch. "Goddamn, Sadie."

My head is swimming, no doubt from the alcohol, but mostly from the fact that I have Ashton's dick in my mouth. This moment is too surreal. I'm not this brazen girl who does shit like this, especially in public.

But it feels good to be this girl now. Feels damn good to shatter his sanity, steal his breath, and take what I want.

I have no idea what I'm doing, but I must be doing something right. His thigh is rigid under my free hand, and his groans drift to my ears in choked pleas, as if I'm wrenching them from his throat by force.

He tastes good, salty with the perfect hint of sweet. He smells even better. His light, woodsy scent infuses my nostrils as I work his length toward the back of my throat. I grab hold of his knee to keep from falling over as I impale myself on his erection. The tip hits my tonsils, and the instant my gag reflex kicks in, I begin to panic.

Damn it. I'm losing control. Letting fear seize me. This is the point when I shy away, leaving a trail of disappointment, but with Ashton...I don't want to stop this time. I want to know what it's like to make a man come undone.

I want to know what it's like to reach past my limits, and I want to do it with Ashton. I've known him for most of my life, and I trust him without question. He won't judge or become angry at my inexperience or lack of skill. He won't cop an attitude and act butt hurt if I have to put on the brakes.

His hands guide the tempo of my mouth, the depth of his thrusts, and I gag again. Drawing air through my nose, I pull back the tiniest bit and count the rapid thumps of my heartbeat before sucking him deeper once more. His grasp on my hair tugs at my scalp, taking some of the control away from me. Ensuring I don't pull away again.

God, he's shaking, and something about that excites me. Warmth floods the space between my legs.

Is that me moaning?

Holy shit, it is.

I'm losing myself to the task, enjoying it for the first time ever.

Someone's talking above the music, and Ashton goes still. I'm so lost in him that I don't realize Mandy is back at first. His voice sounds far away as he says something to her.

"Sadie's ah...she's..."

He pulls on my strands one last time before dropping his hands from my head with a shitload of reluctance. I veer back and let his erection slip from my mouth, and horrified at the thought of being caught and having to explain, I wrack my brain for an out. Inspiration strikes, and I fumble with my ear, unhooking an earring as I scoot ass-first out from underneath the table, wiping my lips on my arm as I go. I pray the lighting is dim enough to hide my blazing cheeks.

"I was just...just looking for my earring." I hold up the tiny hoop in question before pushing it through my lobe again. But I can't meet her eyes, and I sure as hell can't bring myself to face Ash.

Shit, I don't have a choice. I face my friend and meet

her eyes with a boldness I don't feel. They're the same sea-blue shade as her brother's.

"Jesus, Sadie. You're about to fall over." Holding the requested fries in one hand, Mandy uses the other to guide me back into the booth. She slides in next to me, and the telltale sound of Ashton zipping up his jeans makes me shiver.

The weight of his stare presses on me like a wet blanket. I'm immovable, and way too fucking hot. He's mere inches from me, radiating heat.

Breathing with jagged desire.

Peeking below lowered lashes, I spy the death grip he has on the edge of the table. Long, heart-pounding seconds pass, rife with arousal and wreckage, before I bring my eyes to his and plummet into the sea of his gaze. I don't think either of us are breathing. The world falls silent as our secret pings back and forth between us.

"What's up with you two?" Mandy asks. "Are you guys fighting or something?"

I swivel my attention to her, relieved to find that she doesn't suspect the truth. Like usual, she assumes we've been arguing over something stupid—the way she and Ashton do all the time. In that moment, it doesn't even cross her mind that I'm seeing Ash in a whole new light for the first time.

My God. I had his cock in my mouth.

Maybe tomorrow, as I bury my hungover head beneath the covers to block out the searing reality of daylight and destructive decisions, maybe then my insane actions will start to penetrate.

But tonight...tonight everything is surreal. Ethereal even. With alcohol still buzzing through my veins, ignoring my mortification is doable. I'm trying to form a response when Ashton beats me to it.

"I cut her off." He slides an arm along the back of the booth, and his fingers brush my shoulder. A tingle of awareness shoots through my system, from the nape of my neck to the aching core of my sex.

I tell myself it's from the alcohol.

I'm *not* breathless and jittery from the heat of Ashton's mindless caress.

"I think she's had enough." Reaching across the table for a fry, he rubs his chest against my arm then brings the golden fry to my lips. "Have you had enough, Sawyer?"

My heart adopts a crazy rhythm as I dip forward and take the offered fry, my lips grazing his warm fingers. As I chew, I meet his eyes again.

There's a challenge in them. A smug glint to match the smirk taking hold of his lips. He's enjoying this too much. With a gulp, I swallow the fry. But I'm thinking about swallowing something else. His focus wanders to my lips, and I know what he's thinking. *He* knows that I know what he's thinking.

My mouth. His cock. Unfinished business.

Fear barrels through my bravado. Real fear. Not the kind one experiences when faced with a what-if or an unknown, but the kind of soul-numbing terror that blasts through your blood when you realize how badly you fucked up. When you realize that fuck-up could be the beginning of the end of something too important to lose.

A lifelong friend...gone in the tatters of the status quo.

This is why I snuffed out any feelings beyond friendship when I hit my senior year of high school. Ashton and Amanda are like family, my sanctuary against my own disapproving flesh and blood. I've witnessed his inability to commit to one girl for longer than a few weeks, and I can't stand the thought of being a forgotten notch on his bedpost. Nausea rises, thick in my throat.

A few weeks of blissful insanity with him isn't worth breaking a lifelong bond.

"I...I think I'm gonna get sick." I nudge Mandy out of the booth before pushing past her to make a beeline for the restroom, wresting my way through the throng of sweaty, moving bodies on the dance floor. Everyone is oblivious to the turmoil rolling in my belly, so maybe if I hide in the ladies' room long enough, Ashton will be oblivious too.

I cast one last glance across the club to our table and find his intense blue eyes on me. That is not the look of an oblivious man—that's the look of a man who has no intention of letting me forget what happened tonight.

three

ASHTON

Sadie comes back looking sicker than she did when she bolted for the ladies' room. Mandy scoots out of the booth to let her back in, but she doesn't budge. She doesn't meet my eyes, either. I have no clue why she pulled that stunt under the table, but I'm still hard as fuck over it, not to mention confused.

"I had too much, guys," Sadie says. "I'm gonna take a cab home."

"Like hell you are." I stand and shoot her a glare. "I'll drop you guys off on my way home." Unlike the two of them, I haven't been drinking.

Willing my dick to settle down, I exit the booth and hand them their coats. The nights in Douglas Falls, Oregon are getting chillier as the leaves change colors, and Sadie is drunk enough to forget her jacket. The last thing I want is for her to get sick.

After they shrug into their jackets, and I settle our tab, I herd my sister and Sadie toward the entrance of the club.

Mandy leads the way, winding a path between the tables and dancing bodies. I take Sadie's hand and pull her along behind me. The place is overcrowded, and I don't want to risk losing her in the throng of people in her current state of fucked-up.

"Party Monster" by The Weeknd blares through the speakers, the bass vibrating under our feet. Glancing over my shoulder, I take in Sadie's appearance. Wild red locks riot around her flushed face, and she's focusing on the dirty floor while we move through the club. I don't have to see her eyes to know they're the sexiest hue of jade I've ever seen.

And that little black dress. She failed to button up her jacket, and damn, she was out for blood tonight when she dragged that low cut scrap of fabric over her body. Has she always had such a sexy-as-fuck rack?

I don't even have to answer that question. I've known for a while what a knockout Sadie has become.

My Sadie.

I want to grill her and find out what she's thinking, but she and my sister share an apartment, so there's no chance for us to work this shit out until tomorrow after Mandy leaves for her weekend job tatting skin. Sadie, no doubt, will be hungover in bed. I plan to attack then and hopefully get some damn answers.

She can't just pull this shit and pretend it didn't happen.

She had her lips wrapped around my cock like they belonged there. And damn it to hell because it *felt* right. Aiming my gaze forward again, I almost groan out loud at the thought of shoving back into her mouth to finish the job. It's been a long time since a woman made me this hot over a blow job, and the fact that it was interrupted is only making it worse.

Fucking hell, this is *Sadie*, I remind myself. She's not some faceless chick I picked up for a night of no-strings-attached sex.

It's Sadie.

I don't know how many times I'll have to repeat that in my mind before it sticks.

Lord knows I've wanted her for a long time. But Sadie has always been and will always be out of my league. She's off-limits. Sweet, sexy, and sincere. Too innocent to subject to my depraved ways. I can only imagine what her reaction would be if she ever found out what I'm like in bed.

The red would never leave her flawless, pale cheeks. Both sets of cheeks, because I'd spank her ass for putting me through this torture.

As we step onto the sidewalk outside the club, Sadie stumbles into me.

"Sorry," she slurs as the chilly wind whips her auburn hair around her shoulders.

The sidewalk is wet with rain, and I'm worried she'll slip and fall. Hoisting her over my shoulder, I lead the way to my car, Mandy steady on her feet at my side. She didn't have nearly as much to drink as Sadie did.

"I've never seen her this smashed," Mandy says, watching me buckle Sadie into the front seat of my Honda.

"Me neither." I grit my teeth, not liking her behavior one bit. I'm tempted to take her home and spank her ass anyway, to hell with the consequences. Tomorrow, we can hash out the impulsive actions and desires—her tempting lips around my dick, and my twitchy hand unleashing retribution onto her bottom.

But fifteen minutes later, I tuck her drunken body into her bed and hightail it out of their apartment before I get myself into serious trouble. I'm almost home when my cell buzzes from the center console. I glance at the screen and spy the name of the girl I dated briefly in high school.

The girl I was stupid enough to hook up with again a few weeks ago.

Corinne Kaldwell is sexy and willing and the perfect example of a bad idea because I'm starting to suspect she wants more than I can give her. That still doesn't stop me from hitting the brake hard and making an abrupt turn down a tree-lined street.

Because I need an outlet for this rampant desire raging through my blood, compliments of my sister's best friend.

Fuck.

I backtrack several blocks, all the while questioning the wisdom of this unplanned side trip. Neat rows of residential houses with perfect lawns give way to the bustle of college living. People litter the sidewalk, coming and going from cafes and bars. Friday nights don't end until closing time, and for those looking to party all night, there are numerous frat parties going on down the road. I pass one such party, throbbing bass spilling out the two-story house, and realize that Corinne might not even be home. She could have called from anywhere.

But the last thing I'm in the mood for is a damn party.

Truth be told, I'm in the mood for one thing and one thing only, and it doesn't involve Corinne. Yet here I am, wheeling the car into the parking lot of her apartment complex. It's pouring rain by the time I climb the stairs and head toward her door, and I'm relieved to see light shining through the gap in the living room curtains. She answers in sporty gray sweats and a pink T-shirt. Makeup free, she's far from dressed up, with her blond hair pulled back in a long ponytail.

I've always been partial to blondes, with the exception of one redhead who has the power to make me crazy.

"Hi," Corinne says before opening the door wider and gesturing for me to come inside.

"Tearing up the town tonight, I see."

She responds to my teasing grin with one of her own. "Got a test on Monday."

"Look at you," I say, reaching out and twirling her ponytail, "staying home to study like a good girl."

Long, dark lashes flutter over her deep brown eyes. "I'm just finishing up for the night. I was hoping we could...if you want to, I mean?" Swallowing hard, she aims her gaze at my feet.

I make her nervous—the kind of nervous that's a red flag for what I already know.

This is more than sex to her.

Walking away should be a no-brainer. A necessity of self-preservation. It's the reason I distanced myself from Corinne a couple of weeks ago.

And I don't want to hurt her. I never set out to hurt anyone, but I'm not a saint either. What I am is upfront.

"If I fuck you," I say, letting go of her hair, "that's all it'll be. I need to know you're okay with that."

"I'm okay with that." Her voice softens. "I just want you."

I grab her by the back of her neck and pull her closer. "You know how I want it."

Heat flushes her cheeks, and something flashes in her eyes, but it comes and goes too fast to put my finger on it. "I do know, Ashton."

Of course, she does. She's known about my ways since high school. Though looking back, I had no business touching her, considering she's two years younger.

But she's not young and innocent anymore. My hand loosens from around her neck, trails down her spine, slaps her cotton-clad ass. I step back and issue a command with nothing more than the heat in my gaze.

As she heads toward her bedroom, I follow, noting the self-satisfied smile she tosses over her shoulder along the way. I'll spank her ass for that alone. We enter the tidy space in which she sleeps. One window, curtains drawn back to reveal the night through rain-splattered glass. Corinne moves to close the curtains.

"Leave them open."

Her hand pauses, fingers itching to shut out the possibility of prying eyes. She glances at me once more, hesitation lining her face, and I stand my ground.

Waiting.

Because she knows what to do.

Facing me fully, she gives the window her backside and grips the hem of her top before shedding her clothes without modesty. Getting naked in front of me isn't a novelty. I point to the desk tucked against a wall, and she bends over the hard surface, sticking her ass out the way she knows I like. I pull the tie from her hair and admire how her blond locks splay across her back.

"Spread 'em wider," I say, nudging the backs of her ankles with my foot as I unzip.

She parts her legs in invitation, but more importantly, total surrender. "I've missed this," she moans, grasping the edges of the desk with both hands. "I need you to fuck me."

"I'll fuck you when I'm ready. First, tell me why you're home cramming on a Friday night. Were you procrastinating, Corinne?"

"Y-yes."

I bring my palm down on her right cheek with a satisfying smack. "Shameful. You know better." I smack her other cheek, using more force this time, and she flinches.

But she doesn't tell me to stop.

This girl lives to take my punishments. She'll do anything to get me thrusting between her thighs, and nothing turns me on more than a red ass. I smack her flesh for several minutes, growing harder with every flinch and gasp. A dip of my fingers into her sex confirms what I already know.

She's drenched as fuck.

"God, Ashton. I'm dying here." With a long, needy moan, she pushes her ass into my waiting palms, silently begging me to take her.

I roll on a condom and nudge her opening, on the cusp of entering her, and that's when I falter.

That's when I see the flaming shade of auburn instead of blond. The memory of Sadie's mouth on me is too potent. Too shattering. Too fucking distracting.

What the hell? My dick has never been so hard and ready to go, but it has nothing to do with the woman spread out in front of me, more than willing. For the first time ever, I can't muster the will to fuck.

Sadie has totally messed with my head, and she's going to explain. She's going to pay for this.

"I can't do this right now," I say, removing the condom. It's one thing to fuck a woman with no strings attached, but it's another to do it while wishing she were someone else.

Letting out a ragged breath, I step away from Corinne and push both hands through my hair as the foolish, confused organ in my chest plays an erratic drumline.

Corinne stands to face me, her features pinched in disappointment. "Did I do something wrong?"

"No. It's not you."

"What the hell is it then?"

"I'm too fucked in the head right now. I shouldn't have come here." Zipping up my pants, I flee her apartment and escape into the downpour.

four

SADIE

Someone's sitting on my bed, their body sinking into the mattress next to my hip. Despite The Little Drummer Boy going to town in my head, I force my lids open, blinking the grit away for several seconds.

Jesus. Why is the sunlight so bright? Have those rays always come through my bedroom window with the power to blind a person?

And why is Ashton sitting on my bed first thing in the morning? As I push my tangled hair from my eyes, everything that I did the night before floods back.

"Oh, God..." I yank the covers over my face.

He pulls them back down. "Wanna tell me why you did that last night?"

Shaking my head with a groan, I haul my blanket over my head again and mutter an incomprehensible "no."

Ashton jerks the comforter below my chin, knuckles turning white from the force of his grip, and I know there's no way in hell he's going to let what happened last night go. And he isn't going away until I give him an explanation. But the truth is too convoluted for even me to grasp. In my drunken state, still hurt over finding Jake with his pants down and another woman's lips wrapped around his cock, I was drawn to Ashton.

For comfort?

For revenge?

Or because...*no.*

"C'mon, Sadie. You can't suck my cock out of the blue and expect me to not ask why."

I let out a frustrated breath. "I caught Jake's assistant blowing him last night."

He quirks an unsurprised brow, but at least he has the grace not to say *I told you so.* Mandy's already given me enough hell about Jake and his *womanizing vibes.*

I sit up, careful to keep the lower half of my body covered, and Ashton scoots over on the mattress to give me more room.

"So you did it to...what? Get back at him?"

"No!" My eyes wide, I temper my voice before continuing. "I was drunk. I'm not sure why I did it."

"How long have we known each other?"

A very long time. Almost too long to remember the exact day I met him. "Years."

"That's right. Too damn long to skirt around this. You know you can tell me anything." He swallows hard, and for a split second, his gaze wavers. "No matter what, Sadie." Something catches in his voice, but I can't put my finger on what it is. Hope? Fear?

Uncertainty seizes my heart, especially since my feelings for him are completely messed up—are nothing more than twisted vines strangling my gut. I bite my lip, deliberating, and finally settle on what little truth I *can* give him.

"I guess I was curious. I'm not...experienced...in that department." Or any department, really. "That's probably the reason he decided to feed someone else his dick." The words come out with more vehemence than I intended.

"So let me get this straight. Jake decided to be an asshole because you wouldn't give him head?"

"Not because I didn't want to," I mumble.

"Jesus Christ, Sadie. Jake did what he did because he doesn't deserve you."

"Doesn't change the fact that I don't know the first thing about pleasing a guy." Groaning, I cover my face with my hands. "I can't believe I'm telling you this."

He grabs my hands and yanks them away from my face. "And I can't believe you tried sucking me off in public."

I gulp.

His icy blue gaze smolders with intensity, roaming my face, studying each nuance of my features. "You confuse the hell out of me."

"I'm sorry."

"For confusing me, or for sucking my cock?"

Every part of me grows warm. My cheeks, my chest, my toes...and everything in between. The fuzzy memory of last night starts an inferno in my veins. I mentally flip through the recollections like TV channels. His steel shaft wrapped in warm, smooth skin. Skin like velvet. His soft tip between my lips, leaking silky desire onto my tongue.

The gagging.

The groaning.

His fingers tightening in my hair, pulling at my scalp. Begging for more. His muscular thigh tense under my hand.

No matter how embarrassing, I can't regret going down on him. It was a ballsy thing to do, a humiliating thing to do. What's done is done, and now my secret is out. Despite my inexperience, I crave things my father would disown me for.

"I'm sorry for confusing you. Last night confused me too. I've never done anything like that before." I try to extricate my hands from his, but he won't allow it.

He leans closer, his lips parting the slightest bit, choppy breaths fanning my mouth. "If it's experience you're looking for, I can help you out there."

Time screeches to a halt. My pulse speeds up, and my hands go sweaty within his grasp. His chest rises and falls too fast.

I *affect* him. Me. The girl he wrestled with in the mud when we were seven. The girl he picked on by pulling my pigtails. But more surprisingly is how he's affecting me. One drunken, thoughtless act shifted the foundation of who we are. *What* we are.

Friends...

More than friends.

It might be undefined and unvoiced, but I suspect neither of us can deny what's happening here. Not after last night.

"I don't think..." Damn, I can't keep my gaze from

drifting to his mouth. My lips have touched his cock, but I've never kissed him. How crazy is that?

"Don't hold back now, Sadie."

"I...it's not...I mean..."

"Not a good idea?"

"Yeah."

Slowly, he lets go of my hands and puts some distance between us.

Why do I feel so disappointed?

"You know I'd never hurt you, right?"

Not physically, but emotionally?

"I have eyes, Ash. You break hearts for a living."

"Are you saying I have the power to break yours?" He seems too interested in the answer to that question.

"I'm saying you're one of my closest friends. I don't want to risk losing you."

"I can be your friend and still be...more."

I read between the lines of his words. Experimenting with him will be safe. He won't hurt me, won't judge, and he won't expect anything more. He isn't the settle-down-in-a-relationship type of guy.

And that's the problem. I don't know myself well enough to know if I can play around without getting my heart involved. The thought of risking what we have, of allowing our friendship to go into turbulent waters, is terrifying.

It's about as *un*safe as you can get.

Deep down, I know I'll only grow closer to him through the act of intimacy. And after he walks away, I'll want to tear out the heart of the next woman he brings into his bed. It doesn't matter that she won't spend more than a few weeks with him. Doesn't matter that he's open about being a manwhore of epic proportions. That's a line that isn't worth crossing.

I open my mouth to say thanks but no thanks.

"Okay."

But that comes out instead. Why does my mouth keep doing things that will get me in trouble?

He sucks in a breath. "Are you sure?"

No.

"I trust you."

"Before we do this, I need you to know something."

"Okay," I say, dragging out the word with caution.

"I like to be in control."

"What does that mean?"

He leans forward, planting a hand on either side of my body, and invades my space in a way he's never done before.

Like he owns the air I breathe. Like he owns *me*.

"It means I call the shots."

I blink, stunned. Ashton's never come across as the dominating type. Okay, well maybe a little. He's always been super protective of his sister and me when we were kids. Truth be told, he still is. And now that I give it thought, he never asks for what he wants. He doesn't have to since he always makes his intentions clear from the get-go. He carries himself with confidence that borders on cocky.

Unless you know him like I do.

Like I thought I did. His words from last night drift

back to me, untainted despite my drunken state at the time.

You couldn't handle me.

One look into his eyes steals my breath. The curve of his lips steals rational thought. The firm set of his jaw steals my will. Against my better judgement—against the warning staccato beat of my heart—I hurtle from everything that's safe and familiar and boring.

"You call the shots. Got it."

"Do you?"

"Yeah, I get it, Ash."

"Okay then. It's settled."

"So..." I despise the way my cheeks flush under his scrutiny. "Where do we go from here?"

He takes my chin between two gentle fingers, his thumb stroking my jaw. His touch sparks something inside me—an ember longing to blaze. It takes everything I have not to let my eyes drift shut and just *feel*. A small sigh escapes my lips.

"We go where I take us."

Now I do close my eyes. This is too much. Things are shifting too fast. I'm still the same girl I've always been, only now I want to drop to my knees and tear at his zipper. And I want him to teach me how.

A long stretch of silence passes. Or maybe it's short and just feels like minutes instead of seconds.

"Look at me," he says, the softness of his voice lifting my lids. "If you want to pleasure a man, the first thing you need to learn is how to pleasure yourself. Do you touch yourself?"

I jerk back, alarmed by such an intrusive question.

He won't let me retreat. "Eyes up here, Sadie," he commands, and that's when I realize I'm staring at his strong jawline. "Answer me."

Holy shit, this side of him both scares and thrills me. What sort of avalanche did I set in motion last night in my drunken stupor?

"I...sometimes."

"Have you ever gotten yourself off in front of a guy?"

He's so matter-of-fact with these questions, we might as well be discussing the ways one could prepare dinner.

"No." I try to shake my head, but his hold on my chin won't allow it.

He seems to consider that for a second. "I want you to get up, shower, and dress. Lying around in bed until noon isn't going to help your hangover." He finally lets go of me and stands. Parting my lips, I allow a tiny breath of relief to escape. But then he tugs on the blanket. With lightning quick movements, I grab hold at the last second, refusing to let go.

"I'm not dressed."

"We're gonna have to go over some ground rules, beginning with your modesty." He steps back and lets go of the blanket before gesturing at me with a sweeping hand. "You're gonna be naked in front of me soon enough, so a T-shirt and panties is nothing. Get up. Now."

"You're so bossy." My words might have sass, but I can't hide the quiver behind them. I've never heard him speak quite like that before—with commanding presence. With *authority*.

Over me.

He is utterly confident that I'll bend to his will simply because he gave the order.

Who *is* this guy? I can't reconcile the version of Ashton standing before me with the guy I grew up with. He's a fucking master chameleon.

"Bossy doesn't begin to describe me. Now get your cute ass out of bed before I spank it."

I climb off the mattress, exposing my half-naked body to his heated perusal. But I can't stop from folding my trembling arms over my chest. Too much adrenaline is rushing through me. Too much *want*.

"Is this what you mean by calling the shots?"

He nods with a frown. "Don't be ashamed of your body." He gestures at my rigid posture. "Lower your arms."

Slowly, I let them dangle at my sides, hating how naked I feel standing in front of him, vulnerable and exposed to the core, despite my T-shirt covering my panties.

"Do you have a problem with me being in charge?"

"I..." My gaze lowers to his feet. "I don't know. All of this is happening so fast."

I'm dreaming. None of this makes sense. How did Ashton and I end up in my bedroom like this? In this situation?

"Do you trust me, Sawyer?"

He's the only one who's ever called me that.

"Of course I do."

"Then I don't see a problem. We'll go over some ground rules so we're both comfortable with this. But in the meantime, I want you to shower and get some food in your stomach." His lips curve into a grin, and that suggestive smile of his warms me all the way to my toes. "Do you have plans tonight?"

"No."

"You do now. Come by my place at seven."

SADIE

By the time I shower and dress, it's past noon, and my headache has settled into a dull annoyance. Normally, wasting the morning away would bother me more, but after last night and this morning's visit from Ashton, I can't bring myself to care. Maybe I'm off kilter from everything that's happened in the last twenty-four hours, not to mention the hangover, so when an unexpected knock sounds on my door, I'm not taken aback.

Maybe part of me even realizes who it is before I pull the door open.

He's standing there holding my picnic basket, face a picture of regret. "I found this last night outside my office."

"Uh-huh." Raising a brow, I cross my arms over my chest.

He narrows his eyes, forehead wrinkling. "Did you leave it?"

"Yep."

Raking a hand through his blond hair, he lets out a sigh. "Can I come in, Sadie?"

"Nope."

"Are you only talking to me in one-word sentences now?"

"I don't know. I guess that depends on how long you've been fucking your assistant behind my back."

His shoulders sag, deflating in defeat. "I'm sorry you had to see that. It didn't mean anything."

I grit my teeth to keep from yelling at the bastard. Maybe I expected an ounce of remorse, but all I'm getting is regret that he got caught.

"Can I come in and explain?"

"At least be honest," I say, glaring at him. "Call your 'explanation' for what it is—a pathetic excuse."

"Okay! You're absolutely right. I have no explanation for what happened, other than to say I gave in to a moment of weakness."

"Sounded like a lot more than just one moment. I believe the words you said were 'you take it like a whore every time.'" I arch a challenging brow at him. Those words are ingrained in my memory, and I just dare him to deny it.

"I'm sorry, Sadie. I tried being patient with you, but I'm only human. Will you forgive me?"

"I might be able to forgive you someday, Jake, but no way in hell will I forget it."

"Don't end things like this," he pleads. "You're too important to me."

I'm too important...meaning my father is the boss, and

he doesn't want things to get awkward at the office since I work there too.

"I didn't mean to hurt you," he adds, a note of desperation entering his tone.

"You didn't." I gesture to the parking lot where his black luxury sedan awaits. "So you can go back to your assistant with a clear conscience."

"C'mon, Sadie. It won't happen again, I promise."

"Don't insult my intelligence."

At that moment, my neighbor exits her apartment. She glances at the two of us for a few seconds before offering a small wave. As she makes her way down the stairs, I don't blame her for getting the hell out of Dodge. The tension between Jake and me is palpable.

"Do you really want to do this out here?" he asks, giving the area a surreptitious glance.

"I don't want to do this at all."

"Your father is my boss. Please, Sadie. Give me another chance."

How ironic that Jake is the first guy my father approved of. Like me, my dad was blind to Jake's true nature, only seeing the front Jake perfected. The mature, intelligent guy with his shit together. Clean cut, no tattoos, well-dressed. Well-mannered. He shaves every day, doesn't miss a day of work, and opens doors for women. He drives a nice car, owns his own home, and would make the ideal husband.

That's all Dad sees.

And once I started dating Jake, all I saw was how my father began looking at me with warm pride in his eyes again. It had been a while since I'd felt good enough in his presence, since I'd felt worthy of his approval. I might not be on my way to becoming a lawyer, but at least I'd snagged one.

Jesus, I feel stupid. I swallow bitter laughter at what a joke this relationship turned out to be. I've had some shitty boyfriends in the past, but none of them treated me with such blatant disrespect—they just dumped me and moved on to someone willing to spread her legs.

They didn't do it behind my back.

I wonder what my father would think of that. I already know I won't tell him. The last thing I want is to stir up chaos at the firm. Doing so will only accomplish a shitty work environment.

"Let's just call this a mistake and move on."

Jake shakes his head, his jaw forming a stubborn line. "We have to work this out."

"If you're worried about your precious job, don't be. I won't tell my father what a douchebag you are."

He winces at my harsh words. "I know I screwed up, but I care about you. As far as I'm concerned, this isn't over."

"As far as I'm concerned, it is." Without giving him time to argue further, I slam the door and turn the lock. Of course, he doesn't go away that easily. For the next fifteen minutes, he pounds on the door, pleading his case through the barricade keeping him outside.

Tiring of his bullshit, I threaten to call the cops, prompting him to at least leave my doorstep. It isn't long after when my phone starts ringing, again and again as his too-handsome face flashes on the screen with that smug smile I used to find sexy. Growling under my breath, I switch it to silent.

I don't have the nerves for this today, considering my... date tonight with Ashton. Thinking of it as a date doesn't set right with me, but calling it a casual get together with a friend isn't going to cut it, either. My stomach ties itself into knots as the day passes, bringing me closer to seven. I don't think my apartment has ever been so clean. I'm sure Mandy will appreciate my lack of concentration.

I can't eat. All I can do is think about tonight...and Ashton touching me. The thought of putting my mouth on him again makes my panties wet. It sends my heart into overdrive.

Jesus. My palms are sweating something fierce. But I don't want to analyze the reasons why too closely. If I do, I might find something I don't want to face.

Ashton is *only* a friend. Nothing more, and that's the way it has to be.

So why am I doing this?

A vision of Blondie on her knees flashes through my mind, and that thought alone is what gets me out of my apartment and on my way to Ashton's. Maybe I have no self-respect, but I want to be like her—sexy and confident enough to take charge.

I don't want to spend my life as a spinster because I can't get past my hang-ups. If Ashton can help me, then I have to take the risk. There has to be some reason I crawled under that table last night. On some subconscious level, I want him to lead me down this road.

By the time I'm standing on his doorstep, I'm shaking

in my boots. Maybe not literally, but it sure feels like it. A curious vibration buzzes through my body, originating between my legs. I've been turned on before, but nothing and no one has ever gotten me so worked up as he managed to, which is *insane*. It's like our history turned to dust, and the illusion of friendship was snuffed out in the process.

Not knowing what awaits me on the other side of that door makes me feel more alive, more turned on, than I ever have in my entire life, and instinctively, I know I made the right decision in coming here. Letting out a shaky breath, I raise my hand and knock.

And I realize as I do how ridiculous this is. I never knock on Ashton's door—I *always* walk in. He and Mandy are my family, and we've had an open door policy for years. How can the idea of intimacy change everything in the blink of an eye?

The door swings open, and the first thing I notice is the frown on his face. "Why are you knocking? You know you're always welcome here." He opens the door wider and ushers me inside before taking my coat. I swallow a sigh as his fingers trail over my shoulders.

"I'm just nervous, I guess."

"No reason to be," he says, his tone softening as he hangs up my jacket in the closet by the door. "Bryce is gone for the night," he adds, referring to his roommate, "so we have the place to ourselves."

As I follow him through the two bedroom house into the dining area, he glances at me from over his shoulder. "I made dinner. I figured we should eat first."

"Yeah. Okay." The table is already set, and the smell of food has my stomach rumbling with the reminder that I haven't eaten much today. He pulls a chair out for me.

"About Mandy," he says as I slide into the offered seat. "I think the less she knows about this, the better."

That's one thing we can agree on. Mandy wouldn't understand, and I doubt she'd approve of my arrangement with her brother. Mandy and I don't have secrets...except now we do.

Ashton disappears into the kitchen, leaving behind heavy silence. I'm not sure what I'm doing here, yet I can't bring myself to move from this chair and bolt. He returns a few moments later, carrying a serving dish in each hand.

Leaning forward, I take a peek after he sets the food on the table, and I can't help but shoot him a grin. "Mac and cheese, and broccoli? Some things never change," I tease.

"Mandy stole the cooking gene," he says with a sheepish smile. "I can teach you to suck cock like a pro, but this is all I've got in the cooking department."

I burst out laughing. In some strange way, his bold statement sets me at ease. This is the same old Ashton I've known most of my life. Sweet, endearing...even if he is a manwhore. He's never failed in the friend department.

We fill our plates with food, stealing glances at each other every few seconds. "Why haven't you settled down with a girl yet?"

He pauses, fork halfway to his mouth, and the intensity of his stare steals a beat of my heart. "None of them were the one."

"So 'the one' is something you believe in?"

"Yes." He says it matter-of-factly, without hesitation, before shoveling in a bite of mac and cheese.

Several seconds pass, rife with things left unspoken. "Hmm, that's...interesting."

"Why's that?"

"I figured you were gun-shy of commitment."

"No, Sadie. Commitment isn't my issue."

"So what's the issue then?" It's a bold question, and if I didn't want to know the answer so badly, I wouldn't have dared ask.

"My dad cheated on my mom for years before he finally left. I won't make the same mistake. I want to be certain I'm in it for the long haul before I throw around promises."

"So no serious relationships until you're sure it's going somewhere?"

"Exactly."

"And you haven't found that yet." It's more a statement than a question.

He shakes his head then points at my plate with his fork. "Eat up."

Eat up...so we can get on with the rest of the evening. Nerves barrel through me with a vengeance, and each bite is a tasteless swallow as I force it down my throat. I help him clean up the mess from dinner before he takes my hand and leads me to his bedroom. Stepping into the place where he sleeps—where he screws an abhorrent amount of women—has a stripping effect on me. We aren't friends in this space anymore.

We're not talking and laughing over mac and cheese at

the dinner table. In this room, everything changes. We cross over into stupid territory, become insane people playing with each other's lives...each other's hearts. More importantly, we're risking a friendship we've built since grade school.

"What are we doing, Ash?" I hug myself, suddenly feeling way too self-conscious in front of him. Another new development. Since when do I feel awkward around him? He's the other half of the two people I trust most in the world.

Since you got on your knees and sucked his cock.

"We'll do whatever you want, Sawyer." Reaching out, he twirls a lock of my hair around his finger. "Or we don't have to do anything at all. It's up to you."

"I thought you said you were calling the shots?"

"Oh, believe me, I will. But not until you're ready."

"That's kind of my problem. I should be far past ready."

"You either are, or you aren't. There's no shame in that." He lowers his hand, and my hair slips through his fingers. But he doesn't move away. The heat of his body blasts me from where he stands.

Much too close.

Not close enough.

I distract myself by taking in his bedroom. Of course, I've seen it before, but never under these circumstances. His bed is huge and takes up most of the space. The slatted headboard is a nice accent against the wall. A black and gray comforter covers the mattress, and I can't help but wonder how soft it is. The color suits him.

He's obviously not a slob. The floor is clean, his bookshelves are neatly organized, and every drawer in his dark oak dresser is closed, no sign of overstuffed clothing spilling out. I wonder how many women have been in here.

The number is probably something I want to remain in the dark about.

My gaze lands on him again, and I catch him watching me, ensnaring me in the eye of his arctic stare. My fingers twitch, aching to push his hair out of his eyes. It's been a while since he's had a haircut.

"This is weird," I say, wringing my hands.

"It doesn't have to be. This is new territory for us, but we have an advantage here."

"What's that?" I fold my arms across my chest again. I've never felt so naked in front of someone, despite being fully clothed. I can't comprehend how I'll feel if...*when* I take my clothes off for him.

"We have a strong friendship. We know where we stand going into this, so just try to relax and follow my lead." He steps closer and slowly pries my protective arms from across my chest. "Let me show you how amazing sex can be."

"No. No sex."

He tilts his head. "Mind telling me why?"

Hell no, I don't want to tell him why. Not only am I a virgin, but I know if we get too intimate, I'll lose myself to him—and that would be a travesty because with Ash... there's no hope for a future.

Only friendship.

Because of that some lines can't be crossed.

"I'm a virgin, Ash."

His eyes widen. "Seriously? You've never...?"

I shake my head. "Came close a couple of times, but..." I want to say I wasn't ready, but truth be told, it was never the right guy. Maybe I won't be ready to take that step until I *do* find the right guy.

"Okay," he says softly. "I'm glad you told me."

"Yeah." I pull my lower lip between my teeth, considering for a moment. "So no sex, and...no kissing."

He raises a brow. "You wanted me to kiss you last night."

"This is different. If we're going to do this, I don't want to muddy up our friendship with anything too..."

Intimate.

Understanding dawns on his face, and he seems a little awestruck for a moment, as if my confession told him too much. And maybe it did, but it's the truth. I can't let things go beyond a certain point with him, and sex and kissing...

Unwittingly, my gaze lowers to his mouth. God, those lips.

"So everything else is fair game?"

"Within reason."

He grins, though I'm sure it's more smirk than smile. "That sounds like a free license to me."

"A free license for what?"

"We're wasting time, sweetheart." Settling his hands on my hips, he slowly backs me toward the bed.

six

I've never been so eager to get a girl undressed. "I want you on my bed," I say, inching her toward the end of my mattress with every step. "On my bed and naked."

"Are you serious?" She gapes at me for several long seconds.

"Yes." I bite back a grin. "*Very* serious about wanting you *very* naked. You've got sixty seconds."

"Or what?"

"Or I'll pull your pants down and spank your ass."

Damn, the thought is already giving me wood. The vision of her bent over the end of my mattress, fiery hair trailing down her pale back as I redden her cheeks, is too tempting. Before this night is through, I'll have her laid out on my bed, ass in the air, those fleshy cheeks begging for my hand.

Or maybe I'll pull her over my lap instead.

"Spank me? What am I? Four-years-old?"

"No, thank God, because that's a little young for me."

"Jesus, Ashton. Do you spank all your women?"

"Only the ones that deserve it." Fuck, they all do. Every single time. "That's the way I work, Sadie. Pleasure and punishment. I'll take you places you've never been. I'll teach you how to suck a guy's cock until he's trembling and about to fall to his knees, but we're doing this my way." I nod to her clothing. "As soon as you strip."

My tone is all false bravado. I'm afraid she'll bring me to my knees by the time all is said and done.

"Okay." A breath whooshes from between her parted lips as she kicks her boots off. She brings her fingers to the button of her jeans, and I'm entranced as she lowers her zipper. Keeping her eyes on me, she shoves her pants down her legs. But when it comes to the next step, she hesitates, gnawing on that lower lip again.

"Seconds are ticking away," I remind her.

My tone must have convinced her I'm serious. Springing into motion, she yanks her shirt over all of that fiery red hair, revealing a black bra and panty set. She's wearing lace, and I want to believe she put it on for me.

And I want to see more. God, I want to see so much more.

"Lose the lace. I want nothing between my eyes and your body."

Her hands tremble as she brings them to the front clasp of her bra. Parting the cups, she lets the straps slide down her arms, exposing the sexiest pair of tits I've ever seen. They're not too small, not too big. They're perfect; perky, round, and creamy, with rosy pink nipples forming two buds I can't wait to get my mouth on.

"Your panties," I rasp out.

Her shy gaze falters as she pushes her panties down her thighs and steps out of them.

Naked. Sadie is completely fucking naked in front of me. The moment is too surreal.

I gesture to my bed. "Lie back and spread your legs."

"Spread my legs?" She sounds incredulous, which is kind of cute.

"Uh-huh." A gentle shove sends her onto my bed. "I want to see you."

"W-why?"

God, does she have no idea how gorgeous she is? "You saw me last night, did you not?"

Her cheeks turn pink as she lowers her gaze to the front of my pants, and I know she's remembering. She didn't just see me—she also tasted me.

I wish I could return the favor, but that's not happening. Not yet. Every move I make with her has to be careful and thought-out.

"Now, Sawyer. Spread your legs."

She appears stricken by what I'm asking of her, but she follows my directions anyway. Hell, I can hardly believe I'm letting this side of me out in front of her—the take charge side that few women see, unless they're naked in my bed.

Sadie's trembling as she scoots back on the mattress by a few inches. Legs bent at the knees, she parts her thighs before my hungry eyes, and my breath hitches.

She's already wet.

I fist my hands, clamoring for composure at the sight of

her glistening pussy. I can't fuck this up.

Not with Sadie.

"God, you're beautiful."

"Thank you," she whispers, almost reverently as she locks her jade eyes on mine. We stare at each other for what seems like forever, and I think we both recognize this moment for what it is.

A journey down a rocky path we can't come back from.

"Rub yourself."

She visibly swallows, her gaze taking in my towering form standing between her splayed thighs. I clasp my hands at my back and wait her out, knowing this isn't easy for her. She's inhibited, unsure of herself, and I want her to see just how much watching her can affect a man.

How much it affects *me*.

"Ashton..." Her right hand forms a fist at her side.

"I can smell your sweet scent from here. You're aroused and wet as hell. Touch yourself, Sadie."

Inch by inch, she moves her hand toward her pussy, eyes drifting shut the instant her fingers slide home. But I'm not about to let her retreat into herself. Shedding my own shirt, I toss it across the room then lean over the bed, fitting my torso between her legs. I prop myself up with a hand on either side of her head.

Her eyes fly open.

"I want to watch you come."

"I-I don't...I don't know if I can in front—"

Dipping my head, I suck her nipple into my mouth, and she cuts off her protest with a gasp.

"Jesus!"

"Jesus isn't here right now, sweetheart. It's just you and me." I kiss a path across her heaving chest to her other nipple and gently capture it between my teeth. She's moaning, writhing underneath me, and I know she's finally getting out of her own head, losing herself to impending orgasmic bliss. Glancing down between our bodies, I watch her fingers move fast over her clit.

My jeans are becoming too tight, and the need to unzip is overwhelming, but I don't dare move. One glance at her face has me transfixed. She's straining her neck, chin tilting toward the ceiling, and though her eyes are closed, it doesn't bother me this time because I know she's lost to the touch of her hand.

To the heat of my body hovering over her.

To my mouth on her feverish skin.

She is one-hundred percent here in the moment with me. I drag my tongue over her nipple then blow on it, loving the way it puckers. Loving the way she moans my name.

"You taste so fucking good."

"I'm gonna come." Sweat breaks out on her skin, and she's rolling her head back and forth as she chants *oh God* over and over again.

"You're close," I whisper, brushing my mouth over her collarbone. Barely grazing her skin, I make my way up the smooth column of her neck until I find her ear. "The pressure's building, making you wetter."

"Ashton." The way she cries my name—with a breathless whimper that pleads for mercy—spears straight through me, slicing me in two.

"So fucking sexy. Surrender to it, Sadie."

She cries out as a shudder rips through her body. Spine arching, her limbs held hostage by the waves of pleasure wrapping her in ecstasy, she comes undone before my eyes. An endless amount of seconds go by before she descends from the high. Her gorgeous green eyes flutter open and meet mine.

"That was the hottest thing I've ever seen," I tell her, my voice hoarse with the truth in those words. My breaths are as ragged as hers. Before she has the chance to retreat into shyness again, I shove off the mattress and haul her to her feet. My fingers find their way into her wild locks, and I'm tempted to break the no-kissing rule. But the desire in her eyes pulls me under the haze of her allure, and I drop my hands to her shoulders, needing to feel her mouth on me again too damn much.

"On your knees," I rasp out.

Her eyes are huge and round as she sinks to the floor. I gather her thick mane in my hands and hold it back from her face. "Unzip me."

Licking her lips, she brings her fingers to the front of my pants and frees my erection. I fist her hair, fighting the urge to bring her closer. It takes everything I have not to push inside her mouth and take control.

"God, Sadie. You've got me so fucking worked up." I loosen my fingers, and some of her hair slips through the cracks. "But as much as it's killing me, we're doing this at your speed."

Her gaze veers to my face, full of trust. "Can I touch you?"

"Hell, yes."

Her dainty, hesitant fingers curl around the base of my cock, and my eyes almost roll back at the softness of her warm touch. The sweetness of it. Watching her hand glide up and down my shaft is enough to hypnotize me. I'm so far gone that I don't realize I'm pulling on her hair too hard.

But her wince of pain is short-lived, and she doesn't seem to mind my harsh grip. Tilting my hips forward, I rub the head of my cock along the seam of her mouth, bathing her soft lips in the pre-cum I'm already leaking all over the place.

I remember all too well how perfect the glove of her mouth felt last night. She opened Pandora's box the instant she crawled underneath that table. Her tongue darts out to taste me, making me hiss in a breath between clenched teeth. Hot damn, I've entertained fantasies of her on her knees for years, have never wanted inside a woman's mouth as much as I do now, but I hold back, determined not to rush her or scare her away. I'll wait as long as it takes for her to open her sweet mouth and let me conquer it.

Her jade orbs flick up to my face, and I'm surprised by the bold way she holds my gaze as she parts her lips. Slowly, I push inside and sheath my cock in the perfection of her hot, wet mouth.

Blessed hell.

Her lips close around my shaft, and her tongue swirls the head. She sucks me in like I'm a damn lollipop. I find her inexperience intoxicating, her flushed cheeks endearing, her need to please addictive.

Moving my hand to the back of her head, I urge her forward until she allows me to thrust a little deeper. "That's it. So fucking good." I cover her hand with my own and show her how to stroke me while she sucks.

The instant her eyes drift shut, I know she's getting into it. And I'm lost, moving my hips in a steady tempo, plundering her willing mouth, moving toward the back of her throat with a sense of patience I rarely possess.

But this is Sadie.

My Sadie.

And she's worth it.

"I'm going deeper. You might gag, but just focus on breathing through your nose, okay?"

Our eyes lock, and as she moans her consent around my cock, shooting vibrations of pleasure straight to my balls, the heat in her stare is my undoing. My patience snaps, and I thrust between her tonsils until she's gagging.

"Fuck," I groan, fighting for air. Fighting for control. "Just like that. Don't stop."

She whimpers around my shaft, maybe even whines a little, but one glance at her face tells me she's empowered by this. Her jade eyes are wide, unwavering, darkening with desire.

"You're so beautiful." And I'm so close. As much as I want to come down her throat, I don't think she's ready for that. Fisting her hair until my nails bite into my palm, I moan, and she responds with one of her own.

I'm a goner.

She drags the orgasm from me before I'm ready, and I barely pull out in time to come all over her tits.

seven

SADIE

He finishes on my breasts, and as his release drips down my belly, I suddenly find the floor fascinating. The fact that he didn't come in my mouth tells me everything I need to know. The realization has me fighting back tears.

I'm no good at this.

Without warning, he hauls me to my feet, and his fingers sink into my hair, forcing me to look at him. "Don't even go there, Sadie."

"Go where?"

"To that place in your head telling you you're not good enough. You fucking wrecked me."

"You didn't come in my mouth."

"No, I didn't. Not this time." He brushes his thumb down my cheek. "I don't think you're ready yet. But trust me on this. It'll happen soon, and when I do come down your throat, you'll swallow every last drop before licking me clean to the tip."

His words shatter the rhythm of my heartbeat, sending it out of sync.

"Do you understand?" he asks, his thumb whisking across my lips like a kiss.

"Yeah."

"Good." He lowers his attention to my chest. "I like the idea of you wearing my cum home." The grin he shoots me is absolutely lecherous. "It can be your trophy for the day."

"Jesus, Ash. You're incorrigible."

"I think part of you already knew that, or you wouldn't have crawled under that table last night."

"I was drunk," I protest, shaking my head until he pulls his hands from my hair.

"Speaking of which," he says, taking a seat at the end of the bed, "I need to do something about that." Before I'm able to ask him what he means, he pulls me over his lap, smearing his release all over his jeans, and brings his palm down on my ass.

"What the hell, Ash?" The words are an indignant shrill bouncing off the walls of his room.

Smack!

My skin stings and tingles where his hand lands on my ass. And these aren't playful swats. He's putting a lot of strength into each smack. I can't believe Ashton is *spanking* me, but what I find even more alarming is how it's turning me on as much as it hurts.

My dignity won't let me give in without a fight though. I struggle against his hold, my feet desperate to find purchase on solid ground again. Instead, my fight only aids him in positioning me, and I tilt headfirst toward the floor, ass rising in the air.

His strong, immovable grip keeps me from falling, and he tucks me firm against his abdomen. "Stop fighting me, Sadie. This is the consequence of your actions last night. You want me to teach you? You've got it, but you're getting your ass spanked as well."

"What gives you the right to lay your fucking hands on me?"

"Your arousal, that's what."

"You think this is turning me on?" I scoff, denying the heat wafting off my cheeks—above and below the waist.

"Oh, sweetheart, I know it is."

Another slap of his palm finds its target, making me jerk atop his lap.

"Your breathing is heavy."

Smack!

"Your body is flushed with sweat."

Smack!

"But right here," he says, shoving his fingers inside me, "this is all I need to know. You're wet as hell."

"I'm mad as hell!" Squirming on his denim-clad thighs, I let out a warning growl.

He isn't phased by it.

His fingers aren't helping either. This is the first time he's touched me like this, those digits stroking me to madness, turning me into a drenched mess. He's coaxing my growling tantrum into a series of whimpering moans.

"Fucking hell, Sadie. I don't know whether to spank you, or make you come."

"Second option," I gasp.

"Do you have the slightest clue why I'm doing this?"

I shake my head, beyond caring at this point. I just want his fingers deeper.

"I'm spanking you because you let that jerk get inside your head. Because you ran straight for the club and too many shots of tequila. He didn't deserve your tears, let alone you losing your shit and putting yourself at risk over him."

"Trust me," I grind out between gritted teeth, "it won't happen again."

"It'd better not." He withdraws his fingers then smacks my ass once more. "I'm glad you called me and Mandy, but let's be honest here. You should have called us first. That's what friends do—they lean on each other."

"Right now, the only thing I'm leaning on is your lap."

His stomach vibrates with laughter, and I'm a bit disappointed when he helps me to my feet. He got me so fired up that I'm still throbbing with the need to come. He grabs my clothes off the floor and hands them to me.

"You're sending me home?"

"Yep." He stands tall, feet shoulder-width apart on the floor, and his body is a masterpiece. Broad chest, perfectly cut abs, and a torso that tapers into territory my gaze can't help but ogle. His pants are still unzipped and hanging open. He's hard again, and the realization sends a wave of heat through my limbs.

"Did I do something wrong?"

Slowly, his arms drop to his sides. "No, Sadie."

"Then what is it?"

"I'm respecting your limits by *not* fucking you."

"Oh." I shoot a glance at the bed, imagining us in it. Naked, wrapped around each other, twisted in the sheets and covered in sweat, because sex with Ashton would be a full-body workout. He'd dominate me in every way possible.

Sex with him would be mind-blowing. Life-changing. And I want that more than I thought I would. No guy has ever been inside of me, and suddenly, I want him to be my first more than anything—this sexy man who grew from the boy I remember from childhood.

But then I envision our friendship bursting into flames, turning to ash in the destruction. I can almost hear the inevitable shattering of my heart.

It's just not worth it.

As I pull my T-shirt over my head and step into my jeans, I know deep down that keeping a certain amount of distance between us is crucial. There's a big difference between sucking his cock and letting him inside my body.

Inside my soul.

And maybe that's why I'm still a virgin—no one's ever been important enough for me to want to go there. Though I've certainly tried a couple of times, only to watch it blow up in disaster after I realized I wasn't ready.

In my experience, men are impatient and quick to anger when they don't get what they want. Mandy would tell me that I have poor taste in guys, and maybe she's right. Scratch that—I *know* she's right. But Ashton is differ-ent. He's not angry. He's waiting with patience while I dress, aroused as all get-out and not doing a thing about it. My gaze stalls on his erection.

"Do you want me to...I could...do it again before I leave?" The thought of fitting my lips over him again excites me way too much.

A smirk shapes his mouth. "You want to suck my cock again?" He takes a step toward me. "You can say the words, you know. You won't turn to salt, I promise."

"I-I know."

He invades my space in a way that's becoming too familiar. Taking my chin between his thumb and forefinger, he studies my face. "Go home, Sadie. Tomorrow is another day. You can bet your reddened ass that I'll be seeing you again."

"Okay," I whisper.

He lets me go, and somehow, I manage to escape his place with my heart still in one piece. With my lips unmolested by his tempting mouth. But I'm not a complete fool. We're playing a dangerous game, and I'm kidding myself if I think I can keep my heart out of it.

I'm already in too deep.

eight

SADIE

When it comes to Ashton Levine, *in too deep* doesn't cut it. I run the tip of my tongue across my lips as I approach my apartment, as if I can lick away the memory of his cock in my mouth. As if I can will away the sting from his punishing hand on my ass. The pain is nothing but a phantom recollection, but remembering how he pulled me over his knees and spanked me leaves me conflicted. This whole arrangement with him leaves me confused and uncertain. I already know I can't trust my judgment, let alone my heart, when it comes to Ashton.

To make matters worse, Mandy is going to want answers about my behavior last night at the club. I haven't seen her since I got wasted the night before. She'd already left for work by the time Ashton invaded my bed this morning, demanding an explanation for my insane actions.

Mandy and I have a lot to talk about, but my unexpected...involvement with her brother isn't going to be part of this upcoming heart-to-heart. I can't even entertain the idea of coming clean to her. I mentally scoff at the thought of how that conversation would go.

Where have you been, Sadie?

Nowhere special. Just at your brother's house sucking his cock and getting spanked on his lap.

Yeah. That will go over well.

I enter our apartment, and as I'm locking the deadbolt behind me, Mandy saunters out of her bedroom in a black tank top with a crimson skull on the front. Red and black flannel bottoms hug her curvy hips. Her short dark hair is wet and tangled as if she just got out of the shower. I know she favors tanks since the sleeveless style shows off her tattoos. They're a colorful mixture of hummingbirds and flowers that wrap around her biceps. She's a talented tattoo artist, so I'd expect nothing but the best work on her skin.

She plops onto the sofa then pats the seat next to her. "Let's talk."

I knew it was coming, but I still drag my feet across the room. "I'm all ears," I say, taking the cushion next to her.

"No, *I'm* all ears, so start talking. What happened yesterday that made you want to get shit-faced? I couldn't understand a word you were saying over the phone last night."

"The short version is I caught Jake with his dick in his assistant's mouth." A small pang goes off in my chest. So maybe I wasn't in love with Jake. His betrayal still stings.

Mandy's expression doesn't change. I guess I shouldn't be surprised, since she's been warning me all along about Jake's true colors.

"I'm sorry that bastard hurt you, but I can't say I'm shocked. You deserve better than that."

"You don't have to say 'I told you so.' I'm already kicking myself plenty for the both of us."

"Hey," she says, her voice softening. "I'm not saying 'I told you so.' I'm saying you sell yourself short. You deserve better than these assholes you always end up dating. I swear, Sadie. I think you have some sort of asshole magnetism going on."

I toe off my boots and sit crossed-legged on the couch. "Yeah, well I'm over it. I'm done with guys for a while."

"That's not what I'm saying." Copying me, Mandy crosses her legs under her and turns so we're facing each other. "I'm saying you've been in a rut where men are concerned. Maybe it's time you shook things up a bit. Get outside your comfort zone, you know? Maybe you'll find Mr. Right."

Jesus. I'm so far out of my comfort zone with Ashton, I don't recognize my surroundings. I nibble on my lip for a moment, considering telling her. Because I need someone to talk to about all of this, and she *is* my best friend.

But she wouldn't understand, and no way would she approve. One, he's her brother. Her *manwhore* brother. And two...she'd just see this thing with Ashton as another mistake I'm making. For someone like Mandy, who doesn't have a problem in the sex department, she just wouldn't get it.

She doesn't freeze up with guys. She's not the type to sleep with every guy she dates, but I know she's had several intimate relationships. Obviously, she knows what she's doing.

But I don't. I have no clue what I'm doing.

Maybe it's still true. Here I am, risking my heart with her brother, and for what? So I can blow the next asshole I attract with a shred of confidence?

No, she wouldn't understand that.

"I think I'm going to swear off boyfriends." I pause, giving it even more thought. "No, actually, I'm going to swear off boyfriends *and* dating. How's that for shaking things up?"

"That's not exactly what I had in mind."

My eyes narrow, and I scrutinize her with a good amount of suspicion. "You're up to something."

"Okay, you caught me. I want to set you up with someone."

I shake my head before she can finish speaking.

"C'mon, Sadie. You remember Brett?"

"The guy you were talking to at the club last night?"

"Yeah, him. Well Brett's brother would be perfect for you."

Of course, Mandy can't stick to finding herself a man— she has to find one for me as well.

"You know I hate blind dates."

"I know. Normally, I agree, but I think you and Shane will really hit it off. You know I wouldn't set you up with a loser."

I'm not convinced. "This sounds like a disaster waiting to happen."

And so does Ashton—a fucking disaster waiting on the

horizon. Most people run in the opposite direction of a tornado. But me? I'm running straight for that twisty funnel of heartbreak. Maybe if I date someone, casually, of course...maybe it'll help to keep things real with Ashton. Keep things in the right perspective.

Ashton equals friend. He's not even a friend-with-benefits. He's a...teacher. Someone I can trust with my body. My heart, on the other hand, is another story. But this guy Mandy knows, well he could end up being Mr. Right if I give him a chance.

Couldn't he?

"Let me think about it, okay?"

And that's when Mandy gets that look—the one I always dread because I know she's about to say something I won't like.

"I kinda already set it up."

"What?" I jump up from the sofa, my voice a shrill echo through the apartment. "Mandy!"

"You'll thank me later," she says in a sing-song voice, then the little shit bolts into the safety of her bedroom, slamming the door behind her. She switched the lock, which means I'm not talking her out of this tonight.

Looks like I gained an ex-boyfriend and an ex-best friend all in the same weekend.

nine

ASHTON

I tossed and turned for hours last night, unable to get the image of Sadie out of my head. I can still see her red hair fisted in my hands as she sucked me to oblivion. And the breathlessness of her voice as she rubbed herself to orgasm won't stop haunting me. I can no longer deny that I've got it bad for her. Deep down, I've known it's true for a long time. But Sadie never gave me any indication she might feel the same way, so I put her out of my mind and resorted to having meaningless fun with other women.

I'm good at compartmentalizing shit, and when it came to Sadie Sawyer, she had her own special compartment in my heart, locked down tight with an unbreakable padlock.

Until she crawled under that table and unlocked those dormant feelings by unzipping my fucking pants. It took me all night to figure it out, but I finally came to a decision.

I'm going to date her.

While she's too busy focusing on learning all things related to sucking cock—and then some—I'm going to sneak in and get under her skin in a way she won't be able to ignore. I'm going to risk our friendship for a shot at more, so much more, and the idea terrifies me because I can't stand the thought of losing her.

Glancing up at the sky, I mentally bargain with the clouds threatening on the horizon. They can spew rain all they want if they'll just hold off for a few hours. Because I have a plan, and it involves Sadie on my bike, her hair rioting around us as she clings to my waist. It's been years since she's been on the back of my bike. She hasn't come near it since her father screamed at me for 'risking her life on that deathtrap' during our senior year of high school.

If there's one thing I know about Sadie, it's that she rarely stands up to Joseph Sawyer. She possesses a strong urge to please people; the trait is inherent in the fiber of her being. Some might see her as a pushover, a doormat. A weakling.

I think she's stronger than fuck—she's strong enough to put other people before herself time and again. She might have a potty mouth and the sexiest rack you'll ever see, but underneath the veneer, she's pure sweetness.

And holy hell, do I want a taste.

Her apartment complex is dead quiet. It's just past ten in the morning on a Sunday, and most people are sleeping in. Mandy has already left for work, which is in my favor as that means Sadie is alone. We've never had to hide spending time together before, but I feel the need to do it now.

Agreeing to give Sadie the sexual experience she wants is akin to opening a can of worms, and I don't need Mandy lecturing me on how I'm going to hurt her best friend in the process. People in this town might know me as a heart breaker, but the last heart I want to shatter is Sadie's.

I try turning the knob, but it's locked, so I rap on the door to her apartment. Several seconds pass, and I'm about to knock again when I hear footsteps. The deadbolt switches over, and she answers, rubbing sleep from her eyes as her hair frames her face in adorable dishevelment. Her skin is free of makeup, bringing out her freckles. I know she hates them, but I've always secretly loved those tiny spots dusting her porcelain skin.

"Get dressed," I say, my tone leaving no room for argument.

Sadie blinks several times then raises her brows. "Aren't you bossy this morning."

"You're gonna see my bossy side a lot more, so you might as well just accept it."

She opens her door, gesturing for me to come inside, and I give her a teasing grin. "Besides, you know you love it, Sawyer."

The truth in that statement flushes her cheeks. "The jury's still out on that." She heads into the kitchen and picks up the carafe of coffee I'm guessing Mandy made before she left, because Sadie obviously just fell out of bed.

"Want a cup?" she asks.

"No, thanks. I already had my daily dose." More like three, considering I barely slept last night.

She pulls down a mug that says *Redheads Do It Better*. As she prepares her coffee, I lean against the counter and cross my arms, quietly watching her. Hell, I've watched her for years, but now it's different.

Now I know what it's like to have her mouth on me. I know what her throaty moans sound like when she's about to come. I'm getting hard just thinking about it.

Raising the mug to her lips, she trains her jade eyes on me and takes a cautious sip. "So, I'm guessing you've got something up your sleeve for today?"

"Thought we could go for a ride."

"What?" Her eyes widen, and she lowers the mug. "Seriously? You brought your bike?"

"I did," I say, biting back a smile at her excitement. "Think I can get you on the back of it without getting my ass chewed out this time?"

"Heck, yeah. What my dad doesn't know won't hurt him."

I want to argue that point with her, since she's a grown-ass woman living on her own, but I let it go. For now. If I ever get the chance to call her mine, that's one thing that will have to change. She should have the freedom to make her own choices.

Outside the bedroom, anyway.

While she finishes her coffee and gets dressed, I scroll through social media, biding my time. Corinne messaged me, demanding an explanation for running out on her the other night. Eventually, I'll have to deal with her, but today is not that day.

Today is all about Sadie.

Sometime later, she returns dressed in jeans and a

black and white flannel shirt. Her wild hair is tamed into a ponytail.

Pocketing my phone, I cross the few feet separating us and pull the tie from her locks.

"Why'd you do that?" She reaches for the black band, but I slip it onto my wrist before she can steal it back.

"I love your hair."

"It's a disaster. I don't want to know what it'll look like after the wind whips the shit out of it."

"Mmm, sexy as fuck," I say, wrapping her thick mane around my fist. "That's how it'll look." I think she's going to fight my hold, but she doesn't. Her startled gaze locks on mine, and her mouth parts, releasing a quick breath.

"Have you always thought of me like that?" Nerves shake the question off her tongue.

Tightening my grip on her hair, I lean closer until we're breathing the same air. "I've had dirty thoughts about you long before you decided to get a taste of me."

"Did these thoughts happen before or after you fucked every woman within a fifty mile radius?"

"Better watch it, Sawyer. That sounds a lot like jealousy."

"Sounds like a question to me." She jerks her head back, and I let her hair slip from my fist. "Are you taking me for a ride, or are we going to stand here all day flirting with disaster?"

A smile twitches at the corners of my mouth. She's sassy today, that attitude a shield for the defenses hiding behind it. We're barely two days into this *arrangement*, and already, I'm rattling her composure.

No kissing. No sex.

If she thinks those rules will protect us from changing the foundation of our friendship, she's delusional. Things are already shifting—she set the inevitable into motion when she crawled under that table two nights ago and unzipped me.

ten

SADIE

Riding on the back of Ashton's bike again is exhilarating. A sense of freedom overcomes me as we fly down the two-lane highway. On either side of us, trees whiz past in a mural of burnt oranges, bright yellows, and flaming reds. The further we get away from Douglas Falls, the more beautiful the scenery. A hint of rain is in the air, and if Oregon had a signature scent, it would be the freshness of rainfall.

The skies can open and pour on us for all I care because I feel alive. My long hair whips around my face despite the helmet Ash made me wear, and though it'll be a tangled mess by the time we arrive wherever he's taking me, I'm not bothered by the wind in my hair. I'm more interested in our destination.

He wouldn't tell me. It's a *surprise*, he said with that smirk-like grin of his.

As the road curves, Ash leans with it. And I lean with him, my hands clasped tightly over his abdomen, my thighs warm against him. I'd be lying if I said being so close like this isn't affecting me. I grow hot between my legs, and it's not just from the heat of his body. I rest my head against his back and close my eyes, enjoying the thrilling sensation of flying.

Several minutes later, the bike slows, and I pop my lids open to find we're pulling into the parking lot of a diner. It's an out-of-the-way place I've never been to before, and plenty of miles from Douglas Falls. No chance of running into anyone we know here.

He parks the bike then helps me off, and as we head toward the entrance, Ashton takes my hand in his. The place doesn't look like much from the outside, with its grimy windows and fading brown paint, but once we cross through the doors, my mouth waters at the wafting aroma of pancakes and bacon hitting my nostrils. The interior of the restaurant has been updated. I like the rustic feel, with the wood flooring and knobby oak tables and benches. We pass by a sign instructing customers to seat themselves, and Ash leads me to a booth in the back.

"Have you been here before?" I ask, sliding in across from him. The privacy of the booth isn't lost on me.

"A few times. The crew stopped here for lunch over the summer when we were working in the area."

"Do you like your job?"

"Sure," he says, taking off his jacket. "Better than being trapped inside all day long."

As I pick up a menu, I eye his arms and chest. He's wearing a black thermal shirt that fits him to perfection. No doubt, his muscles got their definition on the job. I don't know much about what he does for a living, but I've noticed how ripped he's become since he started working for the Forest Service a couple of years ago. He smells like the outdoors most of the time, and it's a scent I've come to associate with him. A scent I've always loved.

The waitress stops at our table to take our order. She's tall and curvy with a generous chest. Blond, just the way Ash likes them. She smiles at us both, but her expression turns appreciative when she gives him her full attention. I flick my eyes in his direction, expecting to find him returning her interest, but his ice-blue eyes are on me.

"Know what you want, Sadie?"

Him. The realization hits me hard, stealing my breath. I've always been attracted to him, but this is different. This feeling is new and scary because I can see us hanging out like this all the time.

Talking and laughing.

Touching and feeling.

Feeling so much.

I lower my attention to my menu. "I'll have pancakes."

"Same for me," Ashton says.

The waitress picks up our menus, and Ash and I are once again left alone. I'm having trouble meeting his eyes as these disconcerting feelings blaze through my blood. So much has changed between us in such a short amount of time, and I'm having trouble catching up.

Having trouble making sense out of it. Before Friday night, I had a boyfriend I was ready to take the next step with, and now I'm sitting across from a guy I've known since grade school, practically drooling over him. I'm not sure how I got from there to here.

I blame the tequila.

"What about you?" he asks, bringing my gaze back to his face. "Do you still hate your job?" He knows I do, and the smirk on his face is proof. Ash has always enjoyed getting a rise out of me. When I was a girl, he did it by picking on me. When I was a teenager, he got under my skin by picking on my dates.

"I still hate it as much as I did the last time we had this conversation." I glower at him, not appreciating the reminder that I have to go back to work tomorrow and deal with Jake.

"Then quit. Life's too short to be miserable."

"It's not that simple, Ash."

"Sure it is. You walk in and say 'I quit.' Just like you did with law school."

I scoff. "My father would have a heart attack."

"Your father will get over it." Ashton clenches his jaw. "It's time to grow up. You're a college graduate living on your own."

"That's right," I say, voice rising. "I am living on my own. Which means I have bills to pay, such as rent." Although splitting housing costs with Mandy definitely cuts down on the bills. Truth is, I could afford my own place if I wanted to move. But maybe I'm comfortable with my living situation as part of me *does* want to be able to quit at a moment's notice. Plus, I wouldn't leave Mandy in the lurch like that.

"So find another job first. Find something *you* want to do."

"I wouldn't know where to start." Because I never got the chance to think about what *I* wanted to do with my life —I was too busy toeing Dad's line of expectations. Not for the first time, the idea of going back to school to explore my options flits through my mind.

"You won't know until you try." He pauses, his expression more serious than usual. "I just hate watching you waste away in that place. It's not you, Sadie. You shouldn't settle for a job at your dad's firm because he wants it. I don't care how much pressure he puts on you."

"It's job stability." God, I sound like my dad. Maybe Ash is right.

"It's boring, and I know it weighs on your spirit to watch criminals get off scot-free all the time."

"They're not all guilty," I argue.

"You know they're not all innocent either."

I let out a long sigh. "What do you suggest I do? Plant trees like you?"

His lips curve up in a smile. "If it makes you happy."

"I am happy." I fold my arms across my chest.

"Happy? No." His blue gaze wanders over my face. "If you were happy, you wouldn't be so defensive."

"I'm not fucking defensive."

He raises a brow. "Really?"

"Yes, really."

"You sure sound fired up to me." His eyes are practically grinning at me. "I kind of like you this way."

"What way is that?"

"Passionate."

"It's called irritation," I say through gritted teeth.

"Irritation is still passion."

"In my book, irritation is irritation."

A devious grin spreads across his ridiculously gorgeous face. "I don't think so, Sawyer. Irritation is a form of anger, but you're not the least bit angry. If anything, verbal sparring gets you hot between the legs."

Shit. I press my thighs together, thankful he can't see them underneath the table. My flaming cheeks, on the other hand, are out of my control. They're probably as noticeable as the wild state of my red hair.

Ashton shoots a glance around our surroundings, then he leans forward. "Touch yourself."

"What?" I had to have heard him wrong.

"Unbutton those sexy jeans and slide your fingers into your pussy."

"Are you crazy?"

"No crazier than you were the other night."

"I was drunk. What's your excuse?"

"Payback?"

"I'm not doing this here."

He settles against the bench seat, looking laid back without a care in the world. "Don't have the courage, huh?" He's purposefully baiting me. I *know* it, but my hackles rise anyway. If this isn't outside my comfort zone, I don't know what is.

But isn't that the whole point? I meet his gaze head-on as I unbutton my jeans and slide down the zipper. His eyes darken and sizzle under hooded lids, and those too-kissable lips of his part the slightest bit. I dip my fingers underneath my panties, cheeks burning as I delve into the most private part of myself in the middle of the day in a restaurant.

This isn't me, but it sure feels good to be whoever this girl is.

Especially when Ashton is looking at me the way he is now, with determination in his eyes. With undiluted want.

"Make yourself wet." His voice is raspy with desire, and it shoots straight to my core.

"What if I already am?"

"How about I come over there and find out for myself?"

"Don't you dare!" I swing my gaze around the restaurant, horrified at the thought of someone catching on to what's going on underneath the table. If he moves to my side of the booth, we'll only draw more attention.

"Then touch yourself like you mean it." He leans closer, his hands forming two fists on top of the table. "Run your fingers over your clit until you can't keep quiet."

His gaze holds me captive as I stroke myself into a wet mess. Someone leaves the diner. Three more people enter. The waitress is zigzagging back and forth between the counter and the tables on the other side of the place. All the while, I try to keep my expression blank.

It isn't easy, with the weight of his stare on me, and the pressure of my fingers on my clit.

"You planned this, didn't you," I accuse, and I know it's true. I can see it in the smirk of his mouth. The satisfaction in his warm gaze. He picked this booth for the modicum of privacy it gives us from prying eyes.

"Maybe I did."

My breathing grows choppy, and I chew on my lip to keep quiet. He shifts on the other side of the booth, and one hand disappears under the table.

"Am I making you hard?" The words are a wispy string of need rolling off my tongue.

"You have no idea, Sadie. Feel like crawling underneath any tables today?"

I bite back a smile, a bratty retort on my tongue, but the stroke of my fingers almost sends me over the edge. A moan strangles from my throat as my eyes drift shut.

"God, you're breathtaking like this," he says, the hoarseness of his voice bringing my lids up. "Sadie, stop. I don't want you to come yet."

Part of me wants to argue with him, but the other part of me is grateful he's not pushing it. Much longer, and I'm sure we'd get caught. As if on cue, the waitress heads in our direction, two plates in her hands, just as I'm pulling my hand out of my pants. I cross my arms over my waist to hide my unbuttoned jeans.

But there's no need for me to worry. She only has eyes for Ash as she sets our plates down.

"Can I get you anything else?"

Ashton darts a glance in my direction, and I swear I can read his mind, can tell exactly what he wants.

His cock in my mouth, pronto.

"We're good," he mumbles.

She leaves us be, and the silence that follows is maddening. Neither of us touch our food.

"Sadie," he says, breaking the stalemate. "I want a taste."

My eyes go wide, and he completely shatters the tension with his deep laugh. "Chill out, Sawyer. I'm not gonna crawl under the table." He reaches out an arm. "Give me your hand."

I inch my trembling fingers toward his, and he grabs hold of my hand before closing his lips around my wet digits. I'm so drenched I could put out a fire. With slow strokes of his tongue, he licks my fingers clean. And I can hardly believe I'm sitting in a diner with Ashton as he licks the taste of me off my own damn fingers.

He lets go with a popping sound. "I don't know about you, but I'm famished." With that, he picks up his fork and digs into his pancakes.

eleven

SADIE

It's pouring buckets by the time we pull into the parking lot of my apartment complex. We rush up the stairs, racing each other as our laughter rings through the air. I unlock the front door, and goosebumps break out on my skin. I tell myself it's from the rain, and that's part of the reason, but I'm way too aware of the sudden quiet between Ash and me.

A single moment can change everything. The sky from overcast to pouring. Laughter to dead silence. Easy-going fun to sexual tension. It was different when I was on the back of his bike. Of course, being so close to him affected me, but there were too many other stimulations to let this buzzing awareness take hold of my throat—cinching until I can hardly breathe.

The smell of the rain, the wind on my cheeks, the roar of his bike in my ears. Now all that's left is him and me in a quiet apartment. I swallow hard as I turn up the heat.

"When's Mandy supposed to be back?" he asks, peeling off his soaked jacket.

"Around five. We have a few hours." I look up in time to watch him pull his T-shirt over his head. Letting my eyes wander down his ripped abs, I stall on the V low on his abdomen. Too many seconds sneak by, and when I bring my gaze back to his face, his lips are curved into a knowing smile.

"Like what you see?" he asks, unbuttoning his stonewashed jeans and lowering the zipper.

I'd have to be dead not to.

He slides all of that denim down his muscular thighs, exposing his hard cock.

"What are you doing?" Why does my voice come out so high-pitched? I've seen his cock before. For fuck's sake, I've had it in my mouth.

"I'm undressing," he says, kicking off his boots. He picks up his wet clothes and takes a step in my direction. "You need to do the same."

"Why?"

"We're going to take a shower to warm up while our clothes dry."

"Oh," I mumble, my cheeks flaming from my ineptness. It's like the sight of him annihilates my brain cells.

"And you're gonna suck my cock."

Liquid desire floods the space between my thighs, but I ignore it, instead shooting him a vexed look. "Wow, Ash. Try asking next time."

He closes the distance, and I hold my ground, even as he begins unbuttoning my flannel shirt. "Isn't that the point of this, sweetheart? Your mouth needs more prac-tice." He pauses long enough to glance down at his erec-tion. "And I don't know if you've noticed, but my cock is happy to oblige."

I smack his chest before retreating a step. "Jesus, you're horrible," I say, biting back a smile as I finish unhooking the buttons on my shirt. His dirty sense of humor is some-thing I've secretly loved about him for years. I remove my clothes then clutch them to my chest, shivering. It's chilly in the apartment, but that's not the only reason I'm shaking like a leaf.

He takes my bundle of soiled clothing and leads the way to the compact laundry room off the tiny kitchen, where he throws our things in the dryer for a cycle. The machine has barely started tumbling when he grabs me and throws me over his shoulder.

"Ashton!" I'm about to pound on his back and demand he let me down, but the sight of his naked ass grabs my attention. God, it should be criminal to look as good as he does. His back is a canvas of hard muscle and smooth skin tapering down to a toned ass. How in the hell did I manage to be around him all of these years and not know what he was hiding underneath his clothes?

Because I hadn't wanted to know. Instead of following my heart, I followed my head and buried my attraction to him. Too many years as friends were at stake, and too many women came and went from his bed.

Turning a blind eye to Ashton Levine was pure self-preservation.

With each step he takes toward the private bath off my

bedroom, I self-destruct a little more. The fear of how this will end is too much to bear, so I toss my apprehension into the empty grave in my soul where my feelings for him used to reside.

I'm going to give myself permission to follow his lead. I'm going to give myself permission to fucking enjoy him.

And somehow, I'll find a way to keep from falling for him too hard.

Our teeth are on the verge of chattering by the time he sets me on my feet in the shower stall. He switches on the water, turning the knob to hot, and pulls me under the spray with him.

"Turn around," he says, voice rough with desire. I pivot, facing the wall, and he slides his palms down my arms. Taking my wrists in his hands, he lifts my arms and makes me flatten my palms against the tile.

"Ash?" I can't hide the nervous tremor in my voice—it matches the flutters of excitement going off low in my belly.

"Shhh, just follow my lead." He speaks the words in a low tone, his breath warming my neck. Slowly, he edges my feet apart with his foot.

My hands are on the tile.

My feet are planted on the floor shoulder-width apart.

And I've never felt so vulnerable. Part of me likes this feeling too much.

"Don't move your hands."

A shiver breaks out on my skin, despite the heat from the water, and all I can manage is a muted nod. He shifts behind me, then his fingers are trailing down my spine, sparking zaps of awareness on my skin.

Is that his lips on the small of my back? The undeniable heat of his tongue spreads low on my spine, and my breath hitches.

He's making me light-headed. Dizzy with longing. I bite my lip to keep quiet because I'm about to beg him to touch me. *Really* touch me. The space between my legs is throbbing for his hands and mouth.

He drags his palms over my butt-cheeks before bringing a hand down with a loud smack. I can't hold back a small cry of surprise.

"I like a red ass, Sadie. Can you handle it?"

Can I? I'm not sure, but I'm aching between my legs too much to care. "Uh-huh," I mumble.

"That's not an answer." He lets loose another smack. "Answer me."

"Yes!"

Smack!

The blow comes with more force than the last two, and with a small whimper, I shoot to my toes.

He snakes an arm around my waist and gently pulls me into his body, bending me until I'm arching my spine. Until my ass is raised for better access.

"Perfect," he rasps out. "You've got the finest ass. Anyone ever tell you that?"

"No." Shit, no one's ever touched me like this either. Looked at me like this. And no one has ever wanted to spank me before. The more time I spend with Ash, the more we tumble down the rabbit hole of whatever this is.

Who knew he was hiding this side of him all these years behind that flirty grin?

He spanks me again, and I jump once more with a small gasp. Jesus, I'm surprised I like it so much. His palm comes down over and over, alternating between my left and right cheeks.

Fuck, it's starting to sting, and I can't help but whimper and squirm. The urge to press my thighs together is overwhelming. The longer I stand like this, the more likely my arousal will drip down my legs.

I sense him crouching behind me, his hot breath fanning over my left butt-cheek. He parts his mouth over my flesh and sinks his teeth in.

"Ash." His name is little more than a throaty cry, and I clench my jaw to keep from moaning again. His nibble doesn't hurt. If anything, the location of his mouth is making me wetter. Needier. God, I'm desperate for him to touch me.

He runs his nose down my inner thigh. So close, but so far away. It's pure torture.

"I'm gonna touch you," he says, planting soft kisses on my skin as he grazes my other thigh with his fingers. "Unless you don't want me to."

I've never wanted it more. But getting my vocal cords to work is proving to be impossible. I arch into his touch, hoping he'll get the message.

"No, Sadie. I want you to say the words. If you want my fingers in your pussy, you're gonna have to tell me."

"Jesus, Ash. You're driving me insane."

"I can drive you insane for hours, and I will if you don't say the words."

My pride lets an endless amount of seconds tick by, but eventually, I cave to the need clawing inside me. "Touch me," I choke out.

He slips his fingers inside me, and his touch is different from last night, when he shoved them into my pussy while spanking me. Now, his movements are careful. Teasing. He's taking his time, extracting low moaning cries from my throat.

"You're so wet."

I've been drenched since the restaurant, but I suspect he already knew that. I can still see the smug tilt of his lips as he sat across from me, watching while I engaged in an embarrassing but entirely thrilling display of public indecency.

His fingers dip in and out of my pussy, his pace unhurried, and I'm rocking my hips, moving with his hand in a dance of want and need. My breaths become choppy as water drips off my hair and slides down my face. And his fingers...

God, he knows how to use them.

He glides up to my clit and rubs circles on that sensitive bundle of nerves. "I want you to come."

"Don't stop," I whisper as my lids drift shut. I block out everything—the tile under my palms, the spray of the shower raining down on us, the rapid pace of my thumping heartbeat.

I focus all of my attention on his fingers and what they're

doing to me between my legs. Hot and drenched to the core, I can't stop the pressure from building. That soaring high is almost within reach. A groan escapes my mouth. I'm so close, but he won't touch me the way I need him to.

"I need more, Ash."

He groans. "You're sexy as sin when you're desperate, Sawyer." Pressing more firmly on my clit, he bites into my ass again.

"Please," I whine.

He reaches around and palms my breast. The caress on my nipple, his teeth nibbling in naughty places, and those fingers swirling through my most intimate spot—all of it crashes together, igniting an explosion, and I cry out his name.

The orgasm seizes my limbs, and I can do nothing but stand there with my thighs trembling as my body pulses and contracts around his fingers. Long seconds go by, and my uneven breaths mix with his ragged ones as the shower tries to drown both sounds out.

Ash stands behind me, and the hard length of his cock presses against my lower back. "If I don't get inside your mouth, I might die." He whirls me and pushes down on my shoulders until I drop to my knees. Grabbing the base of his cock, he pushes the wet crown against my lips. There's no waiting for me to take him in this time. Ashton takes control by fisting my hair as he thrusts into my mouth.

My heart beats fast as adrenaline rushes through my veins. Apprehension also creeps in. I want to swallow. I want to know what it feels like to make a guy come in my mouth. He thrusts hard and fast, holding nothing back, and I know this is it—this is the day I'm going to know what it's like to swallow.

To really taste a man.

"Goddamn, Sadie. Feels amazing." He shoves his cock deeper, making me gag, and I jerk back without thinking. He pulls out and places both hands on the tile. He's glancing down at me, his chest heaving, water dripping down the perfect cut of his abs. "Do you want to swallow?"

I nod, but doubt plagues me. "I need you to make me."

He raises a brow. "Are you sure? Because making you swallow my load is a bigger turn-on than you realize."

He likes the control. Likes to call the shots. Right then, I get the sense he's been holding back, and this is his way of warning me.

Make a decision, and be sure about it.

Problem is, I don't think I'll ever be sure. It's one of those things I'll just have to do in order to get past the fear of the unknown.

"I want to swallow." I lock my eyes on his. "Don't let me back out."

"Not a chance in hell, Sawyer."

This is what I wanted, right? For Ashton to teach me how to suck off a guy. From the moment I saw Jake thrust into the mouth of his assistant, I wanted to be the one on my knees, and now I am.

Keeping his hands on the wall, Ash pushes the tip of his cock against my lips again. "Open." It's only one word, but there's an undeniable note of command behind it. Protesting is impossible with that tone ringing in my ears.

I part my lips, and he pushes in again.

"Hands behind your back. Don't move them."

I follow his orders. The pose is one of complete submission. I've never felt so vulnerable. I'm putting my trust in Ashton's hands, counting on him to take what I so desperately want to give.

He pumps in and out of my mouth for a while, his tempo languid as if we have all the time in the world, as if my mouth was designed to be used like this. Each time he shoves in again, my pulse ratchets higher, drumming at my collarbone. Sounding off in my ears.

The way he's drawing this out is driving me crazy.

"Close your eyes," he says in that raspy tone he uses when he's on edge. As my lids drift shut, he grabs my head in both hands.

I start shaking. There's no backing out now.

"Nothing to be scared of, Sadie. Just let it happen."

My heart skips a beat as he starts plunging with purpose. He's got such a tight grip on my head that I couldn't pull back if I wanted to.

It happens so fast.

I gag as he thrusts down my throat. He expels a long series of grunts and groans as he holds me immobile in his grasp. My gag reflex can't take anymore, and I try jerking back, but he won't let me.

"Fuck, I'm coming, Sadie. I'm fucking coming."

I whine around his cock, begging for mercy. Hoping it'll be over soon.

And then it is.

Ashton withdraws, and I glance up to find him

breathing hard, arms shaking under his weight as he props himself against the shower wall.

"You okay?" he asks.

I nod, but before I can speak, he lifts me to my feet. Our chests smash together as he buries his face in the crook of my shoulder. Spearing one hand through my hair, he presses the other against the small of my back, holding me against him as warm water sprays on us.

And I love the way he's trembling—it's a surefire sign that what we just did affected him the way it affected me.

"You bring me to my knees, Sawyer." The words blast against my neck as powerfully as the truth in them blasts through the last of my defenses. Something too strong for me to fight coils around my heart. Rises in my throat.

Fear.

I let out a shaky breath, scared of drawing him closer even as my arms tighten around him. I can't even think straight as I run a hand up between the valley of his shoulder blades and sink my fingers into his hair.

And that's the moment I know we made a horrible mistake.

twelve

ASHTON

I can't get Sadie's deer-caught-in-the-headlights look out of my head. It's especially disturbing because I've seen it plenty of times in the mirror whenever a girl begins showing signs of getting too serious.

It's the same damn expression I wear right before I break things off with whoever I happen to be screwing at the time.

Now that same look is lingering in Sadie's eyes, and I don't like it one bit. She tried to play it off. Tried using the excuse that Mandy would be home soon to get me out of her apartment.

But she's scared, and it has nothing to do with sucking and swallowing. She feels more than she's letting on, and I hate how she's wrestling with herself over this. We're approaching a fork in the road, and it's coming up way too fast for my liking.

If I can't win her over, I'll have to let her go in order to save our friendship.

I know her as well as I know myself. Sadie has always been part of me, but over time that part morphed into this ball of longing in my gut I can't ignore any longer. I'm dying to taste her lips, aching to get inside her body. Not just her body, but her soul.

The realization has been trickling in for what seems like forever, and now it's crashing over me like an unstoppable wave. I fucking want her more than I've ever wanted anyone or anything.

The annoying redhead my sister befriended on the playground when we were young and innocent. The fiery girl who infiltrated my heart before I even realized it was happening.

The stunning woman who has me wrapped now.

I pull into my driveway and cut the engine on the bike. The rain has slowed to a drizzle, and tiny drops collect in my hair and on my coat as I head up the pathway to my front door. I stall at the sight of the shadowy form sitting on my front stoop. Corinne is huddling under the awning, staying dry from the rain.

"How long have you been waiting?"

"Not too long."

Stepping past her, I insert a key into the doorknob. "You should have called," I say, wincing at my harsh tone as I swing the door open.

She rises to her feet. "I would have if I'd known you'd be in such a shitty mood."

"I'm sorry. I didn't mean to snap at you. I've just got a lot on my mind." I switch on a light and gesture for her to come inside.

Corinne follows me into the living room. "I messaged you. Didn't you get it?"

Shit. I completely forgot. "Uh, yeah, I did. It's been a busy day."

She settles a hand on my arm. "Did I do something to piss you off?"

I take in her hunched shoulders and feel my own slump. "You didn't do anything, Corinne. I just wasn't expecting you."

Nibbling on her lower lip, she stares at me with hurt in her brown eyes. "I miss you."

And I know I'm wearing *the* expression—the same one Sadie shot my way before I left her apartment twenty minutes ago.

"Look, Corinne, I don't want to hurt—"

"Don't," she interrupts. "Don't say you don't want to hurt me. It's too late for that."

God, I feel like such an asshole for not addressing this before now. "I should've realize sooner that you felt...more. I thought we were just having fun."

"Just having fun?" Her brown eyes are bright with pain, and the accusation in them spears through me, making me feel like the bastard I am. "I thought we had something...I mean..." Lowering her head, she wipes under her eyes. "What did I do? Just tell me so I can fix it."

Fucking hell. I hate this part. I hate hurting people, especially someone as sweet and vulnerable as Corinne.

"You didn't do anything. I'm just not into serious hookups. You already know this."

She raises her chin and looks me square in the eyes. "I'm in love with you. How could you not know that?"

Closing my eyes, I drag a hand down my face. I'm not ready for this—for this girl standing before me, saying she loves me as tears drip from her eyes.

I'm a total asshole.

"I'm sorry, Corinne."

"If you didn't feel something for me, then why'd you worm your way back into my life after all of these years?"

"I didn't worm my way into your life." Taking a deep breath, I temper my tone. "We hooked up at a party. If I'd known you felt this way, I wouldn't have slept with you again."

And again and again.

"I thought I meant something to you." Her mouth is trembling, and I dig deep for an explanation that will make her feel better, but there isn't one. There's only the harsh truth.

"We were never serious in high school. I didn't think this was any different," I say, silently pleading with her to stop crying. If there's one thing that rips me apart, it's a woman's tears.

"It was serious for me!" Pointing her finger, she stalks toward me. "You broke my heart in high school, you jerk." She jabs me in the chest, and I retreat a step. "But you were so caught up in yourself to notice."

I grab her hand before she can do more damage with her finger and its razor sharp nail. "You're right. I *am* a jerk. I didn't realize, Corinne. If I had, I wouldn't have hooked up with you."

Her wet eyes pin me to the spot, like prey she's about to devour in the eye of her pain. "Is there someone else?"

Parting my lips, I will the denial off my tongue, but the lie won't form. Instead, I shake my head. But it's too late. Glaring at me, she yanks her hand from mine. I hesitated too long, and now she knows the truth.

There is someone else, only that *someone else* doesn't know it yet. What a twisted circle of heartbreak I've managed to create here.

"Who is she?" Venom drips from her tone, and something dark flashes in her brown eyes. I revisit my earlier thought that she's sweet and vulnerable.

Because Corinne doesn't look like either right now. If she were a cat, she'd have her claws out, her teeth bared as she hisses her warning. Instead of answering her, I cross to the door and open it. Arguing isn't going to help either of us.

"I think you should go," I say, trying to soften my tone. But as I ask her to leave my house—to leave my life—I know nothing will soften the blow to her heart.

Shit.

How many times have I ended up in this exact spot? Letting a girl down gently is never easy, but usually they leave more angry than hurt because I don't make promises I can't keep.

So where did I go wrong with Corinne? What did I do to make her think that what we had was more than a fun hookup? For fuck's sake, we didn't even see each other every weekend.

There was no dating. No declarations of love. We

communicated over a few texts in between the times we fucked, but that was it.

"I didn't mean to hurt you," I say, hoping my words will get her to move from her motionless spot in the middle of my living room.

She turns pained eyes on me. Damp eyes full of anger and heartbreak. "Ashton...I'm pregnant."

Time doesn't just screech to a halt—it slams into a wall. I can't fucking breathe. A thousand thoughts and what-ifs torpedo through my mind, but it's nothing but incomprehensible chaos. "I don't believe you," I finally say, my own voice strange to my ears.

This isn't happening.

We were careful.

I'm always so fucking careful.

She finally moves, her steps renewed with purpose and power as she nears me. I'm still standing by the door like a fool.

"It's true. Wishing otherwise isn't going to make it disappear." She brushes past me and steps onto the front porch. "And before you even think about asking, I'm keeping the baby."

"I wasn't asking," I say, still shell-shocked. How can a person ask questions when their world is spinning out of control around them? Fuck, I can't even think straight.

"When you're ready to talk about it, you know where to find me." She hurries down the pathway toward the street, seemingly unbothered by the rain. If I weren't frozen to the spot, I'd offer to drive her home.

But I'm doing good to shut the door and plop onto the couch before my legs fail me.

thirteen

SADIE

Monday mornings are the bane of my existence. This Monday morning, however, is ten times worse. Jake's legal assistant—Candace "call me Candy"—is avoiding me like the plague, which isn't the easiest to do since, as a paralegal, I work directly with Jake. If it were any other job, I would have thought about walking out by now because dealing with Jake trying to corner me at every turn is getting old.

Working for my father is a pain in the ass. I wish I *could* just waltz into his office and say "I quit." But I've only gone against my parents a handful of times, and one of them was when I refused to give up my friendship with Mandy and Ash in the tenth grade.

My parents—my father especially—aren't the biggest fans of the Levine twins. They disapprove of Mandy's body art and the various jobs she works to put herself through school. She doesn't have well-to-do parents to send her to college like I did. Her father split when she and Ashton were young, and her mother worked two jobs to make ends meet.

I have mad admiration for Mandy. She's almost done with her business degree, and what my parents don't realize is that she has plans to open her own tattoo parlor. Her future is wide open in front of her, unimpeded by parental expectations since she didn't have parents who put her through college.

She didn't break their hearts by deciding not to go to law school.

"Sadie, can I see you in my office for a moment?"

"Sure," I tell my dad. "I'll be right there after I put these away." I hold up the files I was working on, and he gives me a brisk nod. As I make my way through the office, I wonder if this impromptu summons has anything to do with Jake.

News broke this morning that Jake Jennings—or JJ, as my father calls him—is getting his precious promotion.

I return to Dad's office and find him and the other partners, along with Jake, seated in leather high back chairs. The space has a masculine atmosphere, with tall mahogany bookcases lining one side of the room and an executive desk situated on the other. Floor-to-ceiling windows offer a view of the city.

One glance at the ornate clock on the wall tells me the lunch hour is almost upon us, and though everyone at Sawyer and Bennett—from the partners to the lowly assistant staff—have a habit of taking working lunches, today is obviously not one of those days.

The men are holding amber-filled tumblers. Even the lone female partner is seated, legs crossed at the ankle as she clutches a glass between her manicured fingers. She probably needs the booze to survive the testosterone in the room. Jake rises to hand me a drink. I gaze down into the liquid and wrinkle my nose.

"Now, sweetheart," my father says in his deep, booming voice, "I know bourbon isn't your drink, but we've got cause for celebration. I figured you'd want to be here to congratulate JJ on becoming the latest junior partner at Sawyer and Bennett."

Jake aims a wide smile at me, his teeth perfect and whiter than the paint on the damn walls. He drapes an arm around my shoulders and raises his glass. "To new beginnings."

"To new beginnings." The toast echoes through the room amongst clinking glasses. I tap my tumbler against Jake's before moving out of his reach. To make my father happy, I take a small sip, then I wait a couple of minutes until they're deep in conversation before setting the glass onto a table.

"We're putting on a celebratory dinner this Friday night. JJ has worked hard for this, so I hope you'll all attend." He trains his brown eyes on me, and I don't miss the flash of reproach in them. "That goes for you as well, Sadie. JJ should have your support."

With narrowed eyes, I glance at Jake, who is suddenly avoiding my gaze. Shit. I promised him I wouldn't air our dirty laundry in front of my father, but he obviously didn't feel the need to do the same. I can only imagine how he spun the story in his favor.

"Of course," I agree, hoping no one notices the slight tremble in my voice.

One by one, everyone in the room rises to leave, shaking Jake's hand on the way out. Once it's just my father, Jake, and me, the tension in the room is so thick you could slice it with a knife.

"You've done good, son," my dad tells Jake, slapping him on the back. It's not often that I let my father's disapproval get to me, but seeing the pride in his expression for Jake burrows under the scars of my youth.

My father will never forgive me for not going to law school.

"Thank you, sir," Jake says, his wide grin still plastered across his face.

"Sadie, don't be rude. Congratulate JJ. Now's not the time to allow hiccups in your relationship to impede on such an important accomplishment."

Jake pushes his hands into his pockets. He's still unable to return my stare.

"Congratulations," I say, my voice monotone. "I know this is what you've always wanted."

"Thank you. It is." He tilts his chin up then, and a rock of dread falls to the bottom of my gut. The smile is gone from his face—in its place is a formidable line of determination.

He hasn't given up on us yet.

"I need to speak with my father in private."

"Of course, Sadie." As Jake passes by, he leans down and brushes his lips across my cheek. "We'll talk later."

If I have my way, we won't, but I don't voice that intention. His confident, quiet steps carry him out of the office, and he closes the door with a small click.

"So Jake told you what happened, I take it?" I have no doubt he kept several details hidden, but I want to hear the tale he spun to my father.

"Sit down, Sadie." He gestures to one of the many chairs in his office.

I consider standing my ground, but one look at my father's rigid posture has me sinking into soft, malleable leather.

"JJ did come to me about this problem the two of you are having."

I raise a brow. "Is that what he's calling it? A problem?"

"I'm not going to defend his actions, but a man under the type of pressure JJ endures is bound to make mistakes."

Unbelievable.

"Now, sweetheart. The question is what do we need to do to fix this?" My father brushes his thick hair back. He's a handsome man, appearing younger than his fifty-two years, with dark hair sprinkled with the first signs of gray, and vibrant, sometimes vicious brown eyes. I certainly didn't get my looks from him.

Some say I'm a spitting image of my mother. I'd have to agree—right down to her inability to say no to my father. He's always run our household with an iron grip. And my mother and I have always fallen in line.

Not this time.

"It can't be fixed."

"Nonsense. Everything can be fixed."

Meaning he never fails to find a way to get what he wants. It's the lawyer in him. Being a defense attorney isn't just a job to my father. It's a passion. A calling. A way of life.

And if his only child won't follow in his footsteps, the least she can do is marry an attorney of his choosing. I can already see it coming, and my skin breaks out in a cold sweat at the realization.

"He's been fucking his assistant," I say, my tone flat and disinterested. Because I am. Jake was attractive for a hot minute, but the moment I watched another woman go down on him and failed to feel my heart crack told me everything I need to know. His betrayal hurt and angered me, but it didn't break me. "I caught Candy giving him a blow job in his office the night of his birthday."

"There's no need to use such obscene language, Sadie."

Oh, for fuck's sake.

I bite my lip since arguing with him never helps anyone.

"He's a good man, Sadie. He made a mistake, but he's owning up to it. He's willing to do whatever is necessary to make it up to you."

My jaw slackens. Jake actually told him the unvarnished truth, but my father is still defending him. I'm utterly stupefied as I rise from the chair, more hurt over my dad's reaction to Jake's betrayal than I am the actual betrayal.

"I should get back to work," I say, blinking to hold back the threat of tears.

"That's my girl," he says, a note of pride entering his

tone. "Don't forget. This Friday. JJ will pick you up at six sharp. It's a formal gathering, so use the credit card to buy something appropriate."

As I leave my father's office, I have trouble drawing a deep breath. Jake and Friday and appropriate formal wear —all of it tightens around my neck like a noose I can't escape.

ASHTON

Three days go by with no word from Corinne, and Sadie... well, I'm pretty sure she's avoiding me. I've texted her a couple of times, but she hasn't responded. I'd be lying if I said a small part of me isn't relieved. The thought of telling Sadie about the situation with Corinne is turning me into an irritable ass.

I don't want to believe Corinne is carrying my child.

I don't want to believe Sadie is avoiding me.

So I'm burying my head in the sand by throwing myself into work. My newfound appreciation for my job was doing the trick until Sadie shows up at my house Thursday night. She's wearing sweatpants, no makeup, and no way in hell do I miss the dejection lining her beautiful face.

"What's wrong?" I usher her inside and take her coat before hanging it up in the closet. I can never resist pulling at her layers; lately it means I end up with her naked in front of me.

Or on her knees at my feet.

"It's this dinner party at my parents' house tomorrow night."

"They're having a party?" There's mild surprise in my tone. I don't recall her mentioning a party—not one that would call for her looking this upset.

"It's a work thing."

Work...

Oh.

"Work, as in Jake's involved?"

She nods.

I try swallowing the bad taste in my mouth that speaking that bastard's name leaves behind, but it's impossible. Considering how my feelings for her are morphing onto the edge of serious, it makes sense that speaking of her scumbag ex is like poison on my tongue.

"Jake finally got his promotion. Of course, my father is putting on a celebration."

"I'm sure your parents will understand you passing on it." I fold my arms across my chest. "I can't believe your dad promoted him. After what the asshole did to you, I'm surprised he hasn't been fired yet." Especially knowing Joseph Sawyer the way I do. He's overprotective, overbearing, and over-ridiculous.

An uncomfortable glint passes through her jade eyes as she wrings her hands. "I didn't tell him what happened. But Jake did."

"And?"

"And my father says Jake will make it up to me."

I'm stunned speechless for a few moments. Then the implications of her words really sink in, and disbelief roils in my gut, anger right on the tail of it. "You aren't serious. Tell me he isn't taking that asshole's side?"

"Jake can do no wrong in his eyes."

The hurt shadowing her face is too much to bear. I clench my hands, fighting the urge to pull her into my arms. "You can't go to this dinner. Jake doesn't deserve your presence there after what he did."

"I can't *not* go."

"Why the hell not, Sawyer?"

"I...you wouldn't understand."

I refrain from gritting my teeth. Barely. "Try me."

"It's only one night. I'd rather go and get it over with than disappoint my dad. I just wish Jake would leave me the fuck alone."

"He's still bothering you?"

"He's got it in his head that I'm going to give him a second chance."

"Trust me, Sadie, I can correct him on that misconception. Just give me ten minutes with the prick."

"C'mon, Ash! I didn't come here so you could go all Tarzan on your chest. I just needed..."

Letting the tension ebb from my shoulders, I close the distance between us and tilt her chin up. "What is it?"

"I needed a friend."

It's a simple confession, and maybe that's why it hits the bullseye of my heart. People often overlook the small things in life, but it's the little things that keep you going.

Like Sadie coming to me because she needed someone. Not Mandy, but *me*.

That has to mean something.

"I'm always here for you. *Always*." I want to tell her she's so much more than a friend to me, but now isn't the time. The dread in my gut solidifies as my issues with Corrine come sneaking back in. Sadie and I are close to... something.

I can feel it heating up at the center of my being.

And Corinne could ruin everything. If she's really pregnant, I'll step up. There isn't another option, but I despise the idea that this might drop a huge roadblock between Sadie and me.

"I have to attend the dinner," she says, breaking into my tumultuous thoughts. "My dad is having Jake pick me up at six. But I think he's only going to use this dinner to insert himself back into my life."

"There's an easy solution to all of this. Tell your father you won't go."

With a sigh, she steps back, and I drop my hand, instantly missing the heat of her skin.

"Dad and Jake are close. Failing to show up won't change anything." She pauses, giving me a considering look. "That's why I need you to go with me...as my date."

I never knew a person could feel such anger and elation in the same breath. But that's what I am—outraged at her need to play charades in order to avoid conflict, and utterly excited at the prospect of being with her for a night, no pretenses or excuses.

If only her obstinate parents and ex weren't part of the picture.

"Yes to the date, but no to your parents uppity shindig."

She arches a brow. "Uppity shindig? You really don't like my parents, do you?"

"I can't say the dislike isn't mutual. But I'm serious. Let's do something else tomorrow night. Let me take you out on a real date." I shoot her a grin. "It's the least I can do, considering what a good job you've done at sucking me off."

Despite her eye-roll, her cheeks warm to a rosy hue. "Please, Ash. I know how you feel about my parents, but I need you for this."

"To hell with how I feel. The douchebag cheated on you with his fucking assistant. Your father should be on *your* side, Sadie. You need to stand up to him."

"I will," she says with a downcast stare. "As soon as things calm down, I'll talk to my father and make him understand."

I don't believe her for a second.

"Now just isn't a good time," she continues. "The partners from the firm are going to be there, and they expect to see me there too." Her mouth twists in disdain. "I don't want to walk in there with Jake. Please, Ashton. I need a buffer."

"Tell them *no*. It's not hard to do."

She darts her fingers through her red hair. "It is for me."

I advance on her by a couple of steps. "Do you always do what other people tell you to do?"

Her gorgeous green eyes widen at the challenge in my tone. "Not always."

Another step forward. Four more inches of space eaten

up by my invading body. I'm going to invade the fuck out of the bubble she hides inside. "Prove it. Tell *me* no."

She cocks her head, her perfectly arched brows narrowing in confusion. "No to what?"

"To kissing you." I close the last few inches of space between us and slide my hands along her cheeks. "I'm going to kiss you, Sadie, then I'm going to push you to your knees and make you do very, very dirty things to my cock."

Her pupils dilate. She swallows hard, struggling to speak the word I'm challenging her to say. "No" is on the tip of her tongue, but the way her chest rises and falls gives her true feelings away, not to mention the blatant want and need blazing in the depths of her eyes.

She wants me, and that gives me hope.

This no kissing, no-getting-too-intimate bullshit has to end. Putting rules up as a barrier won't save either of us from what we want, and it's as clear as her flawless, kiss-able skin that we want each other.

"I want to kiss you, Sadie."

"Why?"

My grin is a bit incredulous. "Have you really not figured it out yet?"

"Enlighten me."

"I'm fucking crazy about you."

Damn, there's that look again. She's the beautiful doe caught in the blinding path of my light. I brush my thumb across her lips, and my heartbeat accelerates. My jeans tighten to the point of pain.

"Let me kiss you," I whisper.

She won't say no. Her entire life revolves around

pleasing others, and I'm just enough of a bastard—just that pathetic and desperate—that I'll take advantage of it. I'll exploit the fuck out of it.

She blinks several times. "Okay."

I settle my hands on her shoulders and dip my head, hesitating as her warm breath drifts across my mouth.

And I know if I taste her lips, it won't be enough. I'll want her underneath me, her skin covered in sweat, her nails digging into my shoulders. My cock finding heaven between her legs.

"What if I want more than a kiss?"

Her tongue darts out to wet her lips. "I'm not sleeping with you."

Rejection has never hurt so much. Not because she won't let me into her bed, but it's the tone behind it. I'm not good enough to be her first. Not worthy enough.

Instead of kissing her, I graze a path to her ear. "Then I guess I'll have to settle for your sweet mouth wrapped around my cock. If I can't fuck you, at least I can shoot my load down your throat." My tone is harsh, cruel even. I'm frustrated and taking it out on Sadie, and some small part of me kicks myself for being such an ass, but she's getting under my skin like no other woman ever has.

It's driving me fucking insane.

Her shoulders become rigid underneath my hands. "Let me go," she says, her voice mangled by hurt.

"Unlike you, I have no problem saying no." I back her into the nearest wall and cage her petite body between my arms, refusing to let her escape. "After you swallow every drop I give you, I'm gonna watch you play with yourself, but this time..." I trail off, meeting the challenge in her fierce gaze. "This time I won't let you come. In fact, I'll make you edge until you *finally* learn how to put yourself first for a change."

Shoving against my chest, she gains a few inches of ground and glares at me. "No," she says, and that single word comes out with such conviction, I'm both frustrated and proud of her.

"What exactly are you saying no to?"

"All of it. We agreed to keep this..." She halts, her cute little nose wrinkling the way it always does when she's searching for the right word. "Whatever this is, we agreed to...to..."

"Spit it out, Sawyer." I know what she's getting at, but damn, I can't help but goad her when her face flushes like that.

"Things weren't supposed to get so complicated."

"Life's complicated. Especially when you're twenty-two and still allowing your parents to dictate your life." The asshole in me rises, demanding to take over. Demanding that I demand things from her. I shoot a hand out and curl my fingers around her tiny wrist. "I should punish you for that alone."

"Let me go."

"Who's calling the shots here, Sadie?" With a gentle tug, I pull her to the couch and make her drape over the arm.

"You seem to think you are," she bites out.

Gathering her wrists in one hand, I hold them at the

small of her back as I shove her sweatpants down her thighs.

"Are you challenging my authority?" I'm crossing a line here, but I can't stop myself.

If she were mine, this is exactly what I'd do, so I guess I'm staking my claim.

"Answer me. Are you challenging me?"

"Kind of hard to do that when you've got my arms trapped behind my back and my pants down, isn't it?"

Fucking hell, how I love that tone of hers.

"You're giving me a hard-on, Sawyer. When you stand up for yourself, it's a free invitation for my cock to stand up as well."

"Ugh! You're infuriating!"

"And you're so goddamn sexy it drives me insane." Taking a deep breath, I let my fingers drift over her bare ass, my palm twitching to make contact. Before I give in and spank her, I let her go.

I won't punish her. Not yet.

I'm still holding out hope that she'll stand up to Joseph Sawyer. What kind of father puts anyone above his own daughter? Especially a man who cheated on her. The whole situation is disgusting. If she doesn't give her father a piece of her mind, I might do it for her.

She stands, straightening her spine, and shoots me a defeated look as she pulls up her pants.

"I can't talk you into going with me, can I?"

"I'll go with you." I pause, drawing this out. "Under one condition."

She sighs. "I already told you—"

"I don't care what you said. Tomorrow night, you're going to tell your father to shove his expectations up his ass. It's way past time, Sadie."

"And what if I can't?" Her voice is high-pitched. Distressed. To me, I'm not asking much, but to Sadie, I'm asking everything. I'm asking her to stir the pot, to disrupt her tidy little life.

I'm asking her to upset her father, and that's something she avoids at all costs.

"If you don't do what I ask, then I'll punish you, and I'm not talking about an innocent spanking."

"Punish me how?"

"And ruin all the fun? I don't think so."

She grinds her molars, and I know she's fighting the urge to argue with me. And part of me wants her to. Part of me wants her to give me a reason to show her who she's dealing with. I'm getting harder just thinking of what it would be like to take away her control. To bend her to my will.

Her mouth drops open, then she clamps her lips shut and stomps to the coat closet. Sadie shoots me a glare as she yanks her jacket from the hanger. I can't help but watch her in amusement as she shoves her arms into the sleeves.

"Punish me however you like. I'm not making a scene tomorrow night." She slams the door, and in the wake of her tornado-like exit, I can't decide whether to be angry, or excited.

Tomorrow night, I'm going to put all of my cards on the table.

fifteen

SADIE

"Are you holding out on me?" Mandy meets my gaze through the reflection in the mirror. She's standing in the open doorway of my bedroom, her dark brows more severe than usual.

"What do you mean?" I ask as I add another coat of mascara.

"You're taking a lot of care in the makeup department." She shrugs. "I guess I find it strange you'd go to so much trouble for a guy who cheated on you." Leaning against the doorjamb, she crosses her arms. "Unless you've got a hot date to this thing at your parents' house you're not telling me about."

I hide my nervousness behind a small laugh. "I've got a real hot date," I say, infusing sarcasm into my tone. "I roped Ash into going with me. I thought he could help fend off Jake." Now, when Ashton shows up at the apartment I share with his sister, I have a valid reason for him picking me up.

Just play it cool, Sadie. She doesn't need to know just how hot of a date Ash really is.

Her shoulders sag. "Oh. You had me excited there for a second. I thought you were up to something interesting."

"Nope. Just a boring work-related dinner."

And the promise of Ashton's "punishment" hanging over my head because no way am I going to do what he wants me to do. Standing up to my dad is an inevitability —he's right about that—but tonight isn't the time, and a work function isn't the place.

I'm not the sort of girl who makes waves, especially at work events.

Especially at my parents' house.

As I twist my hair into a neat up-do, Mandy saunters into the room. "You should wear it down. You've got gorgeous hair. I'd kill for it."

I wrinkle my nose. "It's a wild mess."

"I should know better than to argue with you about your hair by now." She flings my closet open and begins rifling through my clothing. "By the way, Brett and I are going out next weekend with Shane. We think you should come along."

"Who?" I ask, distracted by the curls escaping around my face. After a few seconds of trying to get them to behave, I decide to leave them be.

"Brett's brother?" she says, her tone implying I should know who she's talking about.

Right. The guy she's trying to strong-arm me into dating.

"I don't know, Mandy."

"Why not? We'll call it a double. We haven't done that in forever." She pauses, brows scrunching in thought. "And I don't think we've ever gone out with two hot brothers. It's just one date, Sadie. You've gotta come with next weekend. Unless you have plans?"

Knowing Ashton, he'll keep me plenty busy. A memory flashes through my mind of how his cock filled my mouth as he gazed down at me, biceps bulging as he propped himself up in the shower. God, thinking about the way he took control and came down my throat makes me wet between the legs. I can't imagine going out with anyone right now—not while feeling this way about a guy I have no business having feelings for in the first place.

And maybe that's why I should do it.

"It'll be fun," she adds, sliding one...two...three hangers to the right. "And Brett's brother is hot and loaded."

"I don't care about money. You should know me better than that. Last thing I need is some bossy rich guy telling me what to do." I already have enough people dictating my life.

"He's not like that. Shane's very down to earth."

"I don't know. Let me think about it, but keep this between us, okay?"

"Jeez, you're a hard sell."

If she knew about Ashton, she'd get it, but confiding in her isn't an option right now. I rise from the stool in front of my makeshift vanity—a white oak desk with a mirror hanging on the wall above it—and watch Mandy raid my closet. "What are you doing in there?"

She casts an assessing look my way. "Finding a dress for you."

"I *am* wearing a dress." I tilt my head down to inspect the dark green number I'd chosen, with its wide spaghetti straps and sweetheart neckline. My father insisted I use his credit card to buy something "appropriate." So I spent a fortune on it to spite his demand that I attend this dinner. It's stylish, simple with a hint of sexy, but most of all, it's *safe*.

"Just because my brother is taking you to this thing doesn't mean you shouldn't look good. If you're going to paint on a killer face, you should dress to kill too. Hit Jake where it'll hurt the most." She fingers a plum-colored dress that drapes open in the back. It's slinky yet classy and barely reaches mid-thigh. "I think this will do the trick."

It's most definitely *not* safe.

Dad will have a fit if I show up in that. But more importantly, one glance at me in that dress, and Ash will lose his mind.

I'm not sure if that's a good thing or a bad thing.

"I can't wear that," I finally say, my voice thick with indecision. It was a Christmas gift from Mandy last year, but I haven't had the guts to wear it yet.

"Oh, yes you can. You can't let such a sexy dress go to waste." Decision made, she slides it from the hanger and stalks toward me. "C'mon, let's see it on you."

I gulp. My undergarments will be a dead giveaway that I'm out to impress. Mandy and I have never been shy about dressing around each other, so I pull the zipper down and let the material slide to a puddle around my feet.

Mandy whistles. "Are you sure you're not going on a hot date?"

My cheeks must be as bright as my hair. "Too much?"

I know it's too much for a work gathering, but I can't tell her I put on the black balconette bra and matching thong with her brother in mind. I feel my nipples harden in the see-through lace cups.

"Too much? No way, but you'll have to lose the bra if you're gonna wear this." She shoves the dress into my hands. Apparently, I don't have a choice. With a sigh, I drape the garment over the stool before removing my bra. As I shimmy into the dress, Mandy searches my closet for a pair of shoes.

"Wear these." She tosses a pair of black stilettos onto my bed. My feet aren't looking forward to those shoes for the next few hours, but it's a quarter to six, so I put them on anyway. I reach for my black clutch when someone rings the doorbell.

And that's when my heart starts pounding with equal amounts of apprehension and excitement.

Apprehension because I told Jake I wasn't going with him and I'm worried he'll show up anyway. And excitement...because it could be Ashton on our front step.

My spirit takes a nosedive as I realize that if it were Ashton, he'd probably just walk in. Mandy beats me to the door, and when she pulls it open, my heart skips a thousand beats.

Ashton is standing outside, wearing dark slacks and a gray button-up that makes his ice-blue eyes pop. He left the shirt untucked, and the cuffs rolled-up, displaying his rebellious side. His gaze warms my body from head to toe, but with Mandy as our audience, he wipes his appreciation from his face after a couple of seconds.

"Why did you ring the doorbell?" Mandy asks. "It wasn't locked."

His teasing eyes clash with mine. "A gentleman doesn't walk into his date's apartment without ringing the bell."

Mandy rolls her eyes, and I let out a relieved breath that she didn't catch on to the truth. As far as Ashton is concerned, this is definitely a date.

"We better get going," he says, holding a hand out to me. "Unless you want to stick around and find out if the douchebag is gonna show?"

"No," I say, sliding my hand into his. "Let's not and say we did."

"Works for me."

"You have her back by ten now," Mandy teases.

Ashton reaches out and ruffles her sleek dark hair. "Yes, Mom."

She waves us off, shouting after our retreating forms for us to drive safely.

Ash leads me to his car, his warm hand leaving a tantalizing impression on the small of my back, and as soon as Mandy disappears into the apartment, he pushes me against the passenger side door.

"You're asking for trouble in that dress." Cupping my chin in his hand, he steps closer until I'm trapped between his hard body and the car.

"It was Mandy's idea."

"Don't get me wrong, Sawyer. I like it." His gaze lowers

to the plunge of my neckline, and his eyes darken. "But you've been forewarned."

Desire clogs my throat, so I don't even try to speak. Slowly, he lets go of me, and I step out of the way so he can open the door. Ashton might have a reputation as a manwhore, but he's a gentleman when it comes to opening doors for women.

Always has been.

"Thank you," I murmur as I lower into the seat.

Seconds later, he slides in behind the wheel. "Really, Sadie. You're gorgeous. I could eat you up tonight."

I'm tempted to let him, which is just stupid.

"You look pretty good yourself."

What an understatement. As he pulls onto the road, I openly ogle him, from the sexy mussed-up state of his dark hair to the way his clothes hug his body. I can't help but flirt with the idea of leaning over the console and tearing at his zipper. I'm getting addicted to the sounds he makes in the back of his throat as he's shoving his cock down mine.

I love the power of knowing I can make him come undone. It's the most exhilarating feeling in the world.

"In the mood for more practice, Sawyer?" He darts a glance my way, and I don't miss the teasing curve of his mouth. The nighttime cloaks us in shadow, but it does nothing to dampen the sexual tension flowing between us.

If anything, the darkness only heightens it.

We're ten minutes from my parents' house when Ashton pulls onto the side of the highway. He cuts the engine, and the rain tapping out a melody on the wind-shield seems to match the pulse at my throat.

The throb between my thighs.

The internal alarms going off in my ears.

"What are we doing?" My voice is a breathless whisper, strangled by the urge to be close to him.

Instead of answering, he leans over the console. My eyes adjust to the lack of light, and his blue gaze comes into focus. Time suspends as he pulls my hair free of the careful up-do I decided on for the night. Holding my stare, he settles a palm on my thigh.

And I forget all about my wild, hard-to-tame hair, or the fact that we're parked on the side of the highway.

"Spread your legs. I need to touch you."

Jesus. He almost made me come from words alone. I part my thighs, allowing him to slip a hand underneath my dress. He dips his fingers beneath the scrap of panties providing the only barrier to his touch and slides his digits inside me. His mouth lingers inches away, lips slightly parted as he probes my pussy. Our breaths grow heavier with each second that passes.

"You're so goddamn beautiful."

A whimper cuts loose of my throat. Unashamed, I spread my thighs and arch into his touch, wanting...no *needing* to feel him deeper. Needing to be full of nothing but Ashton.

"You're making me hard, Sawyer."

I move my hips in a subtle motion and bite back a moan as he thrusts his fingers in and out of me. His gaze lowers to my mouth, and I lick my lips.

"You want my cock in your mouth, don't you?"

"Uh-huh…" I can't verbalize more than that, which is probably a good thing because I want so much more.

I want things I shouldn't want.

God, I want his cock inside me.

"I love watching you like this," he says, burying his fingers clear to the knuckle. His touch is driving me higher, and I'm a few caresses away from coming.

"So close," he says, a note of awe in his voice. He slows his pace to a maddening crawl, and I feel his fingers slip in and out of me in measured, wet strokes. He's making a mess of my panties.

"My cock wants in *here*…" He cuts off with a hard swallow. "You're so wet, Sadie. So tight. I want to fuck you more than I've ever wanted to fuck anyone."

"Ashton—"

"Don't bother arguing your reasons. Trust me, I'm well aware of them." He withdraws his fingers, and my traitorous mouth lets my protest be known.

"Take off your panties," he orders as he settles into the driver's seat again.

I reach under my dress and pull at my thong. Refusing him doesn't even cross my mind. In the darkness, I sense the weight of his stare as I work my panties down my thighs, past my trembling knees, and free of my stilettoed feet. I hand him the scrap of lace with jittery fingers.

And I stare at him in stunned silence as he brings the undergarment to his nose and inhales. Without another word, he shoves my panties into his pocket then turns the key in the ignition.

What the hell just happened?

Is he seriously going to walk into my parents' house carrying my panties in his pocket?

Jesus. That's exactly what he's going to do.

Fuck, I'm in trouble.

sixteen

ASHTON

Sadie's scent has taken over my sanity. It infuses my nose with a subtle vanilla and a hint of citrus. She smells good enough to eat, and I'm so inebriated that I'm not sure I should be driving. The rest of the short trip to her parents' place passes in a blur. I don't recall getting from A to B— from that spot on the side of the road, where the sensation of her sex clenching around my fingers dragged me into a frenzy of lust—to her parents' massive house on the outskirts of the city.

I'm downright dizzy from the scent of her arousal, and I've never wanted her more. Continuing this charade with Sadie is going to be nothing but pure, bittersweet torture.

Several luxury sedans are parked in the circular driveway of her parent's place, and I can't help but wonder if Jake swung by Sadie's apartment, thinking he could weasel back into her good graces, or if he actually listened when she told him she wasn't going to this dinner with him.

I know my presence is going to be a surprise because I'm certain she didn't tell her father she was bringing a date, let alone me.

He's going to shit bricks, and I'd be lying if the thought of watching him go red in the face as he tries to hold on to his precious control doesn't tempt my mouth into a devious grin.

There is no love lost between her father and me. Joseph Sawyer has always looked down his nose at Sadie's friends, and that's especially true of Mandy and me. I can handle his dislike, but his obvious disdain for my sister is another thing. Mandy is the sweetest, most kind-hearted person you'll ever meet. Sure, she can be a royal pain sometimes, but her gentle spirit puts my womanizing reputation to shame.

I can't even claim innocence. Lord knows I've had my fair share of women over the years. I eye Sadie from the corner of my eye. But this fiery redhead is changing everything, and she doesn't even know it.

No...she doesn't *want* to know it.

Killing the engine, I let a few moments of solitude pass before I swing the driver's side door open. Those stolen seconds of quiet will probably be the last for a while. This dinner has disaster written all over it.

If I have my way, it'll be far worse than I'm anticipating. I want to buy a front row seat to watch Sadie put an end to this bullshit, once and for all. She shouldn't accept the way Jake treated her just to appease her father, and she shouldn't give two fucks about Jake. But that's Sadie for you—too kind-hearted for her own good sometimes.

I pull her door open and offer her my hand. As she slides her palm into mine, her large, jade eyes look a little jaded. She's skeptical of how tonight is going to end, and I can't blame her. I meant every word when I said I'd punish her if she doesn't have a good heart-to-heart with her old man. She's not in high school anymore, and if she wants to continue to act like it, then I'm happy to punish her ass like the bratty, stubborn girl she is.

The bratty, stubborn, infuriatingly sexy girl I'm falling hard for.

Jesus, what am I getting myself into? If I thought I could go back to the way things used to be—to the time before she unzipped me and put her bewitching mouth on my cock—I would. I'd scroll through the hordes of women programmed into my phone and fuck this ridiculous fascination with Sadie Sawyer into oblivion.

The fact that I have no desire to do so says everything. Sadie has ruined me for all other women, and I haven't even fucked her yet.

I say *yet* because I'm optimistic.

And fucking determined.

As we approach the double wooden doors to the place where she grew up, she squeezes my hand. Maybe the move is subconscious. Either way, it's comforting to know that she needs me. After all, isn't that why she came to me to begin with?

She wants me here with her. Maybe part of her actually *wants* me to step up and defend her since she's incapable of doing it herself.

I'm expecting her to just open the door and walk in—

like Mandy and I do when we visit our parents, or each other, for that matter.

But Sadie rings the doorbell.

That doesn't just make me angry; it makes me sad. Suddenly, I want to whisk her away from here, want to save her from yet another episode of her father's disapproval, and her mother's acquiescence to Joseph Sawyer's "my word is law" type of attitude. The only good things Sadie got from her old man is his strength and intelligence.

Mrs. Sawyer answers the door with a gracious smile plastered on her face. She's impeccably dressed, as always, in a modest green suit that compliments her auburn hair. She draws her daughter into a hug, and Sadie's hand slips free of mine. But at least the embrace is one-hundred percent genuine. I like her mother a little more in that moment because I can tell she really cares about Sadie.

"Thanks for coming, sweetie." Mrs. Sawyer's green gaze turn to me. "Hello, Ashton. I didn't realize you were attending tonight."

Before Sadie can speak up and make excuses, I jump in. "I'm her date."

Mrs. Sawyer's brows wrinkle in confusion. "That's...a bit surprising." She returns her attention to her daughter. "Jake's been waiting for you. Your father is beside himself over this announcement." Her mother takes her hands in her own and squeezes. "We're so proud of you, Sadie."

"Okay...Mom, is there something I need to know?"

"Don't worry about a thing. You just enjoy this night."

Before I can reclaim Sadie's hand, if only to give her a lifeline of support, her mother whisks her into the hubbub of high-priced attorneys, overbearing parents, and one smug bastard ex-boyfriend who looks like he's still got the feathers of a helpless canary in his disgusting mouth.

This doesn't bode well.

No wonder Sadie pleaded with me to come with her.

I catch up to Hurricane Sawyer—as I'm starting to secretly call her mother—and grab Sadie's hand again. She came here with me, and she'll sure as hell leave here with me. Every person within these walls will get that through their thick heads.

Her mother introduces me as Sadie's *friend* to several people, and Joseph Sawyer stops short when he sees me. His gaze lowers to our joined hands, and something dark flashes in his eyes.

"Sweetheart, can I have a word with you in private?"

"Of course." Sadie lets go of my hand, and when our eyes connect, I issue her a challenge. She won't find a better time than now to set her father straight.

"I'll be right here waiting," I tell her.

I watch her follow her father through the small crowd of people cluttering the immaculate living room. Her mother offers me another one of her gracious smiles before going off to see to her guests. As soon as Joseph and Sadie disappear into his office and shut the door behind them, Jake comes to a stop at my side.

"Ashton, right?"

I give him a side glance. "That would be me."

"It's good to put a face to the name. I've heard plenty about you and your sister."

I bet he has, and he's so self-involved that he doesn't remember meeting me the first time a few weeks ago.

But I remember him.

"Did you hear about me from Joseph, or Sadie?" I look him up and down as I speak, taking in his slicked-back blond hair and perfect suit.

"Both, actually. It's obvious you and Amanda are important to Sadie." He shifts, hands going behind his back. Chest puffed out. "So that makes you important to me."

I raise a brow. "And why is that? She isn't your concern anymore, so you should have no vested interest in her friends."

"Sadie is very much my concern."

I want to stuff a dirty sock into his mouth to quiet that superior tone of his. Then I want to land a fist into his equally smug face. Fucking chump in a high-priced monkey suit. I can't for the life of me see what Sadie ever saw in this self-important prick.

"She broke up with you," I point out.

"That was a misunderstanding. We're working through it." He pauses a beat. "I want to make myself clear. You're just a friend. I'm the man her father approves of."

I can't fucking help it. A grin twitches at the corners of my mouth. "Let me make myself clear. You're just the asshole who cheated on her. I'm the guy she comes to for mind-blowing orgasms." I stuff my hands into my pockets and finger her panties. "She's quite insatiable, if I do say so myself." I imitate his smug expression and give a mental fist-pump when the superiority melts from his face. "Nice catching up with you, Jack," I say, purposefully using the wrong name. "I should probably mingle." I turn on my heel before he can reply.

If I were wearing a tie, I'd have it removed by now. This place is suffocating enough all on its own. Caterers move around, preparing for the elaborate meal in the dining room, and this portion of the evening must be happy hour, Joseph Sawyer style, since guests are situated in small groups, nursing cocktails and beers as they talk about their importance in the grand scheme of things.

Jesus. I want out of here.

And I want to drill Sadie about every aspect of her relationship with that asshole. How far *did* she go with him? Suddenly, I want to know every detail. The thought of him touching her paints my vision with nothing but red.

I'm jealous as hell, and that doesn't happen often.

A waiter passes by, and I grab a drink off the tray, unmindful of what it is I'm about to guzzle like a lifeline. But damn, a guy needs a drink to get through something like this. I settle against the wall in one corner of the room and down half the bubbly.

Definitely not my usual poison, but it'll do.

Jake has reinserted himself into the crowd as the center of attention. But he's not immune to me any more than I'm immune to him. Between sips of his drink, and gruff laughter interspersed with serious discussions of God-knows-what, he keeps shooting me death glares from across the room.

The hard lines on his pretty-boy face say it all.

I'm about as welcome here as the underbelly of this city.

A few minutes pass before Sadie returns on the heels of her father, and as she follows him like a sheep across the room to fucking "JJ," I don't miss the apologetic look she aims in my direction.

She didn't stand up to her father.

I don't have to ask to know it's true. The guilt is written all over her beautiful face, her porcelain skin marred by self-disappointment.

Her father picks up a flute of champagne from a passing tray. "Attention, everyone!"

The room falls silent, and in that moment, I understand Sadie a little better because Joe Sawyer's commanding presence is unshakable.

"I'd like to congratulate JJ on all the hard work he's put in at Sawyer and Bennett these past five years. He's the youngest to make junior partner in the firm's history, and we're all proud of him. To JJ," he says, raising his glass, and everyone else follows suit, their voices a collective echo of Joseph Sawyer's toast.

"Thank you, Joe. It's an honor to have learned from the best." The suck-up sidles up to Sadie and wraps an arm around her shoulders. "I have an announcement of my own to make. As most of you know, Sadie and I have been dating for the past couple of months, and though this might seem hasty, Joe has given me permission to ask for this extraordinary woman's hand in marriage."

People's lips move. Glasses clink together. I hear none of it, and I suspect Sadie doesn't either. She's too busy staring right at me with that look I hate so much, her body rigid at Jake's side.

There my girl is again, caught in the headlights.

Unable to stomach any more of this twisted game of elitist charades, I set my half-empty drink down and exit the room.

Because if I stay in there for another second, I'm going to lose my shit.

seventeen

SADIE

Jake's announcement winds around my throat like a boa constrictor. I sneak a glance at my father and feel like throwing up because he looks too damn thrilled. More like ecstatic. But what slices me to the soul is Ash.

I watch, frozen in this twilight zone of a reality, as he leaves the room with a look of disgust and anger tainting his handsome face. I want to call out to him. I want to tell my father and Jake they can shove this absurd marriage idea up where the sun don't shine. I want to do something.

I *need* to do something.

Instead, I do nothing.

My heart is beating too fast, threatening a panic attack. Voices swirl around me. More congratulations, followed by intrusive questions.

Have we set the wedding date yet?

Are we going to have a traditional church wedding, or something less extravagant?

Will the ceremony be intimate, or something more newsworthy?

The whole time, I refrain from arching incredulous brows. But on the inside I'm screaming *are you fucking kidding me?* I never even said yes. Fuck, he never even *asked*.

Unable to take any more, I break away from Jake, ignoring his protests and the disapproving eye of my father, and go after Ashton. I leave the din of voices behind and enter the hall to find him leaning against the wall, arms crossed and head down. I spare a glance behind me, but my father and Jake are both distracted by the praise and attention of the guests. So is my mom. She's got the hostess persona down to a science, and her face is glowing as people congratulate her on her daughter *snagging such a good catch*.

I might barf after all.

Drawing in a deep breath, I move toward Ashton. "Please don't be mad," I say, coming to a stop in front of him. "You know how my father is."

He lifts his head, and I'm taken aback by the fervor in his ice-blue eyes. "You just let them walk all over you, Sawyer. I don't understand it."

Cheeks flaming, I dip my head. "Bad habits die hard, I guess. But there's no way I'm getting engaged to Jake. It's not happening."

He points in the direction from which I just came. "Then go tell them that."

"Not now, Ash."

"When? On your way down the goddamn aisle?"

His caustic tone makes me flinch. "Of course not."

"Come here, Sadie." His heated gaze pins me to the spot, and my lungs work extra hard to pull air in. He raises a hand and crooks a finger. "Now." The undeniable command in his tone has my feet eating up the space between us. He takes me by the chin and whirls us until my back is against the wall.

"What are you doing?" My voice trembles too much in his presence lately and now is no exception.

"I'm debating."

"Should I be scared to ask about what?"

"Yeah, I think it's fair to say you should be scared." He reaches to the right of us and turns the doorknob to one of the guest bathrooms on the main floor. A small push later, and it swings open. "I'm going to make you come right here in your parents' fucking house, with your new *fiancé* just a few feet down the hall."

I clamp my lips shut. Arguing with him is futile, considering how his words just soaked my core. I press my thighs together to keep from dripping down my legs.

"Do you have any objections?" He lifts a brow, and I'm positive he can smell my arousal pooling at the apex of my sex.

"My only objection is that you took my panties."

His mouth tilts into a grin. "Are you worried you'll soil your parents' spotless floor?"

"Maybe," I say, breathless.

He dips his head, lips brushing my ear. "Beg me to take the ache away." His voice is a throaty caress, chock-full of seductive promise with a dangerous undercurrent of *dominance*.

I inch back and hold his gaze. "Please, Ash."

Hoisting me into his strong arms, he carries me into the dark bathroom. The door closes behind us, and I detect the unmistakable sound of the lock clicking into place.

Ash doesn't bother turning on a light. A streetlamp shines through the frosted window, providing just enough illumination to make our way to the counter. He lets me slide to my feet, and I sense his lips hovering close to mine, can hear his heavy breathing and feel the heat of it on my face.

"How far did you go with that jerk?"

"Not far."

"Not a good enough answer, Sawyer." His arms cage me in, and his chest brushes my hardened nipples. I can practically taste his lips.

"What do you want me to say? You already know we didn't sleep together."

"Did you go down on him?"

"Ashton, please."

"Tell me. Did you suck him off?"

"No! I mean I tried once, but I..."

"You what?"

"I couldn't do it." For fuck's sake. He should already know this by now, considering he agreed to teach me.

"Did he touch you?"

"Yes," I say, not liking his possessive tone.

"Where?" He brings his hands to my breasts and flicks his thumbs over my hard nipples. "Did he touch here?"

"Y-yes."

Slowly, he trails a hand down the front of my dress and grasps the hem. "Did he put his mouth on your pussy?"

"Uh-huh," I mumble as his hand disappears under my dress. He's rendering me incoherent.

His finger draws a shiver-inducing path up my wet slit. "Did you come?"

"No."

"I love that answer." The scruff along his jaw chafes my cheek, and more warmth floods my core. We're too damn close.

"Did he kiss you?"

"Yeah." The word glides off my lips, little more than a sigh.

"God, Sadie. *I* want to kiss you."

And that's when I know it's going to happen. Maybe not now in this bathroom, or even later after we leave. But eventually, we're going to cave.

I'm going to cave.

His mouth teases the corner of mine, and my vocal cords freeze. I want to tell him to stop, but all I manage is a choked moan. He veers to the sensitive spot below my ear, and sharp disappointment rips through me. I don't have time to dwell on it. Next thing I know, he's grabbing me by the ass and lifting me onto the counter. Something crashes to the floor and shatters, but I can't bring myself to care about my mother's perfectly staged home, or how inappropriate our behavior is.

Nothing matters but Ash shoving my thighs apart until I'm spread before him. "Kissing is against the rules, so I guess I'll have to taste you elsewhere." He drops to his knees, pushes my dress up, and drags his tongue straight down the center of my slick pussy.

"Ash!" I grip the counter, squirming against his mouth, my poor excuse of a dress gathering around my hips. His hands are hot on my skin, palms sliding up inner thigh, fingers digging into feverish flesh. Keeping me spread wide open for his hungry mouth.

Oh God.

This might not be the first time someone's gone down on me, but it is the first time I'm not too self-conscious to enjoy it. Everything around me fades, save for Ashton's dark head between my legs.

The wet heat of his lips lightly sucking.

The tip of his tongue stroking my clit.

The press of his fingers, demanding I submit to his mouth.

My head falls back, and a whimper escapes me. I'm as hot as the sun, blazing several million degrees past an inferno. Sweat tickles my brow. My nipples tighten. Limbs tremble and grow heavy. I can't hold the pose anymore. Ashton grabs my legs and hauls them over his shoulders, and I tilt back toward the wall.

I'm spread out before him, a buffet of sexual offerings.

He catches my gaze, and the glint in his arctic stare is brimming with power and ownership. In this moment, no matter the rules or emotional walls between us, I have no doubt that I am *his*.

"Try not to make too much noise," he says, mouth tilting in a cocky smile as he lowers his head to the apex of my sex again. Pumping his fingers between my legs, he flicks his tongue back and forth over my clit, launching me so high I can't breathe.

Moaning. *My* moaning.

It's all I hear.

And Ashton Levine is all I feel.

My head's swimming. Stars explode behind my eyelids. I'm a fissure, split down the middle from the force of his will. It's stronger than my fear. I've never been so vulnerable and exposed in my life.

So out of control.

So unashamed.

So fucking free.

Cries burst from my throat, and he smothers my mouth with a hand just as someone knocks on the door.

"Sadie?"

Jake. Dammit.

"Are you in there?"

Ash lets loose a displeased growl against my clit, and the vibration of his lips sends me over the edge. Even though Ashton's warm palm muffles my cries, I'm positive Jake can hear every uncontrolled moan.

For a few seconds, I don't care.

For a few liberating moments, I manage to cling to all the don't-give-a-fucks in the world. It's just me and Ashton and his talented tongue driving me insane between my thighs, working my body to perfection for what seems like forever.

Until the last wave of pleasure shoots me soaring

before sending me into a gliding free-fall toward ground zero.

To the tune of reality knocking on the door.

"You taste so fucking good." Ashton licks me clean before rising to his feet. He removes his hand from my mouth, and we're face-to-face once more. The nearness of him, the smell of myself on his lips, the rise and fall of his chest—all of it binds me to him, keeps me tethered to the ethereal plane of existence he sent me to.

A fist pounds on the bathroom door, and I slam back to reality, my mind hitting concrete. How are we going to get out of here without Jake knowing exactly what we were up to?

"Jesus Christ, Sadie. I can't wait to get my cock in your mouth again."

Obviously, Ashton isn't worried about the wolf pacing outside our stolen haven.

"We can't," I say.

"Not here, I know." His words heat my collarbone as he runs his lips over my skin. "I want you in my bed, taking your time with that sweet mouth of yours."

"Ashton?"

"Hmm?"

"How are we gonna get out of here?"

"Walk out the fucking door?"

Jake calls my name again, and now he's resorting to trying the handle.

"He'll know."

Ash veers back, and even in the dim light, the scowl on his face is unmistakable. "I don't give a fuck who's out there. You brought me here as your date, so who cares if your ex catches us fooling around?"

There's no way I'm going to make him understand. And maybe he's right because part of me doesn't understand this feeling of shame crawling over my skin either.

Five minutes ago, I had no shame.

But that's the problem with reality—it shines a spotlight on the things you don't want to see. Sticks needles in the things you don't want to feel. Croons a song in your ear about the things you don't want to hear.

And I don't want to witness the possessiveness in Ashton's eyes. Don't want to experience the shifting foundation of what we are. Don't want to listen to the truth in his words because it shouldn't matter who's on the other side of that door, attempting to intrude upon our stolen moments in my parents' bathroom.

Jake is the one who cheated, so why do I feel like the guilty party here?

"I just don't want him knowing," I finally say, for lack of an explanation that makes sense. "What I do isn't his business."

It's not my father's either.

"You're right about that." Ash pulls me off the counter, and I barely have time to straighten my dress before he hauls me to the door. I dig in my heels.

"No! Ashton, wait."

"I'm not hiding in the dark with you." With that, he unlocks the door and yanks it open.

Jake takes one look at us—our laced hands and the

flush that is undeniable on my cheeks—and his eyes go wide.

"Did you need something?" Ashton asks.

"Unbelievable." Jake darts his gaze between Ash and me. "Are you doing this to get back at me?"

The fact that he even thinks I'd do this because of him digs under my skin. "Not everything is about you." I pull on Ashton's hand, desperate to get away from the accusation in Jake's eyes.

As if *I* have anything to explain.

We return to the sitting room, as my mother refers to it, and find that guests have begun trickling through the open French doors leading into the formal dining room.

And I'm certain I have a sign on my forehead that reads *just got eaten out in the bathroom by hot, perverted friend.*

Jesus, my face is flushed. It feels like a hundred degrees in my parents' house. I let go of Ash's hand and make a beeline for two open spots at the other end of the table from where my father usually sits. My legs are shaking as I dip into the seat. I shoot a glance at Ashton as he slides in next to me, hating him in that moment for making me a nervous wreck during this dinner.

He leans down, lips lingering near my ear. "Just breathe. We'll be out of here soon." Under the table, he takes my hand and squeezes, and any trace of anger I harbored toward him vanishes.

This is the part of Ashton I love.

Love.

That word sticks in my mind like a fly to a glue trap, just buzzing there, trying to break free. My heart thuds to the bottom of my gut, and I know I won't be able to eat much—not with this disturbing, dawning realization that what's going on between Ash and me is growing into something bigger than I imagined.

Something terrifying.

Something out of my control.

"You look like you're about to be sick. Want me to get you out of here?"

Yes. More than anything. But the promise of my father's watchful eye isn't the reason my head is spinning. Ashton is, with his husky voice in my ear, his fingers locked with mine, and his woodsy scent infusing my senses.

His quiet ability to infiltrate my heart despite me trying to stop it.

"No, I'm okay," I say as Jake enters the dining room. His stare is thunderous as he takes a seat across from us.

With a sigh, Ash lets go of my hand. But he sets his shoulders in determination as if he's preparing for a war over a battlefield of gourmet food. And maybe he is, considering he and Jake are locked in a death stare of epic proportions.

My father makes his presence known at the head of the table, and the tension breaks. Jake turns his attention to my dad, his face washed free of the glower that lived there a second ago.

"I'd like to thank everyone for coming tonight," my father says. Servers make the rounds, handing out flutes of champagne. After everyone has their celebratory glass, my dad clears his voice.

"JJ came to Sawyer and Bennett five years ago green behind the ears." He pauses, letting out a gruff laugh. "What he lacked in experience, he made up for with his competitive drive to succeed. Law is in his blood, and we're fortunate to have him onboard. To JJ," my dad says, his voice thick with emotion as he raises his glass.

The toast echoes around the dinner table, but I can hardly speak. Something about my father's speech scraped at the scabbed-over scars on my heart.

He's never once been that proud of me.

Hurt burns behind my eyes, and I blink a few times to keep the tears at bay. No way in hell am I going to cry in front of these people. To mask my fragile emotional state, I take a long sip of the bubbly.

It's as bitter as I feel, and the fizz nearly chokes me.

Just like my father's speech did.

A hand lands on my thigh, and when I tilt my head toward Ashton, I find him studying me with those keen blue eyes of his. He doesn't say anything, but he doesn't have to. His support is there in the warm weight of his palm, the pinch of his lips, the tiny furrow in his brows. His gaze darts to my father for a second, and I swear, if looks could kill, my father would be on the floor right now, bleeding out from Ashton's sharp anger.

I cover his hand with my own, silently thanking him for being here for me. But the air shifts between us, and he inches his hand up my thigh, making my body tingle with heat. My fingers tighten around his, trapped in indecision.

Part of me wants to push him away. The other part wants to urge his touch higher. My legs part by an inch, my body making the decision for me. I don't resist when he drags the hem of my dress up.

Our gazes crash together in a fatal collision of longing. I'm lost, tumbling around and around in the ether regions of this endless loop of a moment.

Ashton draws his bottom lip between his teeth as he slips his hand between my thighs, the warm pads of his fingers stroking me. There's promise in that touch, threat in the heat of his eyes, power in his mere presence.

The unforgiving line of his jaw is a reminder of passion and punishment to come.

Jake's scowl catches my eye from across the table, and suddenly, I know I'd take Ash's punishment any day over the charade playing out in this dining room. I'll bare my ass for Ashton as long as he wants if this damn dinner will just end already.

eighteen

ASHTON

If Sadie's asshole ex glares at me one more time, we're going to have issues. Reserved conversation filters through the room, along with clinking silver on china. I fork in a bite of duck or lamb or whatever this shit is while I stroke Sadie out of her ever-loving mind.

Jake knows exactly what's going on under the table which is why he keeps giving me his eat-shit glare. It's not the barely contained rage on his face that bothers me. It's the possessiveness. The air surrounding him that says he's better than I am.

That expression tells me he thinks Sadie belongs to him.

I've got news for the bastard. Sadie is a goddamn person and doesn't belong to anyone, but if someone is staking a claim here, it's me.

Right now, my fingers are staking a damn memorable claim. I dip one into her wet center, making her grip the edge of the table. An audible gasp puffs off her lips, and I love the way her cheeks deepen in that sexy flush I can't get enough of.

Her knuckles are white, her body stiff with resistance, but her thighs...fuck, she's parting them for me by a couple more inches. I take advantage and finally slide all the way home into her drenched core. Hot damn, she's tight. Pure. I'm desperate to be the first man to push between her legs and steal her innocence.

And I'll treasure it forever.

"You should eat," I say, nodding toward her full plate. "You're gonna be busy later."

She lifts her gaze to mine, and I can't stop the tiny smile from taking hold of my mouth. Her eyes widen as the innuendo behind my words springs to the surface. Across the table, Jake sets his glass of water down with a heavy hand. I don't bother glancing his way; I already know he's glaring again.

"So, Sadie," the wife of some schmuck sitting next to Jake says, "do the two of you have a date in mind for the wedding?" The woman's words ice my veins, and I withdraw my fingers from Sadie's most intimate spot.

What a way to kill the mood.

Sadie stiffens beside me, and I catch the panicked look she darts in her father's direction, as if he can help her. Her trust in that man is misplaced; Joe Sawyer will probably drag her down the aisle, kicking and screaming, if she doesn't put a stop to this bullshit now.

Jake clears his throat. "We're still discussing the particulars, Mrs. Ferris." He settles his possessive gaze on Sadie.

"Though I must confess to hoping for a Christmas wedding."

"That is a fantastic idea, JJ," Joe speaks up from the head of the table.

All the while, Sadie is stone still at my side. Now she's gripping the table with both hands, and if I thought her knuckles were white before, that was nothing compared to now. Her chest is unmoving, and I'm sure she's holding her breath while she stares at her plate.

I swing my gaze between Jake and Sadie's father as they go on about rings and engagement galas, venues, and even locations for the honeymoon.

And I can't take it anymore.

Rising to my feet, I grab my glass of champagne and a spoon, then tap that fucker against the crystal. Everyone falls silent, all eyes on me.

"Forgive me for interrupting this charade, but how about we cut through the bullshit already?" Several people gasp, and Sadie's father...well, I'm sure I'm about to be tossed out on my ass.

It'll be worth it in the end because I can't let them do this to her.

"Sadie has no plans to marry this jerk," I say, pointing to Jake and his reddening face across the table. "Not only did he fail to ask *her* if she wanted to marry him, but he can't keep it in his pants. Just ask his assistant." Setting the glass and spoon onto the table, I step back. "C'mon, Sadie. Let's get out of here." I'm reaching for her hand when her father's booming voice halts me.

"How dare you ruin this night for JJ and my daughter."

He rises and jabs a finger toward the entrance of the dining room, and the front door beyond. "I want you out of my house!"

"Gladly," I say with a barely contained sneer. "But Sadie's coming with me."

She rises to her feet, but Joe's thunderous baritone freezes her to the spot. "Where do you think you're going, young lady? Your mother and I raised you better than this."

I'm waiting for her to tell him she's an adult, her own fucking person, and can make her own fucking decisions. But she doesn't do any of it. Instead, she apologizes.

"I think we should go. I'm sorry if I ruined dinner."

I want to throttle her. No, I want to spank the hell out of her ass. If anyone here should be sorry, it's her father and his favorite chump. Before I can speak up again, she's practically dragging me from the dining room, her desperate fingers curling around my arm.

Only the tears escaping the corners of her eyes keeps me quiet as I follow her outside into the bitter cold.

nineteen

SADIE

As I wipe the moisture from my eyes, the silence in the car is deafening. I know Ashton's angry at me, or at the very least, disappointed. I'm disappointed in myself too, but I'm more angry at him right now for causing a scene. It was unnecessary and far from appropriate.

He doesn't know my father the way that I do, and public displays like that are not the way to get through to him. Calm, logical discussions are the only way to gain any leeway with my father.

Ashton slows the car and makes a left turn, and I realize he's headed toward his house.

"I want to go home," I say.

He shakes his head like the stubborn, obstinate guy he is. "You're coming back to my place."

"I'm not in the mood for this, Ash."

"I don't care. What happened back there isn't going to ruin this night."

"Isn't Bryce home?" I'm grasping at straws, but I don't

have the energy for any more arguments tonight. First, my father laid into me in his study earlier about everything from my dress to my date. And now this.

"Nope. He's spending the weekend with his girlfriend, so we have the house to ourselves."

"I'm not in the mood for this. Just take me home."

"You got to come all over my tongue in that bathroom, sweetheart. Now it's my turn. Besides," he says, shooting me his patented smirk-like grin, "I think you're overdue for another cock-sucking lesson."

Ugh. If only my girly bits wouldn't get so damn excited when he talks like that.

We're silent for the next few minutes as he drives the rest of the way to his place. He pulls into the driveway and cuts the engine. We're both shivering and rubbing our hands together in search of warmth by the time he unlocks his door.

The living room is dark, and the hallway beyond even darker. He grabs my hand and pulls me toward his bedroom, turning up the heat on the way.

We enter his room, and he flips on a soft light before the door shuts all the way behind us. And he wastes no time in undressing me. Considering I'm only wearing the scrap of fabric masquerading as a dress, minus undergarments, it's pretty damn easy for him to get me naked.

"Get under the covers," he says, his fingers working the buttons on his shirt.

"W-why?"

"You're shivering still." He gestures toward the bed. "Don't worry. I'll behave." His edgy tone pricks my heart, but I ignore it as I crawl under the blankets. After he sheds his pants, he slides in beside me, arms reaching.

Fingers grasping, hands pulling, until I'm lying on top of his muscular body with his hard cock between us. I fall into the cold, turbulent sea of his eyes, my breaths shallow.

He raises a hand and thumbs the corner of my mouth. "You feel so fucking good on top of me like this."

"You feel good too." It's a simple truth; one I wish I hadn't confessed.

"I'd feel even better in your mouth."

I start to slide down his body, but he grabs my hair, halting my progress. "I want you to go slow this time. We've done fast and hard, and I've taken control. Now I want you to learn how to tease. Nothing will reduce a man to his knees like the need to blow his load." His gaze traps mine for a few seconds. "The longer you hold it off, the more power you have over him."

His words make my breath hitch. I envision having power over Ashton, and something about that thrills me too much.

"Okay," I whisper, gently yanking on my hair until it slips through his fingers like sand. "I'll go slow."

His hand settles on the back of my head in a guiding move. The covers fall below his washboard abs, and my gaze flicks up to meet his. As I inch my lips over the wet crown of his shaft, he shutters his eyes. I swirl my tongue around the slit, and he sucks in a breath.

And I stop to wait.

For my heartbeat to calm once more.

For him to let loose that breath.

It escapes between gritted teeth, and he gives a push to the back of my head. I soften my lips and slide my mouth down his shaft, and we settle into a lazy rhythm. Up, down, up—my tongue flicking over the slit of his crown before taking a languid journey toward the base. I return to the tip again and place a kiss there.

"God, Sadie. That's it. You've got me on the fucking edge."

The longer I spend teasing his cock, the more wound up he becomes.

The more desperate.

"Shit," he moans. "Your mouth is heaven."

From the corner of my eye, I watch him fist the sheets with his free hand.

"Take me deeper."

His other hand is still unmoving at the back of my head, a constant reminder that he can take control whenever he wants. But he doesn't. He's letting me set the pace. I continue to tease him, and a tremor starts off in his arms before traveling through his legs.

"You've got the teasing part down to the fucking letter."

I pull off his cock and take the sight of him in. *Really* take him in. The hair around his ears is damp from sweat, his mouth is a tight line of frustration, and his knuckles are white as he grips the sheet.

And his body. Jesus, he's shaking with the need to blow his load down my throat.

"Do you react to every woman like this, or is it...?"

Just me.

"Never mind." What a dangerous question. I don't know what I was thinking by asking it.

"Just you, Sawyer. Not that it hasn't been good in the past, but there's just something about you and me..."

He trails off, but I know exactly what he's getting at. We fit together.

But it's time to take the focus off of that idea. "Will other...I mean do you think I've learned enough to...to do this with other guys?"

The look he gives me is alarming. Narrowed brows, icy eyes. The next thing I know, he's flipped us, and I'm lying on my back, staring at the ceiling.

Ash straddles my chest and pins me to the mattress. "Grab the bars."

I hold on to them without protest. He's too on-edge to fling my attitude at him.

He leans forward and props himself up with one hand on top of the headboard. Fisting the base of his shaft, he pushes the head against my lips.

"Open your mouth." Despite the firm pressure of his cock, he gives the order in a soft tone. There's also determination behind it. He wants inside my mouth, and he wants inside now.

I part my lips, allowing him to thrust between them, and push my tongue against his tip to keep him from going too deep.

A low growl emanates from his pressed-together lips. "Let me in your throat, Sadie."

Squeezing the bars of the headboard, I try to edge my head back, but he only follows. And now I'm further trapped, stuck between a sexually worked-up man and a mattress that refuses to give. I'm not sure why I'm fighting him. Taking him deep is uncomfortable and a little scary, but it's also empowering. Maybe it's the position. The help-lessness.

And that's when I realize he wants me helpless. My talk of blowing other guys pissed him off.

"Now, Sawyer. If you don't open your throat, I'll cuff you to the bed and make you come so many times you'll lose count." He cocks a brow. "It might sound like fun, but trust me, it'll be more painful than anything."

My heart skips several beats, and a shiver goes down my spine. I can't decide if it's a good shiver or a bad one. Drawing in a calming breath through my nose, I relax my throat and flatten my tongue.

Ash doesn't hesitate. He squeezes his eyes shut, and his jaw is carved from granite as he thrusts with violent desperation until I'm gagging from the onslaught of his anger. The mattress is bouncing and squeaking under the force of his hips.

And I can do nothing but lie here and take it.

Part of me is ashamed to admit that I like him taking my mouth this way. He's stealing the control from me, and along with that, he's owning the chaos that goes on in my mind when I'm blowing him

There's no time for self-doubt to creep in. No time to wonder if I'm sucking him right since there *is* no right or wrong way when he's in control.

"Close your eyes," he rasps out. My lids flutter shut right as he lets loose a hoarse cry. He jerks out of my mouth, and I feel his warm release squirt onto my lips, hitting my nose, dripping onto my shuttered eyelids.

Wow. He just came on my face.

I'm still reeling from his actions when he thumbs his cum out of my eyes. Blinking several times, I finally settle my attention on him. The coldness in the hard lines of his face is still there. So is the ice in his eyes. He just blew his load all over my face to degrade me.

To punish me.

Intense hurt rises inside my chest, and I fight the burn of tears. I will not cry in front of him. I *won't*. And yet the tears fall anyway. I'm as helpless to stop them as I am from moving underneath his powerful body.

"Get off of me," I say, pushing against his massive chest with blind movements, unable to see clearly through the pain clouding my vision. He grabs my hands and slams them to the mattress on either side of my head.

"Why are you crying?"

"You just came all over my face!"

"That's not why you're crying." His tone softens. So does his grip on my hands. "What's wrong?"

"You did it out of anger."

"I didn't—" He cuts off, his expression stricken. "Fucking hell." He crawls off of me, and I count my way through endless seconds as I get myself under control. When I turn over to face him, I find him sitting on the edge of the bed, his back to me, shoulders hunched. His head in his hands.

"Ashton?" Fear strangles my voice because it's happening. We're ruining our friendship.

He takes in a deep breath then lets it out. "God, Sadie. I'm sorry." The remorse is so thick in his voice that I scramble across the mattress.

"It's okay," I say, kneeling behind him and snaking my arms around his shoulders. In response, he brings his hands to my forearms and holds on to me.

We're holding on to each other, in more ways than one.

"It's not okay. You weren't ready for that." He lets a heavy beat pass. "You didn't *deserve* that."

"I provoked you on purpose." Honesty is the only thing that's going to get us through this.

"Why would you do that?"

"Because I'm scared." The words are a blast to my ears, the echo tainting the room with a truth I don't want to admit.

"What are you scared of, Sawyer?"

"Everything, but mostly...getting too close to you."

Too *attached* is what I should have said.

His chest shakes with bitter laughter. "It's a little late for that. The thought of you with anyone else makes me jealous as fuck."

"Yeah, well maybe that's the problem. You're not supposed to get jealous, Ash. And I'm not supposed to feel so fucking scared. This was supposed to be...uncomplicated." Before I can form my next thought, he extricates himself from my arms. Turning around, he grabs my chin between his fingers.

"Let me *un*complicate shit for you. I'd rather fuck *you* than your pretty mouth." Slowly, he runs the pad of his thumb over my lower lip. "But I'll settle for it." He dips his thumb between my lips, and the salt of his skin infuses my tastebuds.

It's the taste of pure Ashton.

"You should know," he says, his voice lowering to a sexy husk, "that I'll settle for whatever you'll give me."

Stunned by his confession—even though I already knew the truth on some level—I pull back, and his hand falls to the mattress.

"I can't do this anymore. I'd rather have you as a friend than mess everything up because we can't control our hormones."

His eyes narrow, and I know I've said the wrong thing.

"If you believe this is a case of hormones, then you're deluding yourself more than I thought. We're not teenagers in high school. We've known each other too long to write this off as casual."

"You're right," I say with a gulp. "Which is why it's time for us to stop." Scooting off the bed, I search for my discarded clothing. I get as far as spotting the puddle of my dress when he pulls me back, his fingers gripping my chin again in that immovable hold of his.

"I owe you a punishment."

"You can't be serious. C'mon, Ash. You just said we're not in high school. I'm not some little girl that needs a spanking."

"Oh yes, you do need a spanking, but that's only the beginning."

"No, this is the end. You taught me how to blow a guy, so it's time to move on, just like we said we would."

His fingertips press into my jaw. It's not painful, but it

does drive home a point; Ashton is not someone you say no to.

"You've got a punishment coming, but if you still want to call it quits afterward, I can't stop you."

I should say no. This thing between us has gone too far. When tears and jealousy start creeping in, that's never a good sign, and I'd rather preserve our friendship than continue to play with fire, no matter how hard it'll be to walk away from him.

"When?"

Now he does let me go, seemingly mollified by the concession in my tone. "I'll text you."

"That's all you're gonna tell me?"

"Yep. Your curiosity will keep you from backing out. Am I right?"

He is absolutely right, but I'm not about to admit it.

twenty

SADIE

I've managed to avoid Ashton all weekend. But now Monday has arrived, and with it comes the inevitable; I can't avoid my father and Jake forever. I'm standing in my father's office, my sweaty hands clasped behind my back, feeling like I'm fifteen again.

"You are not to see Ashton anymore. Do you understand me?"

"You can't tell me how to live my life. I'm an adult." I've been an adult for nearly five years now. Maybe Ash is right. When am I going to grow a backbone and stand up to the indomitable Joseph Sawyer? Problem is I stood up to him the day I announced I wasn't continuing my education in law school, and I'm not sure I'll survive another confrontation like that.

But marrying Jake isn't an option either, and neither is giving up Ashton's friendship.

"Legally, you're an adult," my dad says, running a hand

through his hair, "but your judgement suggests otherwise. I'm only trying to protect you, Sadie. I don't want you around that Levine kid anymore."

"What do you have against him?"

"Where do I begin?" He rises from behind his monstrous desk and takes a casual stroll around his office, ticking off the reasons on his fingers. "He spent the majority of high school in detention, was arrested for possession, had an absent father, not to mention he's a college dropout." He stops in front of his giant bookcase full of law books, his mouth a severe, disapproving line.

"Well, you've obviously done your homework."

I don't tell him how Ash was arrested his sophomore year because he took the fall for Bryce's pot. Bryce already had a troubled past, and one more charge would have sent him away for a while. Instead, Ashton took community service and probation and helped his friend clean up his act.

I also don't point out that the absence of Ashton's father wasn't his fault, but it did cause him to act out in high school. As for dropping out of college...I'm kind of wishing I'd done the same at the moment. Or at the very least, I wish I'd explored what *I* wanted in college instead of following someone else's plan for me.

"I'm not heartless, Sadie. I see how Ashton has turned his life around for the better. That still doesn't mean he's good enough for you."

And that's when I realize he isn't going to back down, no matter what I say. "If you can't understand that Jake and

I aren't happening, then I might as well clear my shit out of here now."

He clenches his jaw, and I fear that look on his face—all hard lines, unforgiving angles, and a turbulence in his gaze that is all too familiar. "You know how I feel about such language."

"I'm sorry," I say, more out of habit than an actual sense of remorse.

"I did not fight tooth and nail to get you to where you are today just to watch you throw it away on some punk. He's not good enough for you, sweetheart. You need a man with ambition."

"Jake has ambition all right. He's very ambitious when it comes to screwing around with his assistant."

"That is enough!" He takes a deep, calming breath and glances at the watch on his left wrist. "I'm due in the conference room in five minutes. We'll discuss this later." He picks up a pile of folders and hands them to me on his way to the door of his office. "Going through these should keep you busy for a while. Highlight anything with a July date."

I grit my teeth as I take the files from him. It's grunt work—something an assistant would be asked to do. This is my father's way of punishing me.

Seems he isn't the only one with punishment on his mind. I'm mind-numbingly deep into the task when my cell vibrates on my desk. At first I ignore it, but I've read the same paragraph of this boring transcript about six times, so when my phone goes off again, I peek at the screen.

Ashton: We need to discuss your punishment.

Even as a flutter of...something goes off in my chest, I clench my jaw as I tap out a reply.

Me: I'm still angry at you.

Ashton: I thought we put that past us Friday night. What's going on?

Me: My dad is on the warpath. He's not happy about the stunt you pulled at dinner.

Ashton: Be angry at me all you want. What I said to your father is true.

Me: You didn't have to cause a scene.

Ashton: You weren't going to stand up for yourself, so I had to do it for you. If you think I was going to let that asshole put a claim on you, you're insane.

Me: I wasn't about to get engaged to Jake.

Ashton: You weren't about to express your outrage over your old man's underhanded tactics, either. Admit it, Sawyer.

Me: You had no right to interfere. It's my life.

Ashton: It's about time you started acting like it.

Someone clears their throat, and I tilt my chin up from my phone to find a man standing next to my desk. "Can I help you?" I ask.

"Sadie Sawyer?"

"Yes, that's me."

"Got a package for you." He sets a rectangular shaped box on my desk then holds out a screen for an electronic signature. After I scrawl a pathetic version of my name, I thank the delivery guy.

A good five minutes tick by before I find the courage to open the box. It's white with silver embroidery accents, and I'd bet money it's from Ash. I can feel it—especially since he stopped texting me the instant the delivery guy appeared at my desk, almost as if he knew.

Because he sent whatever is in this box.

I lift the lid, and one glance at the contents has me shoving it back on. Cheeks warming, I sneak a peek around the office, but it's just as empty as it was ten minutes ago when I gave in to boredom and started arguing with Ashton via text. Everyone's been holed up in the conference room for the last two hours.

It's just me, the temptation of Ashton's texts, and this damn box.

Me: What did you send me?

Ashton: Didn't you open it?

Me: For like two seconds. Jesus, Ash. You can't send that type of stuff to me at work!

Ashton: What's the matter? Would your father and JJ the Jerk find it in poor taste that I sent you crotchless panties?

My eyes go wide. All I'd seen was a pile of plum purple lingerie—very sexy and expensive-looking lingerie.

Me: What the hell, Ash?!

Ashton: I take it you didn't explore your gift. That's okay. You'll have plenty of time later at the hotel.

Me: What hotel?

Ashton: The one you're going to after work. The key to our room is at the bottom of the box. Room 381.

An anxious butterfly takes flight in my gut. There's something about a hotel room that inspires sex, and a large part of me wants to give Ash my virginity. The other, more logical part of me realizes he's already taken too much of my heart as it is. Every time I'm near him, he chips away at my resistance. Determined to stay strong, I fire off a reply, my thumbs flying over my phone's screen.

Me: I can't do this.

Ashton: Yes, you can.

Me: You know I'm not ready for this.

Ashton: Ready for what?

Me: Sex.

Ashton: Are you saying you might be ready for it eventually?

Me: Well yeah. I don't plan to stay a virgin forever.

Ashton: Let me rephrase that. Are you saying you might be ready for it eventually with ME?

Shit, he would have to ask the tough question.

Me: I can't answer that.

Ashton: I didn't think so. That's why I don't plan on fucking you, so you can chill out.

Me: But you're going to "punish" me.

I hope he can detect the sarcasm in that statement.

Ashton: Fuck yes. And you're going to enjoy every minute of it. Except for one thing.

Me: And what would that be?

Ashton: The part where I don't let you come.

That does sound torturous. So why am I tingling between my legs at the thought? I don't have time to think about it further. The door to the conference room opens, and my father and several of the partners start to trickle out.

I put my phone away and get back to work, determined to keep busy enough to edge out thoughts of Ashton in a hotel room, but there's no amount of willpower in the world that can keep me from wondering what he's going to do to me tonight.

twenty-one

SADIE

Ashton is a pervert, plain and simple. Sure, he's a gorgeous pervert with his endearing cocky smile, hard muscles I want to grope for hours, and the mischievous and sexy glint that lights his eyes when he's turned on.

He's still a pervert.

The lingerie ensemble I took out of the box and laid on the king-sized bed in the hotel suite is evidence enough. Plum colored lace shelf bra—the kind that will leave my nipples exposed—and matching crotchless panties. Not just crotchless, but this scrap of lace opens in the back as well, which tells me one thing.

Ashton's got plans for my ass.

A pair of black thigh-highs and garter belt complete the outfit.

I gaze around the large room, impressed with the suite despite my nerves. The side facing out is a wall of windows dressed in gauzy curtains that flow to the floor. I can imagine them billowing into the room if the windows were left open. A doorway leads into a bathroom that appears bigger than the kitchen in my apartment.

He went all out for this night, which makes me wonder what he's up to. Surely, he could have gotten this punishment thing over with at his house?

So why a hotel suite?

I'm equal amounts intrigued, scared, and excited. As I'm fingering the soft lace, my cell dings from inside my purse on the nightstand. I dig it out, and one glance at the screen kicks my heart into overdrive.

Ashton: Be ready in ten minutes. I want your sexy little body in that lingerie. Wait for me on your hands and knees on the bed. Face the headboard and don't move when I come in. Understand?

Is he serious?

Jesus, he is.

I shoot off a quick "yes" then grab the lingerie before hurrying into the bathroom. There's a jetted tub, and I'd love nothing more than to spend an hour in it, soaking in hot water and bubbles. It sounds like heaven.

But there's no time for wishful fantasies of relaxation. I freshen up quickly before dressing in Ashton's *slut*wear. Even if it is racy, leaving me too exposed and vulnerable, I can't help but admire my figure in the full-length mirror. With my hair cascading around my shoulders—because I know he likes it down—and my breasts spilling over the shelf of the deep purple bra, I've never felt sexier.

What the hell is Ashton doing to me?

Maybe the real question I should ask is what did I do to myself by getting into this situation to begin with? What did I think was going to happen when I crawled under that table and put my mouth on his cock?

Problem is, I wasn't thinking at all.

I was drunk, desperate, and drawn to Ashton. I've been drawn to him for years, but that night, after witnessing what went down in Jake's office, ignoring my attraction to Ashton Levine was impossible.

And though I'm standing in a hotel room, dressed like a slut and feeling like one, I can't regret my actions.

We're gonna be fine. Our friendship is too strong to let this come between us. We're just having some fucking fun, Sadie.

I return to the bed, eye the clock on the side table, and groan. My heart thuds to the bottom of my gut. I spent too much time in the bathroom, and now I've only got two minutes left. Heart pounding a furious tempo in my chest, I crawl onto the mattress and face the headboard, just like he instructed.

Instinctively, I spread my knees and arch my spine until my ass is elevated. I know it's what he wants.

Me, vulnerable.

My pose submissive and exposed.

Air drifts between my legs, reminding me that there's no material covering my pussy and the slit of my ass. My nipples tighten into two hard buds. Jesus, I'm turned on. My breaths come fast and thready, then stall altogether as I hear a card slide into the lock, followed by the beep that signals Ashton's entry into the suite.

"Damn, Sawyer, you're a sight."

I'm tempted to turn my head and look at him, but I don't. *Not* because he told me not to, but I can't muster the courage to meet his eyes while I'm on my hands and knees, dressed like this. His quiet steps bring him closer, and I sense him hovering behind me at the end of the mattress. I can't be sure what he's up to, but it sounds like he's unpacking something.

"What are you doing?"

"Setting up."

"Setting up what?"

"Wouldn't you like to know."

I bite back a growl, but my frustration vanishes when I detect the unmistakable sound of his zipper, followed by the slide of his jeans. He crawls onto the mattress behind me, over me, one hand propping him up while the other brings a black rubber thingamabob to my mouth. The thing is intimidating, especially when he teases my lips with the contraption.

"Open your mouth, Sadie."

"What is that?"

Shit. I know what it is, but I don't want it in my mouth.

"Open your mouth and find out."

I hesitate. He waits me out.

Because he knows me too well—knows how easily I buckle under his demands.

"Will you take it out if I want you to?"

"No."

"What if I take it out myself?"

"You won't be able to."

God, his low tone at my ear sends a gush of liquid desire straight to my sex. I want to press my thighs together, but I don't dare move from my position.

He smashes the gag against my lips, ending our argument, and adds firm pressure until I can't help but part my mouth. He shoves it in, and I feel him shift on his knees between my spread legs as he tightens the strap around my head.

A few seconds later, he wraps what I'm assuming is one of his ties around my eyes, and I'm thrust into blackness. Everything is escalating too fast. He shoves my upper body to the mattress, and I rest my cheek on the fluffy comforter as he pulls my arms behind me. Soft leather circles my wrists, and I realize too late that he's restraining my hands at my back.

"Mmmmfffh," is all I can say. I fight his hold, squirming and protesting in muffled indignation.

That's when he smacks my ass. *Hard.* His palm comes down four more times in rapid succession. "You're not getting out of this, Sawyer."

I don't know what it is about the command in his tone, but I stop fighting instantly. Maybe it's too close to the way my father has spoken to me for years.

Or maybe I just want Ash, and I'll do anything to have him.

"You're so damn beautiful. Seeing you exposed like this is turning me on like crazy."

Yep. Ashton Levine is a pervert. But I am too since I'm wet just from the gruff sound of his voice—from the heat of his knees between mine as the chilly air in the hotel room teases my most intimate places.

And I'm helpless.

Gagged and unable to ask questions or protest beyond a muffled whine.

The ability to touch taken by his cuffs.

My sight stolen by his tie.

The real kicker?

I'm sticking my ass in the air of my own free will, just waiting for him to punish it.

twenty-two

ASHTON

My heart is thrashing against my ribcage. I'm so jacked up on adrenaline, I feel like a lunatic. I crouch between her knees for a few seconds, trying to get myself under control. No one's ever affected me the way Sadie does.

And I'm all too aware of how this might be my last night with her—my last chance to obliterate her will, drive her insane, maybe even make her hate me awhile from the sensation overload I'm planning to unleash on her vulnerable body.

I'm going to destroy her just so I can put her back together again.

My dick is rock hard and longing for the glove of her body. The temptation to sink inside her is too much. I bite my lip until the metallic taste of blood hits my tongue. I might push boundaries, might demand her submission, but she's spread before me, gagged and bound because that's where she wants to be.

No matter how much I want to fuck her, I'd never destroy her trust like that.

Swiveling around, I sit at the end of the bed, then I carefully lie back until I'm gazing up at her sweet pussy. I grab her hips and haul her upright, directly above my mouth, and a muffled gasp escapes her.

"I'm gonna eat you out, and you're gonna be a good girl and not come." As I slide the tip of my tongue through her wetness, she sways forward and almost loses her balance. Steadying her with my hands at her hips, I prop her up, my biceps straining from the effort.

"Can you snap your fingers for me?"

She does.

"Good. When you get close that's how I want you to signal me. I'll stop to give you a short break. But if you come, Sadie..." I lower my voice, and a thrill travels down my spine before reaching the throbbing tip of my cock. "If you come, you'll regret it."

Hell, I have every intention of making her come.

She whines a protest—the first of many I plan to drag from her. I yank her down onto my mouth, and she settles her weight evenly onto her knees. I tilt her body until I'm able to feast on her at the right angle, with firm, constant licks of my tongue.

By the time I'm through, she'll be insane with the urge to orgasm.

This night is all about how far I can push her.

Confident she's steady above me, I move one hand between her legs and dip into her drenched core. Using her body's natural lubricant, I prepare her ass for my finger. As I push into her puckered hole, she goes rigid above me, her mewls high-pitched and erratic.

I'm glad I gagged her. I can only imagine the complaints we'd get from neighboring suites if I left her with the ability to vocalize her pain and pleasure.

She snaps her fingers, and I immediately withdraw my tongue from her pussy.

She snaps again. And again. And again.

And I laugh.

"My finger in your backdoor is staying. That alone won't get you off."

Her breathing quickens, and I think she's cursing at me despite the gag. I can't help but laugh again. I withdraw my finger only to shove it back in, and I love the way she jerks upon the invasion. But if I were really hurting her, she'd be scrambling off of me right now, regardless of her bound wrists. She's so goddamn easy to read. Her body is sinking toward my face again in tiny degrees, her greedy pussy aching for my mouth.

She'll tolerate the intrusion into her puckered hole because she wants more of my tongue. For someone as sexually inhibited as Sadie, she knows exactly how to bring me to my complete and utter demise.

Maybe she couldn't get past her self-consciousness with anyone else because none of them were me. That might sound arrogant, but I feel the same way about her. It's taken me a long time to come to terms with the fact that no other woman caught my attention for any length of time.

None of them were Sadie.

She might be the third leg of the tripod that includes my sister and me, but in all actuality, she's my other half. She's the one girl I can be myself with. The one girl who's burrowed so far under my skin, she's become part of me. I'm not sure when it happened—some pivotal moment in high school I can't pinpoint, but I know it exists.

Maybe it was the night I watched her go to prom with whatever the fuck his name was. As she went off with some jock I couldn't help but despise, arm in arm, all I remember is the jealousy that wrapped around my chest, squeezing until I couldn't breathe.

No wonder Corinne doesn't remember our time together in high school the same way I do. Now that I'm analyzing that night, I realize how all of my attention had been on the fiery redhead across the dance floor instead of on the date in my arms.

Shit, I can't even think of Corinne right now. She called right before I left for the hotel, and I know I can't ignore the pregnancy bomb she dropped on me forever, but for tonight, I need to.

Tonight is all about breaking past the last of Sadie's defenses, and I'll use any means necessary.

"Okay," I say, licking my lips. "Break's over. No coming."

I go after her clit with renewed fervor, tongue sliding between her folds until I find that bud of super sensitive nerves. As my mouth closes around her flesh, I lick her in quick, firm strokes. The wicked digit in her ass sinks a little deeper.

She's lost control of her hips, and she's doing everything in her power to grind on my face. I hold her up with one hand, keeping her from tipping forward as I lick and suck the hell out of her pussy. If she doesn't snap her fingers soon, she's going to come. She's too inexperienced to last much longer without a cooling reprieve.

Just when I think she's tipping over the edge, she snaps her fingers, halting the downward plummet she's craving.

I lift her off of me by a few inches, and my quick breaths drift over her flushed skin. Her thighs are quaking around my head. I slowly roam my gaze up her body, stalling on her pebbled nipples for a few seconds, and find her head tilted back.

Red hair draping her shoulders.

Chest rising and falling with too-rapid breaths.

Drool is escaping her gagged mouth, and the sight of her above me, tense and on the edge, shoots straight to the tip of my cock, making me drip pre-cum. I'm about to pull her back onto my face when I spot tears sliding out from underneath the blindfold.

"Sadie? Are you okay? Do you need to stop?"

A low moan breaks free of the gag, and she shakes her head. I'm not sure what she's trying to say, but her body clues me in. She lowers to my mouth again, encouraging me to devour her with my lips and tongue.

And I do.

We continue this method of sexual madness for an hour or more. I lick her until she snaps her fingers, and every time, she comes back for more.

The unbearable need to orgasm is going to win out—it always does.

And afterward...that's when the real fun begins.

twenty-three

I'm going to come. Ashton is a diabolical ass because he's setting me up to fail, and there's not an atom in my body that wants me to win his cruel game. As his tongue runs the length of my slit, and that damn finger in my ass wiggles, the pressure reaches an all-time high. I'm about to break my fingers from the strength it takes to snap them.

But I can't.

More like *won't*.

My body has taken over, and I'm grinding his face in wanton need. Unashamed, so far out of my mind that the room could be full of people, and I wouldn't care.

All that exists is his hot, talented mouth devouring between my thighs.

More tears drench the blindfold, and some slip free. I'm not crying out of sorrow or pain. I'm sobbing out of pure frustration. I'm not even worried about his *punishment* if I let go and dive into a free-fall.

I don't want to let him win.

It's already too late. My fingers refuse to snap one more time—just one more fucking time—and I come in long waves of ecstasy, my release flooding his greedy mouth. I lose all sense of reality, and any sliver of balance I was holding on to disintegrates. I'm swaying to the side, flopping like a boneless mass toward the mattress, when he grabs me.

He flips us, and I find myself sinking into the mattress on my back. He shoves my legs wide open and brings his mouth to my pussy once more.

And he licks up every last bit of me.

I don't care that I'm a sweaty mess, that my arms are on fire from having my hands restrained behind me. I can't form a coherent thought, let alone worry about my uncomfortable position.

I've never come like that before, on a whole new plane of existence—a level so high I think God himself would have to look up. I'm boneless and disoriented, as if high on drugs...or what I imagine being high would feel like.

He slides up my body and wipes the tears from my cheeks. His touch is so gentle and warm that it makes me want to cry for an entirely different reason.

"You okay?"

Still gagged, I can do no more than nod.

"You're crying." He takes my chin in his hand, his thumb caressing my jawline. "I'd take out the gag, but we're not done yet. As soon as we are, I'm going to hold you for as long as you need, and you can talk to me for as long as you want. Do you understand?"

Another nod. Another bout of tears. I'm not sure I can

muster the energy to speak anyway. I'm overwhelmed by the confusing emotions roaring through me.

He shifts, and I hear a loud buzzing sound come to life. "I promised punishment if you came. I always keep my promises, Sadie." He settles between my knees and presses a vibrator directly on my clit.

The thing is too powerful, making me jerk involuntarily. I bring my knees together.

Or I try.

He shoves them apart again. "Don't move. I don't care how hard it is for you to keep your legs spread. You're going to lie here and come as many times as I want you to." Putting action to words, he adds pressure to that wicked weapon he's using on my most tender, intimate spot, and another orgasm rips through me.

My body is shaking uncontrollably from sensation overload. Something deep, almost animalistic originates from my throat, and not even the gag can smother my howl of pain.

How can something so pleasurable be so painful at the same time? My legs are quaking violently, tensing in cramping agony, and I can't stop my knees from inching together. The thought of him bringing that vibrator to my clit again makes me bite down on the gag.

"Legs open, Sadie. I can tie your ankles to the bed posts if you need me to."

Shaking my head, I spread wide and wait for that horrid method of torture again.

He presses the sexual weapon to my pussy and amps up the vibrations. With a smothered scream, I arch my spine, upper body lifting off the bed. I hang there for a few seconds, suspended in purgatory between wanting to come and *not* wanting to come.

The pulse between my legs goes on for too many seconds—unbearable ticks of the clock that seem endless. Jesus, this is torture.

I want to howl and cry, unhindered by the gross rubber pressing down on my tongue. More than anything, I want to *see* him.

Is he watching me with that dark, lustful look in his blue eyes? Is his cock hard and dripping? I hate that he can see every part of me, feel every part of me, and I can do nothing but take it, sight, touch, and voice taken.

I flop back to the bed. Digging the heels of my feet into the mattress, I scoot up by a couple of inches. The maneuver gets me nowhere. Ashton follows with that vibrator, increasing the pressure on my overworked clit, and draws out another reluctant orgasm.

He does this over and over again until I'm drenched in sweat and rolling my head back and forth. Until my legs are so weak I can't hold them up anymore. They drape open like limp noodles. My heart is thumping so hard, I'm worried I might black out.

"Last time, baby. I promise."

One more time might kill me, but I don't have the energy to fight him. He forces another orgasm, and my spine bows in a torturous arch. My feet cramp—toes curled in a mix of ecstasy and agony. God, it hurts. There's nothing merciful about the way he's playing my body, as if he's the puppeteer of my sex.

He's completely wrecked me. From this point forward, nothing we say or do will erase this night. How can it when he's systematically stripped me of all my layers? My defenses are in utter ruins, and I'm certain our friendship is irrevocably lost.

The word *friends* no longer exists between Ash and me. The only thing left is his sexual web of depravity, and the wings of my useless will caught in his trap.

I am his.

twenty-four

ASHTON

I've never seen Sadie look so beautiful. Some women are hot. Gorgeous. Attractive in a fuckable way. Sadie is that and so much more. Her vulnerability is addictive, and the way she trusts me despite the fear I know is creeping into her mind is disarming.

No one else has this kind of power over me. It's a foreign feeling, yet it's settling with a strong sense of rightness in my gut. If there's such a thing as soulmates, of two halves that make up a whole, then Sadie is my destiny.

Maybe I knew it all along.

Her breathing slows, and I can't take my eyes off of her, spread out the way she is, a sweaty mess with her legs draped open in sexual satiation. Her red hair is wild as usual, splayed around her head on the comforter. I could gawk at her all day like this, but the need to connect with her on another level is too strong.

I need to look into her sensual jade eyes more than anything. Leaning over her, I remove the tie from around

GEMMA JAMES

her head. Her eyes are glazed and red from the purge of
tears. I made her orgasm a total of eight times, and she's
beyond spent, an utter mess over it. Carefully, I lift her and
reach around to free her hands. Then I take out the gag
and pull her onto my lap. I ignore my throbbing erection
and concentrate on giving her what she needs after such
an intense session of pleasure and pain.

I reach for a tissue from the nightstand and wipe the
tears and drool from her skin, brush her wild hair back
from her face, and lock my gaze with hers. And I don't look
away until she comes back to me, if only by a few degrees.

"Come take a bath with me."

"A bath?" she asks, still dazed and high on endorphins.

I scoot to the edge of the mattress and carry her into
the bathroom before setting her on her feet next to the
counter. She waits there, letting the edge of the cool
granite support her as she watches me run the water.

While the tub fills, I lift her left wrist and inspect it for
redness from the cuffs before doing the same with the
right. Then I knead her shoulders, working out the sore-
ness from being restrained.

"Are you upset with me?"

"No." She blinks, appearing to come down a little
further. "I'm not upset, I'm..."

"Whatever it is, you can tell me."

"I'm...on overload. I've never felt...I mean..."

Taking her chin in a gentle grasp, I run a thumb across
her lips. "I know, baby."

That's the second time the endearment slipped out
tonight, but I can't bring myself to care. In this moment,

Sadie isn't my friend. She's not even my sister's friend. She's the girl I just shared an intense sexual experience with that transcended the physical.

She's the woman I'm head over heels in love with.

Lowering my gaze, I run the tip of my tongue across my bottom lip. I'm going to kiss her. She's knows it, and I know it. Just as we both know that nothing will ever be the same between us again. And maybe that's why I brought her here and sent her soaring to a place she's never been. To a place she probably didn't even know existed. I won't stop until she admits that she feels this too.

I lean forward and bring my lips closer to connecting with hers.

"The tub's full," she whispers.

The moment between us breaks, and I step back as sharp disappointment rushes through me. Her guard is fucking impenetrable, but if I have to blast through it with a tank, I'll do it. Taking her hand, I lead her to the spa's edge, and we step into hot, bubbly water. I shut off the faucet then sink into the water until it reaches my shoulders. Sadie settles between my knees and snuggles against me, her back pressed against my chest.

Beyond providing the necessary aftercare, I've never cuddled with someone like this before, have never wanted to until now. Sex has always been *just* sex, but with Sadie it's different, and I haven't even fucked her yet.

We'll get there eventually—I know it in the trenches of my soul. But when we do, it'll happen on a level that's worlds away from a simple lay. As my heart tumbles over its hasty beat, she inhales a long, deep breath then lets it out. Her body is heavy in my embrace, her limbs still weak from the intensity of what I put her through.

And my cock is fucking hard as hell, nestled against the small of her back. She shifts, and I bite my lip to keep from groaning.

"Ash...do you want me to...? I mean, I can...if you want."

A grin takes hold of my mouth. "Are you asking if I want you to get me off?" It's kind of cute how she stumbles over her words when it comes to anything relating to sex.

"Yeah."

"As tempting as that sounds, I just want you to relax. I can wait awhile longer." I cup water in my hands and release it over her tits. She's got beautiful breasts; pale with a hint of freckles in the valley between them. Exquisite roundness that call to my palms. I weigh them in my hands, thumbs sweeping across her nipples until her head lolls against my shoulder. Eyes drifting shut, her lips part on a sigh.

Impossibly, I get even harder.

"Sawyer," I say through gritted teeth.

"Hmm?"

"You realize everything has changed, right?"

Her breath seems to stall in her lungs as she flicks her gaze to my face. "Nothing has to change, Ash."

"Tell me something," I whisper, inching my mouth toward hers. "Tell me that despite the gazillion orgasms I forced on you, tell me you don't want me still."

Avoiding my eyes, she says, "I can't tell you that."

190

"Didn't think so." I push on her shoulders until she's sitting. "Get up."

As she makes it to her feet, legs visibly trembling, water pours down her skin in rivulets, following the sexy contour of her ass. "Do you want me to get out?"

"I want you to straddle my lap."

She glances at me from over her shoulder. Even from where I'm sitting, I spot the gooseflesh on her skin. She opens her mouth, and I know she's about to argue with me.

"I'm not asking, Sadie."

God, she gives in so fucking easy. Next thing I know, I've got her warm body in my arms, her knees straddling me.

Her pussy sliding over my throbbing dick.

Grabbing her by the nape, I hiss in a breath. Our eyes lock. I tug on her neck, bringing her closer, and the tips of her breasts smash against my chest.

"I have *no* words," I begin, swallowing hard, "to describe how watching you come undone made me feel tonight. I've never felt so connected to anyone before." We're breathing the same air, sharing the same choppy breaths. "I know you feel it too."

Her gaze falters, kicking my ire into gear.

"Don't you dare deny it, Sawyer." I watch, mesmerized, as she runs her tongue over her lower lip.

"I won't deny it."

"Then fucking kiss me."

twenty-five

SADIE

Jesus. The thought of a kiss has never seemed so dangerous. I'm transfixed by his mouth, and every nerve ending in my body is on fire.

"Don't make me beg," he says, his grip at my nape tugging me another inch closer. He brings his other hand to my face and sweeps a thumb across my lips. "My cock knows this mouth better than I do. I need to taste you. Fucking *kiss me*."

I exhale my nervousness across his lips, and the next instant, my mouth is on his. That first bit of contact sends a spark through me, trilling through my veins like a live wire. The kiss starts off as a hint of touch, a mere brush of yearning mouths. A prelude of what's to come.

"Ash," I breathe, equal amounts of scared and turned-on.

"Let me taste you," he murmurs.

It's almost too much, feeling him hard underneath me, cocooned by the warm, bubbling water as we approach the

192

forbidden precipice. I'm not sure how we ended up here, but I can't find a single reason to regret bringing my lips to his. Kissing him is as essential as the blood rushing in my veins.

The next few seconds pass in slow-mo. Our lids drift shut—his first, then mine—and only then do I tease the seam of his mouth with my tongue. That's when the spark bursts into an explosion. That's when he closes his fist around my heart. That's when the protective dam inside me splits wide open and lets him in.

His mouth opens under mine, and our tongues come together like desperate lovers. Before long I'm whimpering, moaning, unable to get enough of his kiss, of his taste, of the way he groans in the back of his throat.

As if he'll die if we stop kissing.

He winds an arm around me, ensnaring me inside the cage of his embrace, and moans into my mouth. And I surrender everything that I am, lose the last bits of myself with every sweep of his tongue against mine. I grip his hair as our mouths fight for power, tongues thrashing. Dueling. Mating.

Holding me by the waist, he controls the rhythm of my hips as I slide up and down his shaft, slick with the desire roaring through me. I can't control it any more than I can control how I feel about him.

As he inches back, he catches my lower lip between his teeth before breaking our kiss, and I watch in awe as he rests his head against the tub, his mouth a tight line that smothers a moan, his eyes squeezed shut as if he's in agony.

I've never wanted anyone so much, have never let pure instinct guide me as I do now. Pushing to my knees, I fit my entrance over the crown of his cock and begin to inch down his shaft. I've barely taken in the tip, but the pain is making me dizzy.

"Fucking hell, Sadie. Are you trying to tempt me to death?"

Biting my lip, I shake my head.

The pads of his fingers press into my skin as he holds me still. "God, don't move."

His words accomplish the opposite, and I push off his chest and launch myself out of the tub before I embarrass myself more. As I pull a towel off the rack and wrap the fluffy terry cotton around my shaking body, I sense the onset of tears. They're going to burn something fierce.

Just as his rejection is.

Water sloshes, and he steps out of the tub before winding his arms around me.

"Sadie, don't."

"Don't, what? Everything's fine."

"You're a shitty liar."

I close my eyes and slump against him. He knows me too well—better than my own family does. "I'm sorry. I don't know why I..."

"Why you tried to fuck me in the tub?"

I struggle to free myself from his embrace and turn to face him, tears be damned. "It was stupid. One minute we're kissing, and the next—"

We're kissing.

Just like that, his mouth shuts me up. He thrusts his

tongue inside, again and again until I'm dizzy and breathless. Then, as abruptly as it happened, it ends.

Ash cradles my face between his large hands. "I'm not rejecting you." He pauses, his bright eyes so full of passion that I lose my breath. "When I get inside of you for the first time, it'll be because you're ready." He leans down, an inch from my lips. "It'll happen because you can't stand the thought of it *not* happening."

He's not talking in *ifs*. His *when* is spoken in a tone of certainty.

I feel that same certainty sharpen inside my soul, and I know without a doubt that I want Ashton to be my first. "I want it to be you."

"It will be me, but we're not rushing this. I don't want any regrets between us."

"Me either."

He hesitates. "I don't want a one-time thing, Sadie."

"What are you saying?"

He slants an eyebrow. "I think you know what I'm saying."

"Spell it out for me, Ash."

"I want you."

"I'm giving you *me*. You're going to have a part of me that no one else will ever have."

"I'm not just talking about your body. I want *you*..." He places a hand over my rapid heartbeat. "I want your goddamn heart."

Ducking out of his arms, I seek escape in the bedroom, but he's right on my heels, tugging at my towel until it slides from my body. I turn and glare at him, hands covering my breasts.

His blue eyes are full of turbulence as he drops the towel he stole from me onto the floor with a deliberate motion I can't ignore. Unashamed, he stands in front of me, completely naked.

"Don't hide your tits from me. You've got nothing underneath those hands I haven't seen." He pauses, taking a step toward me. "Touched and tasted." Two more steps brings him within arm's reach. "Come to bed with me. We'll order room service and neck all night."

As I lower my hands, I can't help but laugh. "I thought you said we weren't in high school anymore."

"This is far from high school. This is a hotel room," he says, closing the distance until his chest is brushing my aching nipples. "With a huge, comfortable bed. We're not in the back of a car, and you can be certain I'll call you tomorrow. And the day after that..." Slowly, he lowers his face and brushes his lips against mine. "And every one after that."

Now that I've given in and gotten to know his lips, I can't seem to get enough. Grasping his wet hair, I reel him in the rest of the way and attack his mouth. The groan that rumbles from his throat is an addictive and vulnerable sound I'll never tire of dragging from him. Step by step, he backs me toward the bed, then he scoops me up, naked skin against naked skin, and falls with me onto the mattress. I wrap my legs around him as he blankets my body, his erection hot and heavy between my thighs, just begging for release inside me.

"I want you, Ash." The declaration escapes my mouth with a gasp, and I wish I could yank it back.

"You're testing my will here." He leans his forehead against mine, breaths a rapid succession of shudders against my well-kissed lips. "I'm not fucking you. I want so much more than that."

That scares the shit out of me. Ashton doesn't do relationships. "You're going to break my heart."

"The last thing I want to do is break your heart."

"You might not mean to, but I know you." I draw in a deep breath. "What if we made a huge mistake?"

"We are *not* a mistake."

The hurt in his expression is too much, so I shutter my eyes. "Ash...you're my friend."

"Uh-uh, look at me," he demands, prompting me to lock my gaze on his. "Do I look like a man who thinks of you as a friend?"

He looks like a man who wants to swallow me whole. This conversation is getting too heavy...or maybe I'm just not ready for it yet. I veer my attention to the clock on the nightstand. It's almost eight, and my stomach rumbles, reminding me I haven't eaten dinner. And it's the perfect distraction, the perfect interruption to cool this thing between us before it explodes.

"You mentioned room service."

He studies me for several seconds, gaze wandering over every inch of my face, then with a sigh, he pushes off the mattress. "Okay, Sawyer. We'll do things your way for now, but don't think this is going away." With a smirk, he glances at his erection, making it clear he's talking about more than just the issue of us.

Not that there is an *us*.

As he grabs his jeans off the floor, I go for my dress, but his words stop me. "Don't even think about it."

"I'm not going to sit here naked while they bring in room service."

"No one's seeing a thing. Now get back in bed and let me worry about dinner."

"Are you ordering dessert too?" I can't help a flirty grin from spreading across my face. I settle against the headboard and pull the sheet above my breasts, and he returns my grin.

"I think we both know what's for dessert, sweetheart." Blue eyes sparkling, he zips up his pants but leaves the button undone. He's still hard behind that zipper, and unashamed about it as he picks up the hotel phone to put in our dinner order.

twenty-six

ASHTON

Sadie's licking the honey sauce off her fingers from the wings we just gorged on, and I'm transfixed by the show. Before she sucks her ring finger into her mouth, I grab her hand and close my lips around the sticky, sweet digit. Her eyes darken, and I let her finger go with a pop.

"Tastes much better on you." I lean back on the bed and flaunt my erection, having stripped as soon as the door shut behind the guy who brought us dinner. Clothes aren't needed between Sadie and me.

Not tonight.

We stare at each other for several moments, but eventually she loses the battle of wills. Her attention lowers to my lap, and I watch her watch me, wondering if she'll take the initiative.

Fuck, I hope she does. I want her mouth on me more than anything, but I want her to take the lead this time. At the thought of her lips sliding down my shaft, my cock twitches.

Sadie licks her lips, and a second later, her eyes flick up to meet mine. "Is it painful?"

I bite back a smirk. She's so damn innocent in ways that continue to surprise me. "I'm not answering that. You either want to suck me off, or you don't. The choice is yours."

Her brows form perfect arches. "Thought you said you were calling the shots?"

Christ, I can't help but take that as a challenge. "I am, Sawyer, and the next move is *yours*."

Her bravado slips, and she lowers her gaze to her lap.

I tilt her chin up until she has no choice but to look at me. "What's wrong?"

"Nothing."

I study the wideness of her green eyes, the way she's looking at me without *really* looking at me, the way she's almost tugging on her lower lip with her teeth, and that's when I know she's spooked.

"You're scared to make the next move."

"I'm not scared."

"Prove it. If you want me, you're gonna have to come get me."

Our eyes lock as she reaches out a tentative hand and folds her fingers around me. I draw in a breath, let it out, then swallow a groan. Hell, I don't want to interrupt—not when her hand is gliding up and down my shaft. Every time she reaches the head, she drags her thumb over the slit, and I almost come from that alone.

"Jesus," I groan on her fourth trip to my throbbing crown. There's a new boldness in her expression that excites me too much, and she's got me too fucking close to embarrassing myself.

"You want my mouth on you?" Her voice is soft and coy, all traces of fear gone. Hearing that bit of confidence creep into her tone is more arousing than it should be.

"Hell yes, I want your mouth on me."

Every morning and every night for the rest of my life.

She holds my attention captive as she leans down and closes her lips around the head. The fraying thread of my will breaks, and I push my fingers into her hair, urging her mouth further down my shaft. I've lost control, and now I'm stealing hers.

"God, Sadie. I can't stop this. Gonna...fucking... *daaaamn*."

She holds my gaze as she deep-throats me, and my control snaps. A long moan strangles from my throat. Lids at half-mast, I take in the satisfied curve of her mouth as she drags the orgasm from me with triumph in her eyes. She licks my cock clear to the tip then settles next to me on the bed.

I crook my finger. "Uh-uh. Get your sexy little ass over here," I say before pulling her over my lap. I squeeze her left cheek. "You deserve a spanking."

"Why? What'd I do?"

"You made me blow my load before I was ready."

"That wasn't my fault!"

"Oh, it absolutely was." My hand leaves a firm, satisfying smack that echoes through the suite, but the best part is how she jumps.

"I think you enjoy a good spanking." I land another one, harder this time.

"Ow!"

As she wiggles atop my lap, my semi thinks about growing into a hard piston again. But her mouth isn't going to cut it because I want more.

I want everything.

Before I do something stupid, I push her off of me. And maybe my frustration is apparent, because she protests with hurt coloring her features, the sharp angles of her face an abstract masterpiece of rejection. To reassure her, I lean over and take her by the mouth, and Sadie melts against me, her tongue eager against mine as we tumble to the mattress. Her body blankets mine, surrounds me in her seductive heat, and we become a tangle of limbs, our hands roaming feverish skin, mouths fused together as she straddles my thighs, her tits smashing against my chest.

I'm dying to thrust inside her. The need is a beast clawing my gut.

Get a grip, asshole.

The mating of our mouths will have to be enough for now. The touch of hands, the sharpness of fingernails. She inches back, and her locks fall in a red curtain around my face. "Were you serious about necking all night?"

"If that's what you want." It might kill me, but I'll do it.

Tucking her bottom lip between her teeth, she searches my face. Her hair is wild and disheveled—just the way I like it—but her expression is pure seriousness.

"I want more, Ash."

My dick springs to life. So does my heart.

"What do you mean?"

"I want you."

"You're on top right now, sweetheart. I don't think I'm going anywhere."

"That's not what I mean." Closing her eyes, she sucks in a shaky breath. "I want to be with you."

I lift an unsteady hand and slide it along her cheek, scared to believe I'm reading her right. "You mean a relationship?"

"We can't go back. *Just friends* is long gone."

"Tell me something I don't know."

She's still gnawing on that lip, face pinched in fear, and I hate myself for making her so scared and uncertain about my intentions.

"You've got no reason to be afraid." Lifting my head, I press my forehead against hers. "Look at the affect you have on me. I'm fucking shaking." I run my thumb across her lips. "No one's ever made me feel the way you do, Sadie. I'm yours, all the way."

She blinks the sheen from her jade eyes, then she's laughing as she covers my mouth with hers. Relieved laughter. Happy-crazy-in-love-laughter.

I roll us until I'm on top, and the laughter dies, replaced by moaning. We infuse everything we feel into the sweep of our tongues. At some point, she breaks away, and even though she's pinned underneath me, the seriousness in her eyes gives me pause.

"If you break my heart, I'm gonna break your dick, Ash."

"Ouch," I say, faking a wince to hide the smile that

wants to take hold.

She socks me in the shoulder. "I mean it. Don't you dare break my fucking heart."

I surround her face with my hands. "I've wanted this for a long time."

Her mouth parts in surprise. "What about all the women?"

"None of them were you."

She blinks as if the passing seconds will make my declaration sink in. "Why didn't you tell me?"

"Why do you think?"

Understanding dawns on her face. "Promise me something."

"Anything."

"No matter what happens, promise we'll always be friends."

"I promise, Sawyer. You're stuck with me."

We seal that promise with a kiss that turns into an epic make-out session.

twenty-seven

SADIE

Ashton's embrace is the epitome of security, and I cling to it as doubt and fear of the what-ifs try sneaking past my happiness. I told him I wanted more. I told myself I'd try.

Now I'm scared shitless I made a mistake.

But God. How can I not bask in the sensation of skin on skin, or find solace in the serenity that only the stillness of night can bring? Eventually, we fall into a peaceful doze, wrapped together in the sheets in the aftermath of lust and liberty.

Then something jerks me awake.

I don't know what time it is, but the hotel suite is full of inviting shadows that whisper for me to lay my head back on his shoulder and let sleep claim me. But then I hear it again. Careful not to wake Ash, I sit up, blinking grit from my eyes, and search our surroundings for...something.

Something is making itself known, encroaching on my time in Ashton's arms.

It's a vibrating pulse that goes silent, and I realize it's a missed call. The sound goes off again, this time only once, and my attention lands on his cell on the nightstand. I grab it without thinking, and I'm about to tap him on the shoulder when I happen to glance at the screen. I do a double take since I recognize the name on the text notification pop-up.

Corinne.

The blonde he took to prom. The girl I spied hanging all over him last month at his house during his roommate's drunken birthday celebration. I tamp down the jealousy threatening to rise because Ashton has never hid his manwhoring ways.

But now those days are over. I've been his secret for a couple of weeks, except that's about to change, too. We're a *thing* now. He's mine, and I'm his, and soon, everyone will know it.

So why is this bone-jarring doubt plaguing me? With fear squeezing my heart, I don't question the wisdom of snooping through his phone. I get his passcode right on the first try. It's the same one he's had for the past year, and he's never felt the need to keep it a secret from me. Once I'm in, I pull up the message from Corrine, and my heart thuds to the bottom of my gut.

Corrine: I need you. I'm at the ER. Something's wrong with the baby.

I spring up in bed so fast the room spins around me. The abrupt movement wakes Ash, and he sits up too.

"What's wrong?" Voice thick with sleep, he settles a hand on my shoulder.

I turn to him, evidence of my snooping in my hand,

glowing in the dark. A dead giveaway, but I don't give a shit.

"It's Corinne," I say, barely hiding the tremor in my voice.

He flips on the lamp on his side of the bed, and his focus lands on the phone in my hand. When he flicks his gaze up to meet mine, I hate the guilt I spy there. Wordlessly, he takes the cell from me, and his mouth melts into a frown as he scans the message.

My vocal cords are frozen. I can't ask him what the hell is going on—all I can do is sit and watch while he calls Corinne.

Corinne...with a baby.

She answers, and I detect her panicked voice from where I'm sitting, naked next to Ash in the huge bed where we kissed and touched and admitted there's something real between us. Where I fell asleep in his arms not two hours ago believing we had a future.

I'm gulping down the pain and fighting tears as Ashton's soothing voice fills the room.

"Everything's gonna be okay. I'll be right there." He pauses, and her high-pitched voice comes through the cell again, though I can't make out what she's saying. "No, just stay put. It won't take me ten minutes, okay?"

She says something else, and he must have convinced her since he ends the call. Then his blue eyes are on me, dark and full of guilt but also a plea.

"Sadie," he chokes, reaching for me.

Before he can touch me, I scramble from the bed and search the floor for my clothes. "Just go."

"Goddamn it, Sadie. Don't you dare shut me out now."

"Go!" I shout, launching one of his shoes at him.

"Let me explain."

"You don't have time, remember?" I find his other shoe and toss it to his side of the bed. "Ten minutes, you said."

Raking a hand through his bedroom hair, he exhales a long breath. "Please don't leave like this. At least wait until I come back so we can talk about it."

"You should have talked to me about it earlier, before I had to find out by a stupid text." I find my dress and pull it over my head before wedging my feet into my heels. My face is wet with tears, and I wipe them away in anger before shooting him a glare. "How could you keep something like this from me?"

"I just found out." He finds his jeans on the floor and tugs them up his thighs.

"When?"

"About a week ago." He doesn't look at me as he admits it, and he can't deny he had plenty of time to tell me, especially considering where we've been headed. But he didn't say a word about it, and that makes me wonder what else he's been hiding.

"Are you fucking her?" The thought makes me ill, and I silently beg my heart to stay in one piece as I wait for an answer I probably don't want to hear.

"From the minute you put your mouth on me in that damn club, I haven't been with anyone." He pauses, and a tightness takes hold of his features. "I tried that night, but I couldn't do it, Sadie."

I don't know what to do with that, so I focus on pulling

myself together long enough to get the hell out of this hotel room, to get myself home without having a total meltdown. I grab my purse and head for the door.

"Have you ever known me to lie?" His tone is strained with desperation, and I'm scared to look at him because I'm worried he's on the verge of tears. I've never seen him cry, but I hear the shake in his voice now, the tightness of his words as if his vocal cords are trapped in molasses.

And I've never known him to lie—that much is true.

Settling my hand on the doorknob, I swallow past the lump of hurt forming in my throat. "I need some space, Ash. Just do what you need to do." I try to leave, but he's behind me before I get far, one palm against the door, his bare chest heating me through my dress. His presence cages me in, and I shiver, my resolve threatening to waver.

"Sawyer, don't go." He nuzzles my neck, and his breath is a hot caress on my skin, an unwanted reminder of what it's like to be close to him. "I'm afraid if you walk out that door, we'll never fix this."

My throat thickens at the thought. "What if it can't be fixed?"

"I refuse to accept that."

"Maybe it's a sign we're better off as friends," I say, shaking my head.

He doesn't speak at first, but when he does his words send my heart into an endless tumble.

"I'm in love with you."

And that's when I feel the crack. It's tiny, but it's there, threatening to bust me wide open. I risk a glance over my shoulder, and it takes everything in me to ignore the temptation of his lips only inches away. His ice-blue eyes are shrouded in fear, dark lashes blinking away the pain.

"That's not fair, Ash."

"It's the truth. Running away won't change it."

"Love won't change the fact that you have a baby mamma either." I feel him flinch, and when I move to open the door, he doesn't stop me. I rush into the hall and try blocking out his pleas for me to wait, but as I rush to the elevator, he's mere steps behind me.

"Sadie, don't leave like this. Please."

I jab the down arrow. "If you care about me at all, you'll let me go."

"That's like asking me not to breathe."

The doors slide open, and I escape into the safety of the elevator before turning to face him. Though he doesn't follow me inside, he's still stopping the doors from closing by sticking his bare foot out.

"You're wasting time. Corinne needs you."

The defeat on his face as he moves out of the way almost breaks me, but I grit my teeth to keep quiet. The doors come to a close and shield me from the pain of his expression. Adrenaline is coursing through me by the time I make it to the parking garage, and that's when everything hits me square in the chest. Tears cloud my vision as I unlock my car and slide behind the wheel.

I know Ashton has a past. The night I saw Corinne hanging all over him, I knew he was fucking her. And a few weeks before that, it was some tall brunette girl with a shy smile. The month before that, it was another blonde.

The amount of women he's been with goes way beyond

my fingers and toes. But to think that he got a girl pregnant and didn't tell me about it, even after I gave him my heart...

That's not something I can easily ignore. The guilt on his face when I uttered her name won't leave my mind either. He knew he was in the wrong by not telling me.

So why didn't he?

So fucking stupid, Sadie.

Maybe he would have explained if I'd given him a chance. But he'd been needed elsewhere, and I'd needed to get out of that hotel room so I could breathe again.

So I could push down the panic clawing my gut.

So why isn't it working?

Because this is Ashton, and whether I like it or not, I'm head over heels for him. As I drive down the empty road in the middle of the night, his declaration haunts me.

He loves me.

And I believe him.

But that doesn't change the fact that another woman is pregnant with his child, and I don't know what that means for us.

twenty-eight
ASHTON

I'm an asshole. I deserve Sadie's anger, but acknowledging that doesn't stop it from punching me in the gut. As I drive to the hospital, I'm plagued by the betrayal in her jade eyes as those elevator doors slid shut.

And I'm plagued by the harsh reality of Corinne's frantic words. She sounded so scared over the phone, and that made her situation...*our* situation real. And to think I avoided talking to her for a whole week after she told me the news.

Have I mentioned I'm an asshole?

Not even the rock music pouring through the speakers is drowning out the weight of the mess I got myself into. Fuck, I should have told Sadie. I should have done a lot of shit, like not taking the coward's way out by avoiding Corinne. As I pull into the parking lot of the emergency room and kill the engine, I don't know what I'm going to find beyond the front entrance.

There's only one way to find out, and it doesn't involve

being a coward. I make my way across the deserted parking lot and enter through the automatic sliding doors. Corinne is sitting in the waiting area. The instant she sees me, she spans the distance between us.

Her eyes are tired and red as if she's been crying. "Thanks for coming. My car broke down a while back, and my sister dropped me off, but she's on the graveyard shift, so I'm stuck without a ride home."

"Of course. I'm glad you called. Is the baby okay?"

And that's the moment her pregnancy really starts to set in.

She nods. "Can we just get out of here?"

I dart a glance at the receptionist. "Do they need my information? You shouldn't have to bear the financial responsibility on your own." It's probably too little too late, but I'm hoping late is better than never.

"It's been taken care of. They already discharged me."

"If you want them to send me the bill, I can—"

"Ashton, it's fine. Please, can we just go?"

I want to argue, but the ragged lines of her face are worrisome enough that I decide getting her home is the best course of action for now. We can argue semantics later. As we walk toward my car, she peeks at me from under her long lashes, and I get the feeling she wants to say something.

"Are you sure you're okay?" I ask.

"I'm fine. The baby's fine. The doctor says I just need to take it easy for a few days and avoid stress." She eyes me again. "Will you stay with me tonight? Just in case...I mean..." She lets out a quick breath.

"What is it, Corinne?"

"I'm scared I'll start bleeding again."

Her words jerk the ground from under my feet. Not only is she pregnant, but she might be in danger of losing the baby. I've always known I wanted kids. I just never imagined it happening like this.

But it *is* happening, and no matter the circumstances, there's a fundamental part of me that wants to give this baby the kind of father I never had.

One who sticks around for the long term—the kind of dad who puts his child before himself.

My world seems to spin around me as I unlock the passenger side door and help her into the seat. "I'll stay tonight, but you're gonna be fine, okay?"

"Thank you," she says with a dip of her head. Her blond hair falls forward, obscuring her face. "I almost forgot..." She pulls something from her purse. "They did an ultrasound."

I take the black and white paper with unsteady fingers and study the image under the car's dome light. The baby is tiny, little more than a tadpole-shape nestled in the middle of the photo.

"Wow," I murmur, unable to tear my gaze from the image. In the upper right-hand corner, today's date is listed, along with Corinne's last name. I'm holding the first tangible proof that I'm going to be a father.

And the thought terrifies me. I'll be responsible for another human life, a child whose heart is designed to love unconditionally. A child filled with innocence until the world teaches him or her differently.

"It's amazing, isn't it?" She gazes up at me, lashes fluttering. "We made that, Ashton."

I'm too choked up to say anything, so I hand her the ultrasound image and close her door before rounding the hood and sliding into the driver's seat. We spend the short trip to her apartment complex in silence. Every few seconds, I sense her watching me, but she doesn't say anything until we're out of the car and standing at her front door.

"You don't have to stay," she says, the note of hurt in her voice apparent over the jingling of keys. "I want your support, but I'm not going to force it."

"I'm here, Corinne."

She pushes the door open, and I follow her into the apartment.

"Are you?" Her purse and keys are dropped on a table near the entrance, then she faces me, hands on her hips. "Because it doesn't feel like you're here at all."

"I'm here, okay? I'm just...I'm still processing it all."

She lets out a breath of relief, but I can hardly get air into my lungs. What I don't tell her is how I'm not ready to be a father. Not even a little. But I don't want her to abort, either, and if I fail to do the right thing, or say the right thing, she might consider that option.

"I've just been so stressed." She grasps my hand between both of hers. "I haven't heard from you since I told you about the baby."

"I know," I say, shame taking root in my stomach. "I'm sorry I shut you out. It was a cowardly, dick move. I wasn't ready to face it, I guess."

"You're here now. That's all that matters."

I nod, my throat too thick with guilt to do much else. This is the last place I want to be right now, and Corinne isn't the woman I'm aching for. She's sure as hell not the woman I want carrying my child.

"You have no idea how comforting it is to have you here." She brushes her fingers up my forearm. "I've been so scared."

If my fear is consuming me like this, I can only imagine how she must feel. "Let's get you in bed. Doctors orders, right?"

"Right."

I usher her into the bedroom and fold down the bedding. She kicks off her sneakers, removes her jeans, and crawls in, but she grabs my hand before I'm able to pull away.

"Will you hold me?"

I stumble back, out of reach. "I can't."

"Why not?"

"I'll be here for the baby, and I'll help you with whatever you need, but I need you to know something."

Her eyes narrow, and gone is the scared, fragile lines of her face. "Don't say it, Ashton. I don't want to hear it. I can't take the stress."

And I can't foster delusions, no matter how much she might want me to. Even though I held proof of her pregnancy in my hands, there's still a small part of me that wonders if the baby is mine, especially when she looks at me the way she is now, with calculation in her gaze.

"I won't lie to you, Corinne. I'm seeing someone."

"You're always seeing someone. That isn't a newsflash." A tremor in her voice betrays her nonchalant attitude, and I'm positive she detected the truth in my words.

I reiterate them anyway. "It's serious this time."

She props herself up on her elbows and shoots a pointed glance at her flat belly. "So is this."

"I realize that."

"Who is she?"

"It doesn't matter."

"How the hell can you say it doesn't matter? Our child needs a father. Not a baby daddy."

With a sigh, I push on her shoulders until she's reclining in bed again. "Get some rest. We'll talk about this tomorrow."

She stares at me with her big, brown eyes threatening to spill over. "Are you leaving?"

"No, I'll sleep on the couch."

"I don't want to do this alone."

"You're not alone. I'll be in the next room." I know it's not what she meant, but before she can correct me, I escape into the dark shadows of her living room, and only then do I allow myself to breathe again.

So much for not taking the coward's way out.

twenty-nine

SADIE

I should have taken a sick day. That was the plan. Wake up in Ashton's arms, kiss his gorgeous lips some more, go grab breakfast, then spend the day together discovering the newness of *us*. Instead, I'm sitting in my father's office about to get another of his famous lectures.

The knot in my stomach tightens. Though I left Ashton at the hotel just last night, it feels longer. After I returned home, I tossed and turned for hours, unable to sleep as I was too busy imagining all kinds of scenarios.

Ashton and Corinne together, him touching her the way he touched me, telling her how gorgeous she is, whispering the same words he said to me. I'm green with jealousy, knowing that she has a connection to him that I don't have.

A tie that binds.

Something forever linking them together.

And then I feel guilty for thinking such thoughts because I don't even know if it's true. Her emergency could have ended in tragedy, and the sliver of relief at that idea only adds to my tab of guilt.

"You look tired, sweetheart," my father says.

I cross my legs and settle my hands in my lap. "I didn't sleep much last night."

The hard lines of his face soften—it's the closest to sympathy I'll ever see from my father. "I didn't sleep well either. I realize our conversation about JJ didn't go well yesterday, but I hope you've at least had some time to think things through."

"There's nothing to think through. My insomnia has nothing to do with you or Jake."

"I think it has everything to do with him." With a sigh, he shifts in his seat and steeples his fingers above the desk. "I know he hurt you."

"He didn't hurt me, Dad. He pissed me off."

"I think his mistake hurt you, and I think you're using Ashton to get back at him."

I have to bite back a snicker. He's so off base he's not even on the same playing field. "Ashton has nothing to do with Jake." I lean forward, entreating my father to understand where I'm coming from. "Jake did me a favor. I'd rather find out about his true colors now than later."

My father hardens his jaw. "There's no question he made a mistake."

"Then why are you pushing this?"

He rubs his trim beard. "Every marriage will face hardships. He's a good match with good connections. He'll provide for you."

I count to ten to keep from rolling my eyes. "This is the twenty-first century. I'm capable of taking care of myself."

"I know you are, sweetheart. But who else is going to step into my shoes here at the firm after I'm gone?"

And suddenly, I understand. As an only child—and a girl at that—I'm a massive disappointment to him, especially since I broke his heart by refusing to go to law school. He wants me to marry Jake so he can take over someday. It's all so clear now, and more disturbing than ever. My father cares more about his legacy than his own flesh and blood.

"You owe it to me to fix things with JJ. At least try, Sadie."

I grip the arms of the chair. "How can you put this on me?"

"Your mother and I gave you the best of everything. The best opportunities, the best education. I don't feel I'm asking too much in return."

I jump to my feet. "So let me get this straight. Because you were a good parent to me, financially, I *owe* it to you to marry a cheating bastard of your choosing?"

The instant his nostrils flare, I know I've pissed him off, but he remains unmoving behind his desk, the illusion of his calm facade firmly intact. "All I'm asking is that you give him another chance."

"I don't love him!"

"Is this about Ashton? Do you fancy yourself in love with him?"

"That's none of your goddamn business." I flinch at the anger in my tone.

He stands on the other side of the desk, red in the face. "You might not live under my roof anymore, but I'm still your father, not to mention your employer. I won't tolerate you speaking to me like that."

I don't think I've ever been so furious. The blood in my veins reaches the boiling point as it rushes through me. "I'm done with you meddling in my life." Too many beats pass, heavy with indecision, but eventually, I utter the worlds I've wanted to say for months.

For *years*.

"I quit." I'm not only talking about my job. I'm done being a slave to his demands. It doesn't matter how hard I try to please him—I'll never be good enough. Not unless I'm a lawyer following in his footsteps, or married to one.

"Don't be irresponsible. Quitting your job isn't necessary."

"No, it's absolutely necessary." I leave his office before he can argue further, my decision made. I make a beeline for my desk and clear out the few personal items in the drawers, stuffing them into my oversized purse. Anything else, I'll come back for later.

As I turn to leave, I catch the sight of my father standing in the doorway of his office. I can't pinpoint his expression—it's a cocktail of anger, hurt, and disappointment. My chest aches, the little girl in me silently crying over what will never be.

I know he loves me. I've never questioned that. But he's never been good at showing it. He's even worse at loosening his hold on other people's lives. He's strangely silent as I walk past him toward the elevator, and that stuns me since part of me expects him to use his *father* voice to halt me in my tracks.

To demand I fall in line.

My heart is thumping too fast in my chest when the doors of the elevator slide open, and I escape inside. A deep voice calls my name, and when I glance up, I find Jake hurrying toward me, his long legs covering the distance between us too quickly. I hold my breath until the doors slide shut, and only then do I exhale.

This is twice in the last twelve hours I've made a quick getaway in an elevator. The devastation on Ashton's face from the night before flashes through my mind, and my heart clenches. He's the one person I want to run to right now. But he's the last person I can go to about anything.

thirty

SADIE

A ruckus is coming from Mandy's bedroom. I stall in the front entrance, unsure of what I'm hearing, until a moan penetrates the thin walls, followed by the rhythmic banging of Mandy's headboard.

Jesus. It's barely lunchtime. Either she's skipping classes today, or she and her mystery man came back for a quickie. Either way, I kind of envy her right now. How freeing would it be to forget about everything and just lose myself in the moment?

That's a dangerous thought. I drop my purse onto the couch, take a seat beside it, and lower my head into my hands. My life is falling apart, and I could really use my best friend right now, but she's obviously a little busy.

Now that I've had some time to process what happened this morning, it's starting to hit me for real. I can't believe I quit my job, and even though I need to start the search for employment pronto, I can't bring myself to do it today.

My purse buzzes, and I almost don't pull out my cell

because it's probably Ashton. He's been calling and texting on and off since I left him at the hotel last night. With a sigh, I rub my palms down my face before reaching for the phone.

Ashton: Your silence is killing me.

I tell myself to put the phone away, to deal with this later or even another day, but my actions aren't in line with what my head tells me to do. I reply to his message and end the silent treatment for the first time since we parted ways at the hotel.

Me: Is Corinne okay?

I hope he doesn't take it as a snarky question. I really just want to know how she's doing. It's not her fault Ashton didn't tell me about her pregnancy.

Ashton: She's fine. So is the baby.

I pause, my thumbs hovering above the screen, but before I'm able to formulate a reply, he sends another message through.

Ashton: I was going to tell you.

Me: When?

Ashton: Soon. I wasn't trying to hide it from you. She told me, and I just freaked the fuck out. I hadn't even talked to her about it yet.

Maybe I'm feeling too beaten down and tired today, but I don't want to argue with him. I want to take his explanation at face value. At the core of my being, I want to believe him.

Ashton: Don't let this come between us.

Me: I'm not sure there IS an us.

Ashton: I know you don't believe that.

Hurt wells in my throat, and I swallow it down before shooting out another text.

Me: What does Corinne want from you?

Too many seconds go by, and that only makes my heart pound faster. I tap my foot while I wait for him to reply.

Ashton: It doesn't matter what she wants. The only woman I want is you.

His answer warms me from the inside out, but I know him. Ashton isn't the type of guy to shirk his responsibilities. He'll do right by his child, and I wouldn't expect him to do anything less, especially since his dad split on him and Mandy when they were in the fifth grade. That alone will ensure Ashton goes the extra mile for his child. But I'm afraid he'll realize he wants to do right by Corinne too, and I'm not sure what that says about me.

I'm not sure I care at this point.

I nibble my lip, tempted to throw caution to the wind and tell him to take me away from the mess I've created of my life. I can see myself on the back of his bike, my arms around his waist, holding on for all I'm worth as we zip down the highway. He'd make me forget for a while. *Love* me for a while...love me *forever*.

But I've already met my quota of rash decisions today, and sex isn't going to fix the issues between us. It won't fix my sudden unemployment status either.

Me: The timing is wrong, Ash. I know you don't want to admit it, but this changes things.

Ashton: We aren't just friends anymore. That changed too, or do I need to remind you how hard you came on my tongue last night?

Fuck, like I need *that* reminder. I'm cursing him for fighting dirty when the rapid thumping coming from Mandy's bedroom grows louder. She cries out, and I feel my face heat. Even worse, I can't ignore the tingling warm pressure between my thighs. Listening to her moments of ecstasy is only reminding me of the ones I shared with Ash last night. His messages blur before my eyes, but these are tears of frustration rather than hurt. I want to give in. Now that we've crossed all sorts of lines, I can't imagine not touching him.

I want the line of our friendship to stay crossed because the other side is damn cold without him.

But I can't. If I let my guard down, and he decides to be with the mother of his child, I'm not sure I could survive that kind of emotional wreckage. He's already stolen so much of me as it is—little pieces I'll never get back. Maybe he's been doing it all along, for years and years, only I wasn't paying attention. I thought by ignoring how I felt about him it would eventually go away, become obsolete, and his habit of parading women in front of me helped to shove my feelings for him onto the back burner.

So what made me think crawling under that table was a smart move? I was so fucking stupid. Deep down, I knew going in that this would happen, but I did it anyway. God, I wanted him then and I want him now.

Ashton: *You're thinking about it, aren't you?*

I hear his smug tone in my head. What does he expect? Of course I'm thinking about it. No woman with a pulse could forget riding Ashton Levine's face.

The banging stops on the other side of the wall, and a

squeak of the mattress, followed by footsteps, tells me this is definitely in the camp of a quickie. I send Ash one last text.

Me: I'm thinking about a lot of things, which is why I need some space.

If he replies, I don't read it. I drop my phone back into my bag, and that's when Mandy and her lunchtime special exit her bedroom.

"Sadie?" The draw of her brows betrays her concern, and I know my rough morning is written all over my face. When it comes to Mandy, my expression is usually an open book. It's a miracle she hasn't picked up on what's been going on between Ash and me.

"You're back early," she says. "Is everything okay?"

"I quit my job."

"Oh wow." Mandy glances at the blond guy at her side. "Best friend duty calls." Rising on her tiptoes, she kisses him. "Text me later?"

"Sure will." He kisses her cheek then greets me with a nod on his way out the door.

"That must be the new flavor of the month?" I ask.

"Yep." She crosses into the kitchen and pulls out a pint of rocky road ice cream from the freezer. "You look like you could use this." Settling next to me on the couch, two spoons in her hand, she grins. "I think I can too. Never a better time to splurge than after a horizontal workout."

I laugh. "Who needs a gym, right?"

She pulls the lid off the pint and spoons out a bite. "Exactly."

"You've been into this guy for a while," I say, scooping

up a spoonful of creamy chocolate goodness. "Is it serious this time?"

"Maybe." Her noncommittal shrug doesn't bode well for the guy. "He's good to me, and even better in bed." She points her spoon in my direction. "Enough about my sex life. What's going on with you?"

Shit, where do I start? You'd think we'd be more involved in each other's lives, but we've both been too busy lately to have real downtime—not since the night I got drunk and decided going down on her brother was a good idea.

"Well, I already told you how the dinner at my parents' house ended."

"Ugh. I can't believe your father tried cornering you into an engagement. That's low, even for him. Good thing Ash was there, huh?"

Warmth spreads across my cheeks. I pray to God she doesn't notice. "My dad's still pressuring me about Jake. That's why I quit today. I just couldn't take it anymore."

"You stuck it out way longer than I would have. You're practically a damn saint when it comes to your father."

"I think it's safe to say my sainthood is over."

We fall into a companionable silence for a while, taking turns spooning out ice cream, and I realize I've missed this. We used to be so close that we could tell what the other was thinking with just a glance.

But we're not kids anymore. We're grown ups with jobs and school and boyfriends.

And secrets.

"What's really bothering you?" Mandy asks, breaking

the silence. "You haven't been the same since the night you caught Jake cheating. Are you still hung up on him?"

"No."

"Then what is it? Something's wrong." Her tone is soft, a cajoling melody inviting me to confide in her.

"It's Ashton." Now that his name is out there, I can't pull it back. I'm not sure I want to. I force myself to meet her eyes. "You're going to think I've lost my damn mind, but I'm...in love with him."

She blinks, and the most shocking thing about her expression is the lack of surprise I find there.

"This isn't news to you, is it." It's not a question.

"Well, I'm surprised you're using the L word, but I've gotta say it's been obvious for a long time that there's something between you guys."

"How can you know that? *I* didn't even know until a couple of weeks ago."

She sets the ice cream on the end table and scoots to face me. "Remember on prom night when you were going to give it up to Wes Brantley?"

"Yeah," I say, wondering what this has to do with Ashton and me. I think back to that night. Wes was my date, and he'd gotten so pissed when I changed my mind about sleeping with him at the hotel. But Ash had gone to prom with Corinne, and I'm pretty sure he left with her at the end of the night.

"I can count on one hand the times I've seen my brother jealous over a girl." She shows me her pointer finger. "One time, Sadie, and it was the night you left with

Wes. I had to talk him down from going after you and ruining your night."

"Seriously?"

"Seriously."

I mull that over, recalling how he told me last night that he's had feelings for me for a long time. "I chickened out, so he wouldn't have ruined anything."

"I know that *now*, but at the time, I thought you were really into Wes." She brushes her dark bangs back from her eyes. "I told him to leave it alone, and he did." Forehead creasing, she pauses a beat. "Was I wrong to do that?"

I try to picture Ash and I getting together then. Would we have made it? My gut tells me we needed this time as friends—the years into adulthood when we bonded on a level deeper than the physical. Now that I know how combustible our chemistry is, I'm glad I waited before falling down that seductive rabbit hole with him.

I'm glad I waited for him, period.

"I don't think you were wrong."

"Are you having second thoughts? Is he being a jerk?" Her sharp blue eyes narrow. "Is he pulling his usual bullshit and giving you the 'it's not serious' spiel?" She pounds her right fist into her left palm. "Do I need to beat his ass?"

"No," I say with a laugh. "It's actually the opposite. He said he's in love with me."

Her dark brows creep up under her bangs. "Now that's surprising."

"Gee, thanks," I say, giving her a playful punch in the shoulder.

She laughs. "You know what I mean. I didn't even know Ash knew the definition of the L word."

"It's different with us. Things are...intense."

She leans closer, her gaze roaming my face. "Not that I want to hear about my brother's sex life, but...did ya...you know?"

"No, not...not yet."

"But you want to?"

I feel my cheeks flush with embarrassment. She's my best friend, but this is still so damn hard. "It feels right, like he's the one I've been waiting for."

"You love him, he loves you. What's stopping you then?"

I swallow past the thickness in my throat. It isn't my place to tell her this, but I have no one else to talk to about it. "He was fucking Corinne a few weeks ago."

"This *is* Ashton we're talking about. Is he still screwing around with her? Because then I *will* have to beat his ass."

"He said he's not involved with her anymore." I let several beats pass, and the silence seems to grow louder with each pump of blood to my heart. "But she's pregnant."

Mandy's jaw slackens. "Are you shitting me?"

"I wish. Things were starting to go in a different direction for us and then *bam*! He didn't even have the guts to tell me."

Her lips form a severe line. "How'd you find out?"

"She sent him a text last night after we fell asleep. I happened to see it."

"Was he planning to tell you?"

"He says he was going to." She stares at me for so long that I start to feel self-conscious. "What it is?" I ask.

"He should have told you. There's no question. But maybe you're using this to put up walls. You've done it for years. Intimacy scares you, and the fact it's with Ashton..."

She doesn't need to finish that train wreck of a thought. There's too much risk with Ash—not just his record with women, but the idea of ruining what we have. I've known it from the start. But that didn't stop me from taking the leap toward concrete over him. He could have knocked up a hundred girls, and I wouldn't love him any less.

"I don't know what to do."

"Give it some time. You guys have been dancing around each other for years. I don't think my brother is going anywhere."

thirty-one

ASHTON

"You've been in a shitty mood all day," Bryce says as he pops off the top of his second beer. I've barely put a dent in my first.

I gaze down at the bottle in my hands, not really wanting it but sipping it anyway. If I've been in a shitty mood, it's because it's been a shitty week. Corinne has turned into the clingiest woman I've ever met, and if she weren't pregnant with my kid, I would have put a stop to it before it started.

"What can I say? It's been a shit day."

Not even Corinne's incessant demands managed to get my mind off Sadie, and the longer she shuts me out, the more I want to barge into her apartment and *make* her fucking talk to me. But she asked for space, and I'm determined to give it to her, especially since my sister chewed me out the day after Sadie left me at the hotel. Mandy's pissed I hurt her best friend, and she claims Sadie just needs some time.

But staying away has never been so hard.

And facing fatherhood has never been so terrifying.

"You having issues with the ladies?" Bryce asks.

I can't help but laugh, but it comes out more of a snort.

"That bad, huh?" He takes another long draw from his beer.

"Corinne's pregnant."

His eyes go wide. "Holy shit. For real?"

"Yep." I take a sip of my own beer, but it tastes like piss. Or maybe I'm just not in the mood to muddy shit up with the haze of alcohol. I set the bottle aside.

"At the risk of sounding like an insensitive ass, are you sure it's yours?"

"She says it is."

"Man, that's a tough blow. Is she keeping it?"

"Yeah. It might sound insane, but I wouldn't want her to get an abortion anyway."

"Wow, so you guys are doing this."

"Having a child together? Yeah, but that's it. Corinne and I aren't..." I trail off, unable to say the words. The truth is just...harsh. If I were really manning up about this, I'd try to make it work. It's not as if I don't care about Corinne.

"Still scared shitless of commitment, huh?" He shakes his head before taking another drink. "You're going to be a bachelor until the day you die."

"I'm not scared of commitment. She's not the one, Bryce."

He arches a surprised brow. "I didn't know you believed in that stuff."

"Me either."

Not really. Not on a level beyond the subconscious. Until recently.

I'm about to spill about the mess I've gotten myself into with Sadie when a knock on the door derails my intentions. My heart leaps at the hope it's Sadie, even as it nosedives at the thought that she feels the need to knock. I cross the living room and fling open the door, and the scowling face of Joseph Sawyer stares back.

"We need to talk," he says, then without preamble, he turns around and walks toward the black SUV waiting at the curb.

"What the hell was that about?" Bryce asks from behind me.

"That would be about Sadie."

"Sadie Sawyer?"

"Yep. That's her father."

"What's he doing here? He looked ready to disembowel you, man."

"I'm sure he is." As I grab my coat by the door and pull it on, I eye Bryce. "Because Sadie *is* the one."

Bryce lets out a low whistle as I step onto the porch. "Good look out there."

The thing about Joseph Sawyer? One doesn't need luck to deal with him. One just has to have a strong ass backbone. He's never intimidated me, and that's probably why he hates my guts.

He's waiting by the vehicle, one hand on the open door to the backseat. A mist-like rain falls, but he seems impervious to it. "After you," he says, gesturing to the back of the running SUV, and I toy around with the idea that he's planning to kill me and dump my body somewhere.

I slide in, and Joe takes the seat next to me before shutting the door and closing us off from the chill of nightfall. The driver remains facing straight ahead as if we aren't in the backseat.

"What's this about?" I ask.

"Sadie was foolish enough to quit her job. But I'm sure you already know that."

She finally did it. Pride wells in my chest, and even though his statement is a shock to my system, I feign bored interest as I wait for him to get on with it. Joe clears his throat then pulls an envelope from the pocket of his jacket.

"My daughter is young and impressionable. A bit naïve, which I fear is my fault for trying to protect her from the harsh realities of life." Staring me down, he taps the envelope against his palm. "You're not a bad kid, Ashton. I know your family has faced many hardships, and that's why I'm here."

"I don't understand," I say with a tilt of my head, wishing he would stop speaking in riddles and just say what he came here to say.

"I want you out of Sadie's life."

"Well that's the benefit of being an adult. She can make her own decisions."

"I thought you might say that, which is why I came prepared, Mr. Levine."

"Mr. Levine is my father, and I assure you I'm nothing like him. Get to the fucking point, old man."

My shitty language burrows under his skin like I intended, and his face reddens.

"You, *Ashton*, are a distraction my daughter can no longer afford." He passes the envelope to me, and I take it as if it'll burn me. "You'll find my generosity more than agreeable."

Lifting the flap, I pull out a check with my name on it, and my heart stumbles at the amount of zeroes on the face of it. "What the hell is this?"

"It's enough to pay off your mother's debts and your sister's student loans."

The man is fucking shrewd as hell and knows how to aim where it'll hurt the most. Gritting my teeth, I glare at him. "I didn't ask for your goddamn money."

He merely shrugs. "Consider it payment for removing yourself from my daughter's life."

"You're a special kind of low."

He's unfazed by the insult. "Think about it, Ashton. She'll come to her senses soon enough, and where will that leave you, hmm?" He nods toward the check. "At least this way you get something out of it."

The rage boiling inside me is rampant, nearly impossible to contain. I'm seconds away from ripping the check to shreds and throwing the pieces in the bastard's face, but I have a better idea instead. Taking a deep breath, I slip the check back into the envelope and pocket it. As I reach for the door handle, Joseph grabs my arm.

"Do we have a deal?"

Shrugging his hand off, I turn a dark stare on him. "You'll know soon enough if we have a deal."

"I knew you were a smart kid," he says, and it's all I can do to leave the vehicle without blowing a gasket, especially upon noting his smug expression as I slam the door.

The bastard thinks I'm taking the money.

I put as much distance as possible between Sadie's father and myself before I lose my cool and drag him from the backseat of his overpriced SUV.

Focus, asshole. Take a chill pill.

Sadie needs to know what she's up against, and there's nothing more effective than seeing proof with your own eyes. It's going to hurt like fuck, but she needs to know the lengths her father is willing to go to in order to control her life. Taking cover on the porch from the light rain, I wait for the black vehicle to wheel away from the curb before I text Sadie.

Me: Are you home? I need to talk to you ASAP.

She doesn't answer right away, and I'm growing antsy. Finally, after six long minutes, she replies.

Sadie: You said you'd give me some space.

Me: This can't wait.

Sadie: I can't do this with you right now. I need some TIME.

With a low growl, I pocket my phone, fingers brushing the envelope in my pocket, and set off for Sadie's apartment whether she likes it or not.

thirty-two

My sister is working at the club, so I don't think twice about barging in on Sadie. She's in the kitchen nuking popcorn when she glances up. "What part of 'I need some time' do you not get, Ash?"

I'm distracted by the front door and the fact that it was unlocked while she's in here by herself, looking too damn sexy in PJ's. "I should spank your ass for leaving your door unlocked."

My threat does zero to ruffle her. With grating nonchalance, she pulls the door to the microwave open and removes the bag before carefully dumping the steaming contents into a bowl.

"We already went over this. I'm not 4-years-old."

My gaze falls to her flannel-clad ass. Jesus, her pajama pants are hugging her body to perfection, and my hands twitch with the need to pull her over my lap. She passes me on the way into the living room, ponytail swinging.

Before she gets far, I yank the black elastic band from her hair and pull it onto my wrist.

She rolls her eyes at me, but she doesn't tell me to get lost, so I consider that a win. Taking one corner of the couch, she tucks her legs under her then reaches for the remote control to the TV. "Hope you're in the mood for sappy romances because that's what I'm watching."

My blood simmers in my veins. Despite the walls she's trying to put up between us, she still doesn't have the heart to send me away, and I find that encouraging. "I'm in the mood for anything if it involves you."

As I settle on the other end of the couch, I spy the corner of her mouth creep up. Her father's check is burning a hole in my pocket, but I can't bring myself to tell her about it yet—not when I have her sitting mere feet away in soft flannel, her defenses coming down the way her hair did.

She pulls up the TV menu and begins scrolling through the movies available. "*Serendipity* or *Ever After*?"

"You choose."

Without a word, she selects *Ever After* and the opening scenes begin. As the older woman starts narrating the tale that every little girl fell in love with at some point during childhood, I watch Sadie. Her eyes are on the TV, but the way she fidgets every so often between bites of popcorn, twirling her hair or smoothing a hand down her thigh, tells me she's as aware of me as I am of her. I'd bet her father's check she's growing hot between the thighs.

It isn't until the prince and the heroine meet that Sadie breaks the silence. "You said you needed to talk to me."

She's back to twirling her hair, and now she's peeking at me from her peripheral. "Sounded important."

It is important, but I'm not ready to wreck this tenuous peace with her. If she'll let me sit next to her, watching her watch movies all night long, I'll be happy. "You were right. It can wait."

She lets out a frustrated sigh. "I'm not in the mood to play games."

"Neither am I. We'll talk about it later, I promise. Just let me enjoy looking at you for a while."

Her gaze is full of heat and longing, and I can barely keep from launching across the couch and touching her.

"You're not the type to look and not touch."

If that's not an invitation, I don't know what is. I slide across the sofa, take the bowl of popcorn from her lap and set it on the floor, then palm her cheek. She's soft and warm to the touch, and I've got wood just from the subtle scent of her skin. It's not overpowering like most perfumes. Instead, it draws me in to inhale her essence. Tempts me to taste her. I pull her onto my lap, gripping her by the waist as she straddles me, and the movie is forgotten as the heat between us ignites.

"I've been going crazy wanting you," I say, nuzzling the sensitive spot underneath her ear. Gently biting her flesh, I groan as the taste of her plays on my tongue. Her head lolls back, and I kiss my way down her throat.

"Ash...making out isn't going to fix things between us. Corinne will still be pregnant tomorrow."

"Who's Corinne?" I murmur, then I grasp her by the nape and pull her mouth down on mine. Her defenses bust wide open, and her fingers spear through my hair as she whimpers into the kiss. She's rubbing against my hard-on, rolling her hips in a steady rhythm that's shooting us both higher. I drop my face into the V of her tank and run my tongue over the swell of her tits.

"God, you taste good." I flick my thumbs over her nipples, loving how they harden and poke out beneath the soft material of her pajama top. Her breath hitches, and the next thing I know, she's scrambling off my lap. I think she's going into full retreat mode until she drops to her knees and surprises us both by unbuttoning my pants. Her gaze is pure fire as she slowly drags down my zipper. My erection springs free, and Sadie sweeps her tongue across her lower lip before drawing it between her teeth.

"You know exactly what you're doing to me," I accuse.

"What am I doing to you?" Her tone is all innocence, but the way she's gently raking her nails from the base of my shaft to the tip speaks of calculation.

"Now who's playing games?"

"I don't play games, Ash. Just like I don't lie or keep secrets."

"I never lied to you."

"You lied by omission."

"So you want payback, is that it?"

"Maybe," she hedges, her nails still teasing the fuck out of me.

"Then get your payback, Sawyer."

Our eyes lock, and I'm holding my breath as I wait for her to take me into her mouth, though I don't expect this to end well—not with the way her quiet anger is pulling at her lips. She leans forward, hair tickling my shaft, and lets several seconds pass while keeping me suspended in aching want. This is hell, waiting for her to make her move.

Finally, she does, and I expel a long moan as her hot, wet mouth slides over the tip. I clutch her by the hair, my world narrowed to the sexual beast inside me that aches to thrust deep, but she pulls off my cock and glares at me.

That harsh glance is a kick to the gut, a reminder that she's not doing this to pleasure me, or even herself. This is about the hurt I caused her. This is about taking back the control I stole from her, and considering how upset she was the other night at the hotel, how can I deny her this?

I can't, so I dig my fingers into the cushions and relinquish my power to her.

"I'm all yours." I practically breathe the words, my chest rising and falling fast from the desire she ignited in my veins. Keeping myself in check has never been so hard. I don't let girls get away with this shit, but Sadie isn't just a girl. She's my whole damn world, and if letting her torture me will bring her comfort, or give her some sort of satisfaction, I'll do it.

I'll walk the fuck out of here with blue balls if she'll forgive me for being such a dumbass.

She dips forward again and flicks her tongue over the head of my cock, making it twitch and jump. Her wild hair frames her face, partially obscuring her eyes, and I grip the couch harder to keep from winding those deep red locks around my fist. As if she read my mind, she removes the band from around my wrist and twists her hair into a messy bun.

"If you grab me again, I'll kick you out."

Christ.

My work is done. The woman on her knees is sassy and confident and secure in her skills at driving me out of my fucking mind. As she closes her lips around me again, I shutter my eyes and concentrate on staying still.

Impossible.

Especially with the way her tongue is working the underside of my cock. "God, baby," I groan, gripping the cushions for all I'm worth. I push against the floor, feet seeking better purchase for thrusting into her mouth, and the bowl of popcorn tips and spills across the carpet. "You're driving me crazy."

Shifting between my knees, she wraps her fingers around the base and bobs her mouth on the head, sucking it like a lollipop. Her little moans and whimpers vibrate pleasure straight to my balls. I feel them tighten, feel my cock pulsing in the glove of her mouth.

"Damn," I choke out. "Faster...don't stop...*fuck*."

Her eyes dart up to meet mine, and I swear her lips curve into a smile around my erection.

"You're gonna tease me out of my mind, aren't you?"

She pulls off my dick, but the firm strokes of her hand traps me under her spell. I arch my hips, thrusting my cock inside her fist, my body begging her to fuck me faster with it.

"Maybe." She increases the pace of her strokes.

"Mission accomplished," I groan through gritted teeth.

Now there's no mistaking the self-satisfied smile curving her mouth. "You taught me well."

Hell, that sexy-as-sin mouth has no right grinning at me. Those lips should be wrapped around my cock, sucking me off right now—not taunting me.

"Damn right, I did. I also taught you to finish what you start."

"What if I don't want to this time? Maybe it's your turn to be punished."

"Fucking hell." The back of my head hits the sofa, and I drown in the disappointment of my own making. "Do whatever you want with me, Sawyer."

She attacks with renewed fervor, and her slurping noises and my rapid breaths coalesce to drown out the movie. Impaling herself to the edge of my restraint, she takes me deep enough to trigger her gag relax, and I think *fuck yes!* She's going to show me some goddamn mercy.

Because I'm so close to blowing my load down her throat, secure in the belief that she doesn't have it in her to deny me. So fucking desperate for that sweet completion only her mouth can give me.

That's when my cell buzzes from my pocket.

Sadie halts, lips motionless around my cock, and waits for me to either ignore the call, or answer.

And that's when I resign myself to leaving her apartment with the worst case of blue balls known to man because I know who's interrupting this moment of pure heaven, and Corinne won't let me blow her off. She'll keep calling and texting until I give in and answer.

She's been doing it all damn week.

Why the fuck didn't I shut off my phone before coming here? I want to scream and gnash my teeth and wring Corinne's neck. Instead, I close my eyes and let out a frustrated sigh.

Sadie's mouth slips off my tip. "That must be one important phone call." The bitterness in her voice is unmistakable. She tucks me back into my jeans and jerks up the zipper. Despite the unwanted interruption, I'm still hard, my pissed-off cock straining against the seam of my pants.

"We are nowhere near being done here." I stand, pull out my phone, and set it to silent before shoving it back into my pocket.

"Is that her?"

My non-answer is answer enough.

Sadie frowns. "You should've told me she was pregnant. If you had, I wouldn't have—"

"Wouldn't have what?" I grip her by the shoulders. "You wouldn't have fallen for me? You wouldn't want me still? Is that what you're trying to say?"

She averts her eyes. "I don't know."

Letting go of her shoulders, I cradle her cheeks and close the last bit of distance between us. "Corinne happened before you. And I wasn't irresponsible, Sadie. I've always used a condom. *Always*."

"I never said you were irresponsible."

I tilt her chin until she meets my eyes. "I was going to tell you." My gaze lands on her mouth, and I brush my thumb across her bottom lip. "But you already know that. I think you're using Corinne to push me away." I pause, the weight of those few beats heavy and suffocating as I search her guarded expression for answers. "What are you so afraid of?"

"You," she whispers. "You said you were waiting for the right one." She pauses, guard lowering, and all the hurt and fear she's fighting fills her jade eyes. "What if Corinne is the right one for you?"

"She's not."

"You don't know that. She's going to have your baby, and you could fall head over heels for her."

"I could walk out of here and get struck by lightning too."

"I'm serious, Ash. She's going to be the mother of your child, and you walking out on your kid just isn't possible. It's not you."

I lower my hands and back away. "It doesn't matter what I say, does it? You don't trust me."

"I don't trust the circumstances."

A laugh of irony escapes me. "Your father should have saved his breath and his goddamn money. You're pushing me out of your life all on your own."

"What are you talking about?"

"Daddy Dearest's proposition," I say, fishing out the envelope and handing it to her. "This is why I came over tonight. He tried buying me out of your life."

She takes the envelope from me, and her fingers tremble as she pulls out the check. As she scans the face of it, no doubt taking note of the number of zeroes, her jaw slackens. "I can't believe he did this."

I want to say I'm surprised by Joseph Sawyer's actions,

but when it comes to Sadie, I've learned there's nothing he won't do to get his way.

"What did you say to him?" she asks.

"I wanted to tell him to shove it, but I'd rather you do it. He won't stop this bullshit unless you put your foot down once and for all."

A tear hinges on her lashes then slips free. "I'm sorry about this. He went way too far."

"Don't apologize for your father's actions." I raise my hand and brush the pain from her face. "And don't give up on us yet."

She blinks the tears away with a sniffle. "I think we could both use some time apart. You've got Corinne and a baby to think about now, and I need to fix the mess I've made of my life." She clears her throat. "I quit my job."

"I heard, and I'm damn proud of you." Unable to help myself, I press my lips to hers. "Just don't quit me, okay? Give us a chance."

"I'll think about it."

At least it's progress. Before I do something stupid, like throw her over my shoulder and drag her off to her bedroom, I leave her apartment, determined to give her the space she asked for.

thirty-three

SADIE

I'm sitting behind my father's desk when he walks into his office. Early morning sunlight streams through the windows, painting his masculine desk and bookcases in soft orange hues.

Upon seeing me, he stalls in the doorway. "I knew you'd come to your senses." He saunters into the room and lets the door shut behind him.

Rising to my feet, I hold out the envelope Ash gave me. Inside is the check and my formal *Fuck you, I quit* letter. "I'm here to personally hand you my resignation."

"I won't accept it. This is ridiculous. You belong here at the firm."

"No, you should really open it." I round the desk and thrust the envelope into his hands.

He turns it over for several seconds, almost as if he knows what's inside and doesn't want to face the evidence of his underhanded tactics. Finally, he opens the flap and pulls out my single page resignation, along with the bribery check he wrote to Ashton. "He gave you this?"

Long, turbulent moments stretch between us. "Ashton can't be bought. If you knew him at all, you'd know that."

His face reddens, lips pinched in displeasure, but he remains silent as he stuffs the incriminating check back into the envelope. "You naïve girl. He only did this to squeeze more cash out of me."

I'm buzzing with too much adrenaline, and as we stand in the middle of his office, three feet apart, I clench my hands. "I don't think you understand. This ends now. If you ever want to see me again, you'll back the fuck off and leave Ash alone. Do you understand me?"

"Don't be melodramatic, Sadie."

"I mean it. If I have to, I'll move and change my number. I'll do whatever it takes to get this through your thick head. This is *my life*, and you are no longer part of it." Certain he's not grasping the gravity of what I'm saying, I close the space between us and straighten my spine. And though I have to crane my neck to look him in the eye, I don't dare back down, no matter how much I'm shaking on the inside, quivering like the recalcitrant child he's made me feel like for years. "From this day forward, seeing and talking to me is a *privilege* you'll have to earn back."

For the first time ever, my father is struck silent. His stillness is downright scary, the energy of his overbearing nature slithering under the surface, tainting the air.

I suck in a deep breath anyway. "I didn't want it to come to this, but you wouldn't back off."

"Because I want what's best for you."

"You don't get to decide what's best for me. *I* decide who to marry, where to work, and who to love. I'm not a child anymore." I'm getting caught up in trying to reason with a man who's head is as thick as sludge. Nothing I say will get through, so I'm not sure why I bother trying.

Except he's my father, and I hate the thought of walking out of his life to get him to wake the fuck up.

His jaw is set, the square shape of it unrelenting. The word *stubborn* is synonymous with my father, and his deep brown eyes are resolute with it as he moves past me to claim his throne behind the desk. "I won't condone a relationship with Ashton. I've humored your friendship with the Levine twins long enough as it is."

"What do you have against them?"

"They're not cut from the same cloth as us. I not only expect better for you, I demand it."

"You're a snob."

"Call me what you will, Sadie, but it's my job to ensure your future. If you walk out that door, I'll be forced to rescind your trust fund."

"I don't need your money." Sadness drenches my soul, coils around my heart, squeezes the breath from my lungs. I swallow hard to get my voice to work. "And if your behavior is that of a father, then I don't need one of those anymore either."

His lips move, but I turn a deaf ear to his protests as I barge out of his office. Only after the doors of the elevator enclose me inside do I exhale in relief. Heading downward, I spiral into a sense of despair and disbelief. I can't believe I just spoke to my father like that. Not only the assertiveness, but the harsh words.

And I meant every one of them.

I vow to follow through even though my throat burns from hurt. Even though my eyes are on the cusp of purging it. Empowerment rises inside me, and I wrap it around myself and use it as a blanketing shield.

Still, my heart throbs with regret, and it isn't long before the guilt penetrates. I'm halfway to my apartment when it strikes because my mother might be innocent in this latest scheme, and I don't want to alienate her. At the very least, I need to explain my side of things before she hears it from him. I pull over, shift the car into park, and grab my cell.

The events of the morning roar in my mind, keeping pace with the speeding cars on the highway. A full minute sneaks by before I find the courage to put the call through. She answers immediately, and I'm not sure if that's a good thing, or a bad thing.

Was she on the other line with Dad?

"Hey, sweetie."

"Hi, Mom." I detect movement on her end. "You sound busy."

"I'm in the middle of planning a fundraiser, but I could use a break." She pauses, and I make out the shuffle of papers. "Is everything okay at work?"

She doesn't know—about this morning or the fact that I quit my job last week.

"I'm surprised Dad didn't tell you."

"Tell me what?" More papers. More movement. "Wait!

Did you work things out with Jake? Maybe we'll have that Christmas wedding after all."

She's just as oblivious as ever, content in her sheltered world of organizing events that further Dad's career, cleaning his house, and looking pretty on his arm when required. Instead of feeling angry, I'm just sad. This is all she knows—all she's ever known.

Growing up in a strict family, my mother learned at a young age the definition of *expectation*. My grandparents practically arranged her marriage to my father, whose family not only came from a background in politics, but a long history of wealth.

She never discovered independence, never experienced standing on her own two feet. Never learned to follow her dreams or her heart.

I'm too much like her, and until recently, I'd been as blind to it as my mother. But she won't be blind to what's happened now. Not anymore.

"Jake and I are done. In fact, that's part of the reason I called. I wanted you to hear it from me."

"Hear what? You're starting to worry me."

"I quit my job."

She falls silent for too long, and I calm myself by counting the cars rushing by on the freeway.

A red truck.

A black sedan.

A dark blue SUV.

All swooshing past, oblivious to the pathetic girl on the side of the road trying to hold it together as her life detonates.

"Mom, did you hear me?"

"I heard you, but I don't understand. Why would you do that?"

"Because I'm done. I'm done with all of it. Dad isn't running my life anymore."

"Your father means well. He's just a little overprotective, is all."

"He tried giving Ashton a quarter of a million dollars to stay away from me. That isn't okay." There's dead silence on her end again. God, she has to see how fucked up this is. "Say something," I plead. "Tell me you didn't know about it."

"Honey, I didn't know about it, but I can't say I don't want what's best for you. I'm sure your father had your best interests at heart."

"I don't think Dad has a heart."

"You don't mean that."

"Yes, I do. He tried driving away the love of my life." As soon as the words are out of my mouth, I know they're true.

And they're terrifying. Ashton is it for me, but too much hangs in the balance still.

Corinne and her pregnancy.

And the risk inherent in turning our friendship to more. It's a nagging fear I can't escape because if Ash and I give it a go then crash and burn in the end, losing him will be like losing a huge chunk of myself. The pain will be a hundred times sharper than what I'm experiencing now.

He and Mandy have always been there for me, more so than my own parents. They're a staple in my life. The gravity that keeps me grounded. The electric shock that keeps me alive. I don't know what I'd do without them.

Without *him*.

It's a crippling thought, and that's why being stuck in this neither friends-nor-lovers purgatory hell is preferable to trying and failing.

Ash is right. I *am* using Corinne to protect myself.

"I've gotta go, Mom."

"Sadie, wait. I—"

I hang up, cutting her off mid-sentence, and pull back onto the highway, feeling bereft and parentless. Even worse, I'm heartbroken.

But Ashton isn't breaking my heart. I'm doing that all by myself.

thirty-four

ASHTON

The driveway is a wet blanket of autumn leaves. I trample over them in my muddy boots, tired down to my marrow. The sun set hours ago, and the crew had to clear out of the conservation area by way of flashlights. It took over an hour just to drive home.

The last thing I want is to deal with Corinne. Finding her on my front stoop shouldn't surprise me, and yet the sight of her manages to catch me off guard. Dread pools in the bottom of my gut. I'm in a shit mood, exhausted, and filthy from working in the stormy weather all day, and all I want is a hot shower and a good night's sleep.

I'm not equipped to handle Corinne right now, but it looks like I don't have a choice. If only I'd answered her damn texts, maybe she would have left me the fuck alone for a night.

"What's up?" I ask, keeping my tone neutral as I climb the three steps to my front door.

Arms crossed over her chest, she greets me with a partial scowl. "Where were you?"

I lift a brow at her accusing tone. "Work. Is that allowed?" Now there's no reining in my sarcasm. She's been tapping on my last button since the night I left Sadie's apartment with the hard-on from hell and sharp disappointment slicing my heart to shreds.

"Were you with her?"

She doesn't know about Sadie yet—she only knows there's *someone*. But until Sadie is secure enough in our relationship, I don't want Corinne to know. She might take it upon herself to sabotage us.

"No, but even if I had been with someone, it's none of your business." I jab the key into the knob and turn. Corinne follows me inside, like I knew she would.

"It *is* my business. This girl, whoever she is, will be spending time around our child."

"How about we wait until the baby is born before fighting over it?" I shrug out of my coat and head into the kitchen to look for something quick and easy to make for dinner. I've got my head in the fridge, taking inventory of eggs, cheese, and salsa with an omelet in mind, when her words stop me in my tracks.

"I don't think I can keep the baby."

Shooting her a look of disbelief, I slam the refrigerator door shut. "What?"

"I don't want to do this alone. I told you that last week."

"And I said you wouldn't be alone. I'm fucking here, aren't I? I'll go to every doctor's appointment with you, help with the bills, buy whatever the baby needs. But for fuck's sake, you've gotta give me some breathing room."

She blinks, and my stomach takes a dive once the tears start. I'm a sucker for a girl's tears. "I need more than that. I want our child to have two parents—not visits on the weekends."

"The baby *will* have two parents. They just won't be together."

"Then I can't go through with the pregnancy."

I drag a hand down my face. My head is spinning, and the sickness boiling in my gut obliterates my appetite for food. "Are you seriously trying to blackmail me into being with you?"

"I'm just being honest. I won't go through this without a commitment from you."

"This is insane. We had a fling, Corinne. Rational people don't pull this shit."

"I'm pregnant, not rational."

"That's probably the first logical thing you've said." I close the distance between us and lift her chin. Her face is wet with her vulnerability. I know she's scared, but this seems drastic, even for Corinne, who's always been a bit of a drama queen.

"Why would you settle for something you know won't work?"

"I might've only been a fun time to you, but for me it was different. You know how I feel about you, and I'll fight for us. I'll fight for what our baby deserves."

She's digging in her heels. No matter what I say, logic won't get through to her. Frustration and helplessness grip me in their clutches, and I'm afraid I won't break free from this.

But I sure as hell can't give her what she wants either.

"You're prepared to have an abortion?"

"Yes." She averts her gaze when she says it.

"I don't believe you."

"It's the truth. I won't do this without you, so you're either in all the way, or I'm out."

"This is bullshit. I don't want you to get rid of the baby."

"I don't want to be a single parent."

"Do you really think holding our baby ransom is going to make me want you? It'll only cause resentment." Closing my eyes, I turn away and run a hand through my hair. "I can't believe you're doing this."

She's silent, and when I turn back to face her, I find her gnawing on her lip. Her hands are clasped in front of her, fingers twisting in nervousness, but I can't read her. Maybe she is whacked enough in the head that she'd go through with it. And that's the problem—I have no idea what she's capable of.

If I give her what she wants—no, what she's demanding—I'll never win back Sadie's trust. She doesn't want complicated. She wants what I've always given her.

Security.

The assurance I'll always be there.

Problem is, I need to give those things to my unborn child. There's no question of that, and no alternative I can find in the interim.

Bend to Corinne's demands, or risk her doing something rash.

"You're not leaving me much choice here."

Her face lights up with hope. "You'll give us a chance?"

"What else am I supposed to do here, Corinne? I don't want you to abort."

Eyelashes fluttering, she settles her hand on my chest. Her fingers trail down my abdomen, aiming for the button of my jeans, and I grab her wrist before she reaches her destination.

"I said I'd give us a chance. I didn't say I'd sleep with you."

"Intimacy is part of giving us a real chance, Ashton."

I shake my head. "We're not anywhere close to having a physical relationship. You want a commitment? *Fine.* But the rest will have to wait until I know I can trust you."

"You *can* trust me."

"I don't see how. It's going to take some time."

I let go of her wrist and put some distance between us. "Let's just see where this goes." All I need to do is make her believe the lie long enough for her to pass the point of no return in her pregnancy.

She looks away, her face the picture of disappointment. "I guess it's probably a good idea to get to know the father of my child better. Maybe then you'll realize we belong together."

Fuck, I wonder if she hears herself and realizes how crazy she sounds. Or is she oblivious, too immersed in her fantasy world of love and babies and fucking white picket fences?

I'm not sure I want to know.

"Just promise you won't do anything rash before talking to me, okay?"

"I'll talk to you before making any decisions. We're in this together, right?"

"Right."

"And you'll break things off with her?" Her demanding tone rubs me the wrong way, and I'm tempted to tell her where she can shove her ultimatum. Instead, I use my less-than-stellar past to convince her she has nothing to worry about.

"There's nothing to break off. You were right. It wasn't serious."

She studies me too long as if searching for the answer she hopes to find. "For real?"

Not even close, but I'll lie until my nose grows by a foot if I have to.

"Yes. Over before it started," I say, trying to reel in my clipped tone. "There's no one else."

Corinne relaxes into the lie, the muscles in her body loosening as she exhales. "Okay."

And just like that, she buys it.

For the next couple of months, I'll have to sell it, and after this mess is resolved, I pray to God Sadie will forgive me.

Telling her is going to be hell.

It's pouring again by the time I drop Corinne off at her apartment. She begs me to stay with her, but I use the excuse of being tired from a long day at work.

Even though I'm still caked in mud, exhausted, and it's

late, I detour to Sadie's place on my way home. I'm far from ready for this conversation, but I have to be straight with her since keeping shit from her the first time didn't work out so well, and that's a mistake I won't make again.

I rush through the parking lot of her apartment complex, rain drenching me along the way, and climb the stairs two at a time to escape the downpour. Walking in is second nature, but the door is locked, so I rap on the wood and wait. Footsteps sound, and when the door opens, my sister is standing on the other side.

"I need to talk to Sadie," I say, wiping the rain from my face.

"I don't think she wants to see you right now."

"It's important."

She opens the door wider. "If you upset her, you'll wish you were an only child."

"You need to chill out. This is between her and me."

"Yeah," she scoffs. "You're my brother, and she's my best friend. Shit ain't that simple, Ash."

I gaze around the apartment and take in the empty couch, the dark kitchen, and the muted TV that's showing some program about tattoo artists. "Where is she?"

Mandy points toward the hall. "In her bedroom. I doubt she's asleep yet. I think she just got out of the shower."

My breath hitches, and I imagine Sadie's soft skin under my fingertips and the sweet scent of vanilla wafting to my nose. Her long hair wet and tangled and so fucking tempting that I can practically feel it held captive in my fist.

Focus, asshole.

Stalling in front of Sadie's bedroom door, I close my eyes and inhale. Part of me is hoping I'll catch her naked. The other part knows how foolish it is to wave a red flag of temptation in front of a bull.

Foolish it is.

I knock twice then enter before she can answer. She's wearing a tank top and sleep shorts, and I'm not sure if I'm disappointed or relieved.

Sadie glances up from brushing her hair, fingers frozen around the handle of the wooden hairbrush. "What the hell, Ash?"

"I need to talk to you."

She pulls the brush clear to the ends then sets it on a white desk scattered with beauty products. I find it ironic that she owns so much female junk since she doesn't wear makeup often.

She doesn't need to.

"The last time you said you needed to talk, I ended up cutting my father loose." She takes a seat on the end of the bed, and I settle next to her.

"You finally stood up to him?"

"Yep."

"How did it go?"

"About as well as expected."

I want to touch her. Instead, I clench my hands. If I start touching her now, I won't stop. Her bed is taunting me to strip her naked and spread her out before me, on top of me, underneath me. My willpower where Sadie's concerned is almost non-existent, whittled away from the intense experiences we shared these past few weeks.

"What's so important that you needed to crash my bedroom?"

The explanation lodges in my throat, and I swallow hard before speaking. "Corinne is threatening to have an abortion."

"*Threatening?* Why would she do that?"

"She says she doesn't want to be a single parent."

"What are you trying to say, Ash?"

"I'm saying the situation has gotten more complicated. Corinne will keep the baby if I..."

Christ, I can't say it.

She jumps to her feet, brows narrowing, spine stiffening, and I don't miss the suspicion in her jade eyes. "If you *what*? Just spit it out."

"She'll keep the baby if I commit...to her."

Silence is a weird thing—it can say more than words alone. The utter quiet between us settles over the room like an ominous cloud, thunderous in its roiling presence.

"You gave in to her." There's no question in her tone. Just heart-wrenching certainty because Sadie knows me well enough to know what I'd do if faced with such an ultimatum.

"She was threatening to kill my child. What else was I supposed to do?"

She walks to the door and opens it. "I think you should leave."

"Don't do this, Sawyer. It's only temporary. I just need some time to figure out how to handle the situation." My feet eat up the space between us, and I take her face between my hands. "My heart belongs to you."

"But your obligation belongs to her." She backs away until we're an arm-length apart. "I won't stand in the way of that."

"You asked me for time. Now I'm asking for the same."

"Are you going to fuck her?"

"No way in hell. Do you really think I'd do that to you?"

Lowering her gaze, she stares at my work boots. "Until you straighten this out, I think we should just be friends." She pauses, and I realize I'm holding my breath. "Or maybe we shouldn't see each other at all."

"*Not* seeing you isn't an option, and I sure as hell don't want to be your goddamn friend."

She lifts a shoulder as if this isn't pulverizing her innards like it is mine. "That's all I can give you right now."

Fuck this shit. I grab her by the nape and claim her mouth, making it known with every frenzied dart of my tongue that she's not getting away so easily.

She's *mine*.

Driven by pure instinct, I deepen my possession of her mouth until she's whimpering on my tongue. I'll be damned if this is the last time I get drunk off the taste of her. She can fight me, guns blazing, but in the end, I'll come out victorious.

Before the kiss turns into something neither of us can walk away from, I tear my lips from hers. "There's no way in hell I'm letting you give up on us."

She parts her lips, probably to protest or reason or appeal to me with her annoyingly infallible logic, but I press a finger against her mouth. "Don't bother arguing. You won't win this one."

One...two...three seconds pass before I drop my hand.

I need to leave before I can't. Before her watery jade eyes and quivering lips make it impossible to walk out the front door. Weakness is the ruination of fools, and I'm its bitch because I brush my mouth across hers one last time in a kiss so brief it barely counts.

Because if I truly made it count, we'd end up in her bed, the door to her room shut, clothing a discarded path on the floor, and I'd show her exactly how serious I am about not giving up on us.

For both our sakes, I leave her breathless in the hall and bolt into the rain.

thirty-five
SADIE

"No way," I tell Mandy, my tone leaving no question about my feelings on this. As usual, she ignores my protests as she moves around the wasteland that is my bedroom, picking up dirty clothes off the floor and stacking dishes containing half-eaten food onto the dresser. She's always been on the overbearing side, but she's my best friend, so I let her get away with it.

Not this time.

"I'm not in the mood for going out," I say, crossing my arms.

She wags her finger at me. "Uh-uh. You already begged off once, and I let you since you've been a heartbroken mess, but it's time to get out there again." She starts folding the clothes I left in the hamper a week ago when I mustered enough give-a-fucks to do a load of laundry.

"Comb your hair, brush your teeth, put on some clean clothes—just do *something*."

I've been doing a lot of sleeping. I'm tempted to ask her if that counts, but I bite back the retort.

"I can't stand to see you so depressed," she says, heading over to my closet. "You need to have some fun."

I also need to find a job, but that hasn't been happening either, and my savings account isn't big enough to enable an extended bout of heartache.

Ashton has completely wrecked me.

"I'm not in the mood for fun." And I'm sure as hell am *not* in the mood to go on some blind date.

"It's been three weeks, Sadie. You said you'd at least think about it, remember?"

"I did? When?"

"The night of your parents Jerry Springer style dinner."

"That was before…"

"Before my brother got inside your head and turned you into a moping zombie queen, I know."

"Moping zombie queen?"

"Would you prefer lovesick fool?"

With a wary sigh, I flop onto my bed and hug my pillow. "You said I should give it some time."

"Time, yes, but ever since he barged into your bedroom, you've been a step away from needing Prozac. A little fun won't kill you."

"You're not going to let this go, are you?"

"Not a chance, so you might as well get dressed and turn that frown upside down."

I'm too down in the dumps to laugh at her ridiculous attempt at cheering me up, but the corners of my mouth curve up, despite myself. "I don't want to lead this guy on."

"You won't." She slides several hangers to the side before pulling out a simple charcoal midi dress. Next, she selects a pair of strappy green heels and a matching clutch. A clunky sliver chain belt completes her ensemble. There's no hiding my wince when she marches to where I'm eyeing her from the bed.

"Ashton will get pissed if he finds out." Not only pissed, but any hint of me dating will destroy him. I know the thought of him with Corinne is destroying me.

We've talked via texts a few times since he told me about Corinne's ultimatum, and on the few occasions I left the house to buy groceries or run errands, or—heaven forbid—actually went to a job interview, I happened to spot him around town with her. *Twice*. Each time added another bleeding gash to my heart.

"My brother will just have to deal." She lays the dress, shoes, and accessories on the bed. "There's no reason you should sit at home like a spinster while he's working shit out with his baby mamma."

The term *baby mamma* is like claws on a chalkboard, and I cringe.

"Look," she says. "I told Shane you aren't interested in more than friendship. He understands. He's not in a great headspace for dating either."

"And this is a guy you think I should date?" My tone is more than a little dubious.

"No, this is a guy I think you should meet and have some fun with. It's just a night out with friends. End of story."

I can't believe I'm letting her talk me into this.

An hour later, the four of us enter the place where Mandy works. For a Saturday night, Club Hoppin is low key, though it's still too many people for my anti-social mood. We find a booth in the middle of the club, and I'm glad we steered clear of the tables in the corners, one of which I crawled under and all but attacked Ashton on the night that changed everything.

"Would you ladies like something to drink?" Shane swings his gaze between Mandy and me. The guy's hot as hell, if you go for that clean cut, I-work-in-an-office type of thing.

Until recently, I did.

Until recently, I did a lot of things differently.

From what I can tell, Shane is nothing like Jake, even if he resembles him in style. Then again, I don't really know him, and if my past judgments are anything to go by, I suck in that department.

"What are you drinking?" Mandy asks me, nudging my arm.

"Whatever you guys are having is fine with me."

"Sex on the Beach it is."

I bite back a groan, barely refraining from doing a face-palm. The guys grin, then they're off fetching our cocktails. We settle in to wait, people-watching and listening to the hip-hop pulsing through the club. Eventually, Mandy eyes the dance floor, and I try to sink lower into my seat.

"Don't even think about playing the wallflower tonight. I dragged your depressed ass out to live a little. Let's dance."

I bark an incredulous laugh. "Not happening. You know I don't dance."

"Who cares? We'll have a blast anyway."

"Maybe later, okay? We just got here."

Her breath whooshes out, disrupting her bangs. "All right, I'll let you sit this one out, but if you keep being allergic to fun, I'll drag you out there screaming bloody murder if I have to."

"Who's screaming bloody murder?" Shane sets two cocktails onto the table—Mandy's order of *Sex on the Beach*, I'm assuming—and Brett's standing next to him holding two micro brews.

"Your date will be if I can't get her on the dance floor," Mandy tells Shane, and I shoot her a warning glare. With a shrug, she feigns innocence.

My best friend knows exactly what she's doing.

She's setting me up whether I like it or not, and I walked straight into her we're-having-a-fun-night-out-with-friends trap. I wonder if I can kill her in her sleep without the neighbors hearing.

She takes a long draw from her cocktail, no doubt entertaining thoughts of sex and beaches that include the tall guy with the wild blond hair sitting beside her. It's not long before she tilts her head toward the busy dance floor. "Want to dance?" she asks Brett.

"Lead the way." He's only got eyes for her as he follows her into the fray.

Shane shifts next to me. "You sure you don't want to dance?" He gestures to where his brother and Mandy are getting down and dirty.

"I don't really dance, but thank you." I take a sip of my drink and raise my brow at the sweet, fruity taste. A person could get drunk fast off this adult Kool-Aid.

It sure tastes like Kool-aid.

"I don't either," he says with a shrug. "But I would've gotten out there and embarrassed myself for you."

It's at that particular moment I wish I were anywhere else. It's not that Shane is rude, bad-looking, or has horrible breath. The problem is he's a man I'd be interested in getting to know, if I weren't already in love with someone else, and that makes this night feel pointless, not to mention unfair to Shane.

Despite what Mandy said, I feel like I *am* leading him on.

Music pours through the speakers at a tolerable level that invites conversation, but silence stretches between us as we watch Brett and Mandy bump and grind.

"How long have you guys known each other?" Shane asks, nodding his head toward Mandy.

"Years. It's hard to say when I met her and Ashton. First or second grade, probably."

"Ashton's the twin, right?"

"Right."

"She told me about their childhood."

"She did?" Now he's got my attention. Mandy doesn't talk about that with just anyone. "What'd she tell you?"

"She said their father took off when they were young, and her mother worked a lot. Sounds like they had it rougher than most, but she doesn't let it keep her down." He pauses. "I admire her strength."

I study the profile of his face. Strong jaw. Wide, sensuous mouth that would draw the attention of any woman with a pulse. Maybe even a few men. As if he senses my scrutiny, he swallows hard, Adam's apple bobbing, and drags a hand through his thick, brown hair. All the while, his hazel eyes never waver from the sight of Mandy dancing with his brother across the club.

"Have you told her yet?" I ask, breaking the lull in conversation.

His gaze swings in my direction. "Tell her what?"

"That you're into her."

"I'm not...why would you think that?"

I lift a brow. "Because it's true?"

He expels a breath. "She's my brother's girl."

"I don't think it's serious."

"Maybe not on her end."

I've gotta admire his loyalty to his brother, but I feel bad for him. Probably because I recognize the longing on his face. It sucks not being with the one who makes your heart throb, your body sing, your soul sizzle to life.

"Some date I'm turning out to be." His mouth is a line of apology.

"We're just two friends hanging out, so I wouldn't worry about it."

"Point taken. I don't blame you. I'm rusty as hell at this."

"Why's that?" I'm genuinely intrigued.

"I got out of a long-term relationship a few weeks ago."

"I'm sorry."

"Nah, don't be." He picks up his beer and takes a swig

just as the other half of our quad returns to the table. They slide into the booth across from us, breathing labored and bodies covered in sweat. Mandy wipes away a drop sliding down her temple.

"You guys having fun?" she asks, still catching her breath.

Playing with the straw in my glass, I swirl the ice into a miniature whirlpool. "Yeah. How about you?"

Mandy grins at Brett. "We're having a blast." She presses her mouth to his, and in the next instant, they're sucking face.

And that's when I know Mandy is clueless about Shane's interest because she'd never intentionally do something so cruel. Shane and I exchange a glance, and he mutters something about not being able to take his brother anywhere.

I know the feeling.

I finish the rest of my drink, and I'm about to go in search of another as it would take a saint to get through a blind-date—though not *really* a blind-date—without a good dose of alcohol, and that's when my cell buzzes from my purse. I ignore it at first. If it's not my mother begging me to come home for dinner to "work things out," it's Ashton.

But ignoring the persistent *buzz-buzz* is about as easy as ignoring the suckfest happening across the table. With a sigh, I dig out my phone.

Ashton: *What are you up to tonight?*

Casting a glance around me, I find Shane drinking from his beer, and Mandy and Brett are so tied up in each other, they barely notice my presence. I quickly reply to Ashton's text.

Me: Nothing much. Just hanging out with Mandy.

Ashton: Really? From where I'm standing it looks like you're on a fucking date.

My heart thumps painfully in my chest as I gaze around the club, attention landing on anyone with dark hair. Bonus points if they're wearing black.

But I don't see Ashton anywhere though I'm pretty sure that's Bryce sitting at the bar with his back to me. With a frown, I return my attention to my phone.

Me: Are you spying on me?

Ashton: Meet me by the restrooms.

Oh shit.

Swallowing hard, I tap Shane on the shoulder, gesturing that I need to exit the booth. He slides out so I can scoot to the edge. Mandy and Brett unlock their tongues long enough to acknowledge my sudden movement.

"Whatcha doing?" she asks.

"I need to use the restroom. I'll be right back." I make my way through the crowd and find Ashton leaning against the wall outside the men's restroom.

Either I'm starved for the sight of him, or he's never looked hotter.

Low-slung jeans, faded from working outside. Fitted long-sleeved black shirt that emphasizes the broadness of his shoulders and hugs his abs just right. I have the strongest urge to press against him, to wrap myself in his heat and woodsy smell. As soon as I'm within reach, he grabs me by the arm and hauls me through the back door and into the designated smoking area.

And then I *am* pressed against his chest, my back to the concrete wall as he shelters me from the cool breeze of fall. It's a pure Ashton move, and I'm light-headed and a bit delirious.

He leans down until our lips are inches apart. "Are you trying to hurt me?"

"Of course not."

He slides a palm against my cheek, his touch incongruent with the fervor in his eyes. "You're on a date—a fucking *date*. Do you know how that makes me feel?"

"Do you know how it made me feel to see you and Corinne shopping for groceries together? You two seemed like the perfect little family." I wince at the bite in my tone, but I can't help it.

I'm jealous.

And obviously, the jealousy goes both ways, or he wouldn't have me against a wall in the alley behind the club, staking his claim with the heat of his hands and the determination in his eyes.

Widening his stance, he wraps an arm around my waist and pulls me flush against his body. "I haven't touched her. I only gave her a ride since her car's been in the shop. That's why we were together at the store." He jerks his head toward the back entrance of the club. "What's your excuse for the Jake-wannabe in there?"

"I don't need an excuse. You and I aren't together."

He glances down at our joined bodies. "Could've fooled me."

"It's not a date. We're just friends."

"Like you and I are friends?"

"Not even close."

He shutters his eyes for several seconds. "I miss you so damn much."

I miss him too. More than I can say. "Isn't Corinne wondering where you are right now?"

"She's not my fucking keeper, Sadie." He cradles my face between his warm hands. "This bullshit with Corinne will be over soon."

"You don't really believe that, do you? She'll still be pregnant, and maybe she won't be able to yank on your leash by threatening abortion, but she'll come up with something else. She wants you, Ash, and from what I remember of Corinne in high school, she can be fucking ruthless."

She never liked me, and now I know why. She probably saw what everyone but Ashton and I saw at the time—a close friendship that masked what neither of us were ready to admit.

"So that's it, huh?" Ashton shakes his head. "Are we not worth fighting for?"

"It doesn't matter what I think, or how I feel. You've got obligations neither of us can ignore."

"Try ignoring this." His hand disappears under the hem of my dress, but he stops short of touching me where I'm aching for it the most.

My breath hitches, and I'm instantly on fire.

"You're torturing me," I groan.

"Say the word, and we're outta here." He trails his lips

along my jawline before reaching the arousing spot beneath my ear. His mouth is greedy and wet and so fucking hot against my neck that my knees almost give out. His teeth sink into my flesh with enough bite to leave a mark.

"Ashton, please..." I don't even know what I'm pleading for at this point.

"Tell me what to do, and I'll do it. Just don't tell me to stop loving you because that isn't going to happen."

I've never wanted to give in as much as I do now. My body throbs for him. My heart aches for him. My soul is lost without him. But my head is the loudest, and it's screaming at me to retreat before this goes any further.

Because Ashton Levine will consume me if I let him, and no matter what he claims, he's *not* free to be with me.

We might get our chance, but now isn't it.

"You need to leave me alone," I say, shoving past him.

"Not a chance." He's on my heels as I head back into the club. "Dating other people isn't going to make you forget what we have. You'll still think about me, still want me just as much as I want you. Fucking admit it."

"No."

He grabs my arm, halting my progress down the hall, and we step to the side, out of the way of people coming and going. "Why are you so damn scared to let yourself love someone? To let them love you?"

His words slam into me, and I'm flattened by the truth in them.

"I don't know," I say, my throat constricting.

"I have a theory. Wanna hear it?"

I shake my head, vocal cords frozen.

"Too bad. I'm telling you anyway. Your parents gave you everything you could ever want, but they failed in the single, most important area. Because of that, I know you think you're unworthy."

Sharp pain barrels through me. "Please, Ash."

"I'm here to tell you how wrong you are." He presses his lips to my forehead. "You are so fucking lovable, Sawyer. You have no idea."

Shaken to the center of my soul by his words, I'm on the verge of breaking down. It's imminent, producing an aching lump in my throat. A horrid burn behind my eyeballs.

"I can't do this," I choke out, shoving past him and escaping into the women's restroom. Two girls are touching up their lipstick in front of the sinks, so I enclose myself in one of the stalls until I can regain my bearings.

Ashton spooked me clear to my toes, and I'm still trembling, close to a tearful meltdown in a bathroom stall. Hell, This is the same stall where Mandy found me the night I caught Jake cheating.

This is where it all started.

I close my eyes and focus on breathing, all the while hoping the women hurry up with their primping and get the hell out of here. The door opens and closes a few minutes later, shutting out the giggly girls and the strong scent of whatever flowery perfume they bathed in. I come out of hiding and stumble to the sinks, knees wobbly and threatening to buckle.

Damn Ashton. What was he thinking?

I turn on the faucet and splash water onto my flushed cheeks. The more I think about our stolen moments in the alley, the angrier I become. Even if I weren't terrified of putting this are-we-or-aren't-we-more-than-friends limbo behind us, he's got obligations to Corinne.

I flash back to a couple of months ago when I saw her all over him, her hands in his hair and her lips attached to his. At the time, I'd convinced myself I was oblivious to the tightness in my chest at seeing them together. Now my response to the thought of him with *anyone* else tears at me in such a raw, primal way that I'm not sure our friendship will survive this.

My eyes are red, my cheeks still splotchy from fighting off tears, so I splash more water onto my face and force myself to get a grip, and that's when the door bursts open. All I see is blond hair, a red dress, and someone disappearing into a stall before the door bangs shut. Whoever's in there starts retching, and I consider jumping ship, but my conscience won't let me leave until I know she's okay. A few minutes later, she exits, dabbing her mouth with toilet paper, and recognition hits me.

Natalie, Corinne's older sister.

"Are you okay?"

Natalie nods. "Yeah. It's just morning sickness." She lets out an ironic laugh. "But it happens all day long."

I blink in surprise. "You're pregnant?"

"Yep, about ten weeks, so no alcohol for me."

"Wow...congratulations?"

She laughs again, and the lighthearted sound breaks the tension. "Thanks. It's good news."

As she washes her hands, I dry my face with paper towels. With any luck, Ashton will have gotten tired of waiting and left already.

"So, you and Corinne, pregnant at the same time. That must be fun."

Fun for them. Heartbreaking for me.

Natalie raises a brow. "Who told you Corinne's pregnant?"

"Ashton did. She told him a few weeks ago."

Natalie studies my face as if she'll find the missing puzzle piece there. "You're sure she told him this?"

"Yeah." And then it occurs to me that maybe I just slipped up and spilled something I shouldn't have. "Did she not tell you? Shit, I'm sorry if I'm putting my foot in it."

"There's nothing to tell. She's not pregnant."

I blink, and blink...then blink some more, and a hard swallow clears my vocal cords. "But he picked her up from the emergency room a few weeks ago. She said there were complications with the baby." I'm dumbfounded and sound it.

Natalie shakes her head. "I was the one in the ER. She was there, but it was for moral support."

Why would Corinne lie about something like this? My pulse is throbbing in my ears, and adrenaline rushes through me so fast, I'm dizzy from it.

Ashton's been completely torn up over this—I've been fucking torn up over this—and to think she's been lying the whole time? Why would anyone do something so low? So fucking cruel?

Natalie's expression softens, and I can't decide if it's

sympathy or pity I'm finding on her face. "This isn't the first time she's done something like this. It's an attention thing with her." A buzzing sound comes from the pocket of her jacket, and she fishes her cell out before scanning the backlit screen. "Listen, I'm sorry, but I've gotta go." She heads toward the door then halts long enough to glance over her shoulder. "Trust me. She's not pregnant."

After she's gone, I let the counter hold me up as I process what I just heard. But only two things are on loop inside my head.

Corinne *isn't* pregnant.

And I need to tell Ash.

thirty-six

ASHTON

If Sadie believes ducking into the women's restroom will save her from me, she's mistaken and only delaying the inevitable. As long as she's hanging out with the pretty boy across the club, who's now immersed in an animated conversation with my sister, I'm not going anywhere.

I lean against the wall outside the bathrooms and settle in for the wait, all the while trying to ignore the burning throb of betrayal in my chest. I have no fucking right to feel betrayed—not after asking her to give me time while I pretend to be committed to someone else.

But fucking hell, my commitment to Corinne is nothing more than a facade on my part, and Sadie knows this.

A few women leave the restroom, and one of them I recognize as Corinne's sister. She's too focused on her phone to notice me lurking in the dim hallway like a creeper.

If Sadie doesn't come out soon, I'm going in after her.

Five minutes later, I'm seriously considering it when she finally emerges. All it takes is one glance at her ashen face, and I know something is wrong.

I push off the wall. "Sadie?"

"Can we get out of here? I need to talk to you."

Her complete turnabout is cause for a raised brow, but I'm not complaining. I usher her into the thick of the club, one hand warming the small of her back. "Let me tell Bryce we're outta here."

"I should let Mandy know, too. Plus, I left my purse and coat over there."

"Meet you at the front?" I ask.

She nods before taking off in the opposite direction, and I stand motionless for a few moments, dazed and a little confused as I watch her make her way through the crowd. Twenty minutes ago, she was ready to get rid of me.

Now she's leaving with me. But she's acting odd, and that's got me concerned.

I say a quick goodbye to my roommate before snaking my way through the crowd. Sadie joins me at the front entrance five minutes later, and we duck out into the cold. It's started to drizzle since our interlude in the alley. We rush through the rain, and only after we're inside the dry warmth of my car, and no one's around to overhear us, do I ask Sadie what's going on.

"I ran into Corinne's sister in the bathroom."

"I thought that was her. Did she say something to upset you?" If Corinne is behind this...

"She told me Corinne isn't pregnant."

Whatever I was thinking stops dead in its tracks. Long heavy moments pass, raindrops furious on the windshield.

"What?"

"Natalie's pregnant. She said she was the one at the hospital. Corinne was only there to offer support."

"Natalie was nowhere around when I picked up Corinne."

Sadie shrugs. "I'm just telling you what she told me. She was adamant that Corinne *isn't* pregnant."

I rub a hand down my face and consider the possibility that Corinne's been lying to me all along. The timing is suspect, her news coming on the heels of her wanting more than I was willing to give. Muttering a curse under my breath, I turn the key in the ignition and crank up the heat.

Sadie shifts in the passenger seat, huddling inside her jacket. "Did Corinne give you any proof?"

"Yeah, an ultrasound picture." I peek at Sadie and find her brows drawn together.

"Was her name on it?"

That night is a blur in my mind, overshadowed by the way things went down between Sadie and me, but I focus on the moment I gazed at that photo, overcome with a sense of awe at what I was looking at.

"I remember the date and her last name."

"So it could have easily been her sister's."

Holy shit, she's right.

"I guess so."

"What are you going to do?"

"I'm going to drag the truth from her." What else can I

do? The waiting game is drawing closer to the finish line with each new day. If she is lying to me, then time is not on her side. There will come a point when she'll either have to fess up, or fake a miscarriage.

The thought makes me sick.

"I can't believe she'd go to these lengths," I say.

"Me either. A sane person wouldn't do something like this."

I take Sadie's hand in mine. "Thanks for telling me."

Carefully, she withdraws her fingers from mine, and my heart takes a nosedive to the bottom of my sickened gut.

"We're friends, Ash. That's all we can be right now."

Even as friends, we used to hold hands all the fucking time. Sadie and I never held back when it came to displaying our friendship in a physical capacity.

Hugs, hand-holding, piggy back rides. It's been a while since we horsed around like that.

But none of that matters now since everything has changed, and the only way we're going to find our way forward is by fixing what needs to be fixed.

The situation with Corinne is first on the list.

"I'll drive you home." I shift the idling car into gear, and Sadie doesn't say anything until we're a few blocks down the road.

"Are you going to talk to her tonight?"

There's a hopeful lift in her tone, and I can't help but respond to it on a visceral level. Her hope gives *me* hope.

"This isn't something that can wait until morning. If

she's lying, it's ending now." I give her a meaningful look. "She's already caused enough damage."

Sadie turns away, and neither of us speak for the rest of the drive. Once we reach her apartment, she tries dodging me on my offer to walk her to her front door, but I don't give her the chance.

"Can't wait to get rid of me, huh?"

"That's not it."

"What is it, then?"

"Being around you is..."

I drag a hand through my hair. "I'm not trying to upset you."

"That's not what I was going to say. Being near you is too tempting right now."

My heart leaps at her words, and I have to bite my lip to keep from saying anything as she unlocks her darkened apartment.

She flips on a light and stalls just inside the front entrance. "Will you let me know how it goes?"

I fit my palm along her cheek and brush my lips across the other. "You'll be the first to know."

thirty-seven

ASHTON

Not pregnant. It would make my life a hell of a lot easier if it's true. I'll be able to move on from this shitstorm without worrying about Corinne going straight to the abortion clinic. If it's true, I can walk away, wash my hands of her, and do it without guilt.

I can get Sadie back.

Maybe not tomorrow, but eventually, because we're stronger than this.

I rap on Corinne's door three times. Seconds later, I detect footsteps, followed by a pause in which I'm sure she's checking the peephole. The deadbolt switches over, and there she stands, brown eyes brightening at the sight of me.

"Hey," she says, her voice an octave lower than usual. Softer. Designed to seduce. "I thought you were going out with Bryce tonight." She wanted me to come over for dinner, and when I told her I had plans with Bryce, she wasn't thrilled.

"Change of plans," I say, following her inside. As she clears a pile of textbooks from the sofa, I linger in the center of the living room. "We need to talk."

"Sure. Is everything okay?"

"That depends. I heard something interesting tonight."

Stalling, she glances over her shoulder. "Yeah?"

"I heard you're not actually pregnant."

She drops the books and turns around to face me, eyes wide. "What? Who told you that?"

"That's not even the point. Is it true?"

"Don't I get a chance to defend myself? Who's spreading rumors about me? Is it Sadie?"

Hmm, interesting. I figured she was bound to catch on to my feelings for Sadie, especially after my reaction to running into her around town. Corinne doesn't miss a thing.

"This *rumor* came from your sister."

That steals the sails from her voice, and she opens and shuts her mouth a few times before spitting out her reply. "I haven't told her yet."

"I might believe that, except she says she's pregnant." I advance on her, forcing her back by a few steps. "In fact, she claims *she* was the one at the hospital."

"My sister doesn't know what she's talking about."

"No? You weren't with her at the ER?"

"Well, yeah, but—"

"I don't want to hear any *buts*, Corinne. Just tell me the goddamn truth." My voice thunders through the apartment, and her eyes sheen over with tears.

"I'm...I'm sorry."

"You're sorry?" Sucking in a deep breath, I turn my back on her and drag both hands through my hair.

"I'm *so* sorry," she cries, and I flinch when she places her hand on my back. "I was *so* furious with you, and the lie slipped out...and once it was out there, I didn't know how to take it back without driving you away."

I whirl, seething, hands fisted at my sides. God, how I want to strangle her. "Do you have any idea what you've done? I was willing to rearrange my entire life for this baby —a baby that doesn't even exist!"

Something inside her seems to snap into place, and she lifts her chin a couple of notches. "Do you have any idea what *you've* done?"

"Let's hear your excuses. Tell me what I did to deserve this. Go ahead. Try justifying it."

"You discarded me like trash!" She jabs a finger into my chest. "You made me love you, then you threw me away like I was *nothing*."

"What you are is a lying, manipulative *bitch*."

Her mouth begins to tremble, and I immediately want to take back the words. Even if they are true. She played me, and I fell for it like an idiot.

"I didn't want to lose you," she says, the fight seeping from her bones. Shoulders sagging, she folds her arms in a defensive gesture.

"How could you think we had anything more than a fling? Outside the few times we fucked, we barely saw each other. That's not a fucking relationship, Corinne."

"It could've been," she says, dashing tears from her cheeks. "But I should've known better. It's always been

Sadie this and *Sadie that* with you." The corner of her mouth creeps into a sneer. "You took me to prom—you fucking slept with *me*—but you couldn't keep your eyes off her."

"That was years ago. Let it go, already."

"I'm not just talking about high school!" A beat of silence infiltrates the room, poisoning the air with hurt and lies, and she glares at me. "I thought you finally wanted *me*...but all you wanted was a quick and dirty fuck."

"Jesus, Corinne." I give her my back for a few moments, fingers raking through my hair, then I turn to face her again. "My reputation is no secret. I thought that's what you wanted, too."

"Well aren't you observant."

Her snide statement drains my last bit of patience, and I storm forward until she has no choice but to plant her ass on the couch. "Not observant enough, apparently." Staring down at her, I cross my arms. "But you were counting on that, weren't you? Did you think I wouldn't notice when you failed to pop out a baby?"

"I wasn't thinking at all."

"Bullshit," I say with a shake of my head. "You knew exactly what you were doing."

"I want you to leave."

"How convenient. *Now* you want me to go."

"I don't want to do this anymore. It was a mistake." Face bathed with tears, she sniffles. "I really am sorry."

"The only thing you're sorry about is getting tangled up in your own lies." Keeping my anger in check, I brace my weight on the back of the couch and bring my face close to hers. "You and I are done. Do you understand?"

Blinking rapidly, she nods.

"And stay the fuck away from Sadie."

"O-okay."

Her timid voice burrows underneath my anger, and I pull back, giving her space. "I swear to God I never meant to hurt you." I pause, watching the tears slide down her face. "The next time you get it in your head to yank on some poor idiot's chain, think twice. You're better than this."

She buries her head in her hands, and I take that as my cue to leave. Maybe she really is sorry. Maybe she's not. As I storm out of her apartment for the last time, I really don't give a shit either way.

thirty-eight

SADIE

"How'd it go?" Mandy asks as she settles into the seat across the table from me.

"Good. I start next term."

"I can't believe we'll be going to school together again. I'm so excited."

"Me too." Though I'll be on my own after she graduates next summer. It's a scary leap—starting all over again, exploring what I want to do with my life, discovering who I really am.

It's also exciting. The roadmap of the future is wide open, free of pressure from my father. I can do and be anything I want, and I plan to dabble in all kinds of things until I find something that speaks to me.

The cafeteria on campus is a busy place no matter the time of day, but during the traditional lunch hour, it's exceptionally boisterous. Mandy leans forward and raises her voice to be heard over the collective chatter.

"Bryce is throwing Ash and me a birthday party. You coming?"

I hate how the mention of his name causes an ache deep in my gut. It's hard to believe I used to watch him with all sorts of women without breaking in two, and now I can't even talk about him without feeling like I lost something.

We're still friends, but it's not the same.

"Your birthday is a month away," I point out.

"I know, but I figure if I start badgering you about it now I might wear you down enough by the time the party actually arrives."

"I don't know."

"You can't avoid him forever."

"I realize that, Mandy."

Ever since he showed up the morning after his confrontation with Corinne and told me she wasn't pregnant, I've existed in a state of limbo.

Wanting him.

Not wanting to risk my heart anymore than I already have.

It's been 25 days.

600 hours.

36,000 minutes.

The seconds seem endless.

"I mean, technically, you *could* avoid him forever, but I don't think you want to. And I *know* he doesn't want you to."

"He wants us to take the next step, but..."

"But what? You can't blame it on Corinne this time."

Frowning, she works the top off a plastic fruit bowl. "He's miserable, Sadie. So are you."

"I want to be sure."

Her voice softens. "What aren't you sure about?"

"We jumped into a physical relationship without really considering the consequences...or maybe we did, but we ignored them." I pause, counting the seconds on the huge clock hanging over the entrance to the building. "And it happened *so* fast. One minute we're friends, and the next we're..." I swallow hard. "I don't want to make that mistake again."

"Okay," she says, spearing a bite of cantaloupe with a fork. "What are you worried about the most?"

Glancing down, I push rice and orange-glazed chicken around my plate. "He's never done the relationship thing. It's always been sex for him, so what if we take that leap, and he gets bored with me? You think our friendship is strained now?" My voice wobbles, and I jerk my head back and forth. "Mandy, you guys are my family."

A reality that was driven home over two weeks ago during Thanksgiving. I considered going to my parents' for dinner until I learned Dad invited Jake and his new fiancé. The slimeball didn't waste time.

Mandy begged me to come with her and Ashton to their mother's house, but I didn't want to put a strain on their holiday, so I spent it alone in the apartment, decked out in PJ's in front of the TV.

She sets down her fork. "We're not going anywhere. And besides, it's different with you. Ashton's *never* been like this over a girl. You'd see it too if you stopped picking apart all the reasons why it might not work."

"So in other words, you're telling me to stop being a coward."

"Yes," she says with a smile. "You said it started out physical. What if you guys just dated for a while?"

"We'd end up in bed before the first date was over."

She covers her ears. "Let's not go there. This is my brother we're talking about."

"Hey, you asked."

"I know I did." She nibbles on her bottom lip, lost in thought. "So set some rules and stick to them. Give yourself some time to discover if there's something real underneath the...hormones."

"Hormones?" I ask with a laugh. Oh, the irony, as I recall saying something similar to Ash.

"Hey, it's no secret Ashton is a manwhore," she says with a cringe. "So if you date for a while, keeping things platonic the whole time, that should give you a good idea if it'll work or not."

We had rules before, and they worked...for a while. But even so, her idea has merit, though I'm positive Ashton won't appreciate his sister cock-blocking him.

"So go on some friend dates, is what you're saying."

"In so many words, yes."

"I'll think about it."

"Good."

We finish lunch, Mandy heads to her next class, and I decide to hang around campus for a while, enjoying a rare bout of sunshine in chilly December. Pulling my coat snug around my body, I head down the walkway leading away from the center building. Students rush past, in a hurry to get to their next destination.

I've missed this, and though it won't be easy keeping up with the class load on top of working, the rightness of being here warms my gut.

This feels like *my* life again.

Up ahead, people come and go from a building, its glass angles sleek and sharp, and voices pour through the doors. I venture inside and take in the cathedral ceiling and skylights. Students are gathered in clusters on the couches and chairs while some sort of motivational speech captures their attention.

Finding an empty seat off to the side, I settle in and listen to the guy's deep voice implore students to take charge of their futures. He offers anecdotal stories of struggle and strife, and that's when I zone out.

Because I'm thinking about Ashton again. Hell, I'm *always* thinking about him. Only now I'm considering everything Mandy said.

Before I lose my nerve, I dig out my phone and shoot him a text.

Me: I've got a proposition for you.

Since it's mid-day, and he's likely out in the woods somewhere eating lunch with Bambi, I don't anticipate having to wait long, unless he's out of service.

Ashton: I'm intrigued, Sawyer.

My heart skips behind my breastbone. Twenty-five days seems like a lifetime to spend without seeing him. We've exchanged texts every few days since the morning after the *Corinne Situation* imploded, but he's honored my wish for time and space.

My head tells me we needed this cooling period. My heart tells me I'm still running from what I feel for him.

Me: I met up with Mandy for lunch today.

Ashton: Yeah? I bet you talked about me.

I roll my eyes.

Me: Why? Were your ears ringing?

Ashton: Like crazy.

A few seconds pass, and then he replies again.

Ashton: Seriously, what's on your mind? You've got me on my toes here.

Me: Mandy had an idea.

Ashton: I'm almost afraid to ask.

Me: I think it could be a good thing.

Ashton: I'm open to good things. What are we talking about here?

Me: She thinks you and I should date, but with rules.

Ashton: More rules again? You're killing me.

I suck in a breath then let it out. I don't want rules. I want to give in to the intensity of being with him, skin to skin, losing myself in his touch, finding myself in his kiss.

But I *need* to know this is real, that it'll last and I won't end up another disillusioned girl on the roster of Ashton's flings.

Ashton: Lay your rules on me. You know you've got me wrapped.

Me: We go on several dates, but no touching or kissing or anything else involving my mouth.

Ashton: How about mine? Does using my tongue constitute touching?

Holy hell, he's fighting dirty.

Me: Yes. No touching means no touching.

Ashton: This was Mandy's idea?

Me: Yeah.

Ashton: So basically my sister's being a cock-blocker. You can tell her I said that.

I bite back a smile.

Me: Do we have a deal?

Ashton: That depends.

My heart thuds to the bottom of my gut, and my thumbs tremble as I type out the next message.

Me: On what?

Ashton: If I'm allowed to fall in love with you all over again.

I'm certain my cheeks are pink, and every person in the building can sense the huge grin on my face, but I don't care because something low in my belly is fluttering, growing warmer, siphoning the doubt and fear from my veins.

Me: I kinda hope you do.

Ashton: I'm kinda certain I will.

Me: So we're going to do this?

Ashton: Fuck yes. Can I pick you up tomorrow night?

Me: What time?

Ashton: 10pm.

Me: Why so late?

Ashton: It's a surprise. Don't wear a dress or skirt.

I furrow my brows.

Me: Why not?

Ashton: I've only got so much willpower.

Shit, he's not the only one. I'm about to needle him again about what he has in mind for tomorrow night when he sends another message.

Ashton: Besides, you need to dress warm for this.

Me: You won't even give me a hint?

Ashton: I just did. My lunch break is over. I'll see you tomorrow night, Sawyer.

I stuff my phone back into my purse, giddy and aflutter. This friend date idea is going to require a level of restraint I'm not sure I possess, but I'm going to give it my all.

thirty-nine
SADIE

"I can't guarantee the no touching rule." It's the first thing out of his mouth after he shows up on my doorstep.

"Really? Reneging on our agreement already?"

He holds up a helmet. "Some things require a certain amount of contact."

My lips curve into a smile. Now I understand why he said to dress warm, though being that it's December, I would have done so anyway.

Just to be on the safe side, I dressed in layers—leggings under jeans, a long-sleeved thermal under my shirt, hat and gloves and boots. My hair is in a long, thick braid, and I'll be damned if I let him unravel it.

He's dressed accordingly too, and too damn hot in his faded jeans, black leather jacket, and a dark Carhartt beanie pulled low over his forehead. I grab my coat and let him usher me into the vestibule.

"You're not going to tell me where we're going, are you?"

"Nope."

"Figured as much."

He fits the helmet on my head, we mount the bike, then we're roaring down the street, pressed together in a way that is so against the rules, but Ashton's clever like that. He's doggedly determined when he wants something, and he wants me. I close my eyes and tighten my arms around his waist, shivering from the warmth spreading between my legs at the thought of being wanted by him.

I won't lie. It's an addictive feeling.

He takes us out of town, and about thirty minutes later, I lean with him as he turns onto a county road. It's deserted, curvy, the incline leading us up a mountain. The sky is a blanket of stars, cloudless and moonless, which only makes this night colder.

Wherever we're headed, he'll want to warm me up.

Clever, indeed.

Sometime later, the bike rolls to a stop in a clearing at the top of the mountain. Ashton helps me off before removing my helmet, and my teeth are already chattering as he unfastens the bungee cords on his pack.

"What are we doing here?" I move in a circle, taking in the cold landscape. "*Where* is here?"

"We're about ten miles past the falls."

"Okay...why? In case you haven't noticed, it's freezing out here." My eyes adjust to the moonless night, and I catch him smirking.

"I noticed." Entwining our fingers, he leads me through the scattered brush and boulders to a level spot on the ground.

"Ash, I'm serious. What are we doing here?"

"The Geminid meteor shower peaks tonight."

I let out an excited squeal. "Really! A meteor shower?"

"Damn, Sawyer. Your enthusiasm is a turn-on. I could kiss you right now."

"Against the rules."

He unzips the pack and begins unrolling a sleeping bag. "How about staying warm? Is that against the rules?"

"It's fucking cold out here, so we'll make an exception. But keep your hands to yourself."

"You must think I'm a saint," he mutters as he spreads the sleeping bag onto the ground. He gestures for me to go first. "After you."

I slip inside, snuggling into the thick blanket, and he follows suit. We lie shoulder-to-shoulder, barely touching, kept toasty only by the waves of heat our bodies emit.

And dammit, it's not enough, but there's no way I can tell him that. I need to see this friend date idea through to the end.

"When's this meteor shower supposed to start?" I ask.

He reaches to the side and grabs the thermos he unpacked. "Any time now." He takes a long swig then passes it to me. "Drink some coffee. It'll warm you up."

"Jeez, you're bossy."

"You should be used to it by now."

We pass the coffee back and forth for a while, and instead of settling into a comfortable silence with a friend, I'm painfully aware of his nearness.

The rise and fall of his chest.

The sound of his breathing.

Every subtle move he makes.

The expanse of glittering stars overhead, cast bright from the dawn of midnight, appears to envelope us. Utter quiet amplifies our seclusion, and I feel as if we've been transplanted on another world.

The setting is too...intimate.

I clear my throat. "Where are we supposed to be looking?"

He grabs my wrist. "Point your finger."

I do as told, and he lines up the point of my finger with the three horizontal stars that make up the belt of the hunter.

"See Orion's Belt?"

"Yeah."

Slowly moving my hand upward, he draws a line from the left star in the belt to the bright reddish one at the top of the constellation. "Keep going and you'll find Gemini up there." Just as my finger reaches Ashton's destination in the universe, a star shoots out from where I'm pointing.

"Wow! That was a bright one."

Lulled into a calm quiet, we watch the sky, counting shooting stars, and the whole time, Ashton's got my hand clasped in his. The gentle sweep of his thumb against the back of my hand is burrowing underneath my resolve.

I want to turn into him, snuggle against his side, feel his arms tight around me. But if we do that, we'll start kissing, and then hands will wander. Fingers will work at buttons and zippers. Tongues will trail across skin. Teeth will nip. We'll set this sleeping bag on fire.

I untangle my fingers from his. "For these friend dates to work, we have to follow the rules."

"Friend dates, huh? Did Mandy come up with that?"

"No, I did. And don't mock me, Ash. We were friends long before we fucked it up with too much..." I trail off, unable to find the right words.

Because there are no right words—none without sexual connotation.

"I'm listening," Ashton says, breaking into my mental tangent. "We fucked it up with too much of what?"

"With wanting more."

He shifts onto his side, and his chest comes into contact with my arm. "Is that such a bad thing?"

"No," I whisper, going breathless because his hot breath is at my ear. "But I need to know that our friendship is still solid."

"It's solid. If you need me to keep my lips and hands off of you to prove it, then I'll do it."

I draw in a shaky breath then let it out. "I don't want to keep you at arms-length, but..."

"You need to," he murmurs. "I get it. Our chemistry is explosive." His voice drops to a raspy timber. "It simmers the blood, rushes heat to the groin. Makes the heart pound, the brain delirious." He traces the edge of my ear with his nose.

"Ashton," I warn, though my voice is barely there, stolen by his sensual stanza.

"I'm smelling you. That's not against the rules."

"You have a way of breaking rules."

"Guilty as charged. But I keep my promises. Your virtue's safe with me."

"My virtue?" I can't help it—a giggle escapes me. "I might be a virgin, but thanks to you, I'm far from virtuous."

"Thank God for small favors."

His breath is still a blast of heat to my ear, and I shiver from the chill of night trying to seep in through the sleeping bag.

"Are you warm enough?" he asks.

"Yes," I lie.

"You're shivering."

"I'm okay." Another star streaks across the sky. "Can we just watch the meteor shower?"

"This is bullshit, Sadie. Let me hold you." He doesn't give me a choice. Winding an arm under the back of my shoulders, he pulls me into him, my ass to his groin, and rests his hand on my belly. We settle into a partial spooning position that allows a good angle for skywatching.

"Better?" he asks, nuzzling my jawline.

"Mmm-hmm." This feels *too* good, and I know he's experiencing it too. His burgeoning erection is evidence enough.

"Have you made any wishes yet, Sawyer?"

"No."

"Well get on it. This show only comes around once a year."

I glance up in time to witness the brightest meteor yet, its tail spanning the sky in a brushstroke of cosmic artistry.

"Make a wish," he whispers into my ear.

I wish for the strength to resist him, to give us a foundation that's built on more than the physical. When it comes to Ashton, I want it all with him.

forty

ASHTON

As birthday celebrations go, it's a small gathering. Just Bryce and a couple of friends from work. And Brett and the brother. *The date.*

I'm in the kitchen with Bryce and the guys, bullshitting about work and women over beer and pizza, but I'm only half interested. I can't keep my attention from wandering to the living room, where Sadie is trying her damnedest not to look at me. She's failing miserably.

She and my sister are standing in a small group of friends...and Brett and the brother.

The date.

Fuck, it digs under my skin that this guy is anywhere near my girl. Logically, I have no reason to harbor such jealousy—she told me as much herself the last time we went on one of our "friend dates." But logic and assurances does jack shit from stopping me from wanting to stalk over there and claim her as mine in front of everyone.

We've kept our budding relationship on the down low,

and Mandy and Bryce are the only ones who have an inkling of what's going on. By the end of the night, if my plans play out like I'm hoping, Sadie and I will no longer be a secret.

We'll no longer be stuck in limbo hell, trapped in the constraints of Sadie's unbendable rules.

And it's about time. For weeks now, I've barely managed to keep my hands and lips to myself, and it's been absolute torture.

Laughter filters through the living room, and I find Sadie piercing me with her green eyes from where she stands as she chats with one of Mandy's friends from the club.

I know the brunette...intimately. I can't recall her name, but I remember her colorful ink of butterflies and barbed wire that circle her wrists. She says something that makes Sadie laugh.

Beautiful laughter as melodious as the finest symphony.

The brunette happens to catch my gaze, and there's no mistaking the inviting design of her smile. Sadie picks up on it and falls silent.

Shit.

I've fucked half of the female population in Douglas Falls, so keeping Sadie away from my past conquests is an impossibility. She knows my sordid history better than most, but now that things have shifted between us, I'm not sure how she'll handle the inevitable run-ins with the girls I've hooked up with.

Hopefully, after tonight, it won't matter. There will be

no more doubt, no more insecurities. No more running from something that is scary and a huge step but so fucking worth it.

No more waiting.

The brunette's attention is lured away by Brett, and Sadie takes a sip of her cocktail, meeting my gaze above the rim of her glass. Those jade eyes narrow on me, darkening with a hint of jealousy and a whole lot of awareness. I swear she knows what I'm thinking.

Tonight is the night I'm going to bust through the last of her walls, and she's going to let me. Everyone around us might as well fade away because Sadie and I fall into intense moments of longing, surrendering to the connection that not even a room full of people can shatter. We're going to cross the line tonight. It doesn't even need to be spoken.

"You're totally going to fuck her." Bryce takes a swig of his beer.

"Did your crystal ball tell you that?"

"Please," he scoffs, "I don't need bullshit mumbo jumbo to spell it out for me. If eyesight had the power to strip, you'd both be naked a dozen times over, man." He nods toward Sadie. "Why don't you take her into your bedroom and get it over with?"

"Are you serious right now?" I arch a brow at him, and the other guys laugh before Bryce can reply.

"That's hilarious," says Preston, a guy from my crew. "Ash and Sadie? *Riiiight.*" The guy's buzzed and doesn't mean anything by it, but that still doesn't stop me from socking him in the shoulder. "Don't be a douche. It's my birthday."

"You're pushing fifty now, right?"

"Dude, take that back. Don't make me sic my sister on you."

He throws his hands in the air. "Your sister is scary as fuck."

I'm about to agree with him when I catch movement out of my peripheral. Sadie saunters toward the kitchen, and she's got a sexy, come-hither curve to her lips. I'm powerless against her witchery—she never fails to tempt my dick into a standing ovation.

"Have I told you 'Happy Birthday' yet?" She stops on the other side of the bar and sets down her empty tumbler.

"You might've told me a time or two." I grab her glass and mix her another drink before sliding it into her waiting hands. "Want another piece of pizza?"

She glances down at her drink. "What I want is a little alcohol with the juice. Did you forget I hit the legal age over a year ago, Ash?"

"Nope." As I lean over the bar and shoot her a flirty grin, I'm fully aware the guys have gone quiet. "Maybe I don't want to get you drunk."

She snorts. "Said no man *ever*."

"I can't have my way with you if you get plastered."

A low whistle brings me around to face the guys again. "You got something to share with the class, boys?"

"Nope," Preston says, choking back laughter. "It's your birthday. Who am I to disillusion you?" He tips his beer toward me in a sign of *cheers*. "Keep living in fantasy land."

Setting my beer down, I round the bar and grab Sadie

by the hand before ushering her into the middle of the living room. "I've got an announcement to make," I call out. The chatter dies down, and everyone's attention turns to me. "This incredible, sexy, *stubborn* woman," I say, pulling her snug against me, "is *mine*."

Another one of my coworkers joins in on the ribbing. "How much have you had to drink, Levine?"

"Which Levine are you talking to?" Mandy speaks up, a grin on her face.

"The drunk dude who thinks he's got a chance with Sadie." More laughter, followed by more ribbing from the assholes I happen to call friends. But at some point, everyone realizes I'm being serious, and they go quiet again.

"I'm not kidding. She's my girl, and now you all know it."

Sadie's eyes are huge and alight with the tiniest amount of irritation. I sense an argument on the rise. She's either reverting into retreat-mode, or she's about to give me grief. Before she can do either, I lift her over my shoulder and stride toward my bedroom.

"Ash! What are you doing? Put me down!"

"We've got some private celebrating to do." My house-guests treat us to a tirade of catcalls as I disappear down the hall. We escape into my bedroom and shut the door amid more boisterous laughter.

"You are absolutely crazy," she says as I set her on her feet.

"Crazy for you, Sawyer."

The weeks of no touching, no kissing, no *nothing but*

friends rise between us, and we crack under the weight of desire. We fly at each other, our mouths colliding as if destined to come together in this frenzied reunion. I'm starved for her, drugged by the insistent licks of her tongue against mine. She reaches between us and rubs me through my jeans, and I groan against her mouth.

My response spurs her on, and she unbuttons my pants and tears at the zipper, her movements jerky and desperate and raw with hunger.

Then she's fisting my cock, and I'm the desperate one. Breaking our lip-lock, I glance down and watch her stroke my length.

Jesus, it's been too long, and I've regressed into a pubescent boy experiencing his first hand job. I grab her wrist.

"Take it easy. You're going to end this before it begins."

"What makes you think you're getting lucky?" Her expression is one-hundred percent sass. "I'm just playing with what's mine, Ash."

"Don't deny you haven't been eye-fucking me all night."

"I won't deny it. Still doesn't mean you're getting lucky."

With a laugh, I slide my hands into her hair. "I'm already lucky. More lucky than the luckiest bastard on the planet."

"Well, that's true."

Backing her toward my bed, I kiss a wet path up her neck until I reach the top of her jawline. "Time's up, baby. I'm calling the shots, and I say you're ready for your next lesson."

"You sure about that?" Her voice is a seductive sigh in my ear.

"Oh, yeah."

"What lesson do you have in mind?"

"The one where you give your virginity to the man who's crazy in love with you." I step back and gesture toward her dress. "Take it off."

"You're being bossy again. We'll have to work on that."

"I'm being practical. Clothing will only get in the way."

"In the way of what?" She's baiting me, one eyebrow raised as she unzips the red number that's taunted me all night with its short length and cleavage-revealing front.

"In the way of *your* body and *my* hands."

"You sound pretty sure of yourself." She's putting up a token fight, but with her next breath, she lets go of the dress and it pools around her feet. Next, the heels come off, and she's standing in nothing but lingerie.

Sexy *white* lingerie. I take her in from the crown of her red hair to the pearly polish on her toenails. That shimmery hue matches her lacy undergarments to perfection. Her bra is sheer enough that I spy the dusty rose of her nipples. I lower my perusal and give her panties an appreciative eye.

Lace. Soft and pure, just like she is.

"Damn, Sawyer. I'm pretty sure it's my birthday, and I'm pretty sure you wore that for me."

Her cheeks go pink, and I know I'm right.

"I have one condition," she says.

"Name it."

"I don't want anything between us. I've been on birth control since we started dating, and I trust you, Ash."

I'm blown away by what she's asking and completely humbled by it. The idea that I'll be the first man to get inside of her, and that I'll get to do it bareback, leaves me in awe.

I grab her by the chin, the need to dominate her a force I can't fight. "I also have a condition." We're shuffling toward the bed again, one footstep at a time. "I want you to bend over the end of the mattress."

Her eyes widen. "This is our first time. You're not fucking me from behind."

"I'm not *fucking* you at all. This is more than sex, Sadie." I run my thumb across her lips. "I'm going to share with you what I've never shared with anyone."

She bites her lip, and I let out a low growl. "Head down, ass up. Before we get to our firsts, I need you to submit to me."

So there's no question of who's in charge here, I peel the shirt from my body and drop it on the floor. Planting my feet shoulder-width apart, I hammer home our roles with my rigid posture as I settle my hands on my hips.

My job keeps me fit, and I'm no stranger to the inside of a gym. Next to her feminine, petite form, there's no contest who has the physical advantage.

The longer she stares at me, the more her pupils dilate.

My cock is big enough to choke her, and it has, multiple times. She's probably a little apprehensive at the thought of taking all of me inside her.

"What do you mean by *submit*?"

"What do you think I mean?"

"You want to spank me?"

"Fuck yes."

"But it's *your* birthday. Aren't you getting this ritual a little backwards?"

"Semantics, sweetheart." I whirl her and push her over the end of the mattress. She raises her ass in the language of invitation, and the arch of her spine is graceful, the exquisite curvature of female beauty.

Round bottom exposed, cheeks left bare from the strip of lace running between them. She wore that scrap of lace for me, and that's as good as her begging for my hand.

That first night at the club, when everything between us changed, I thought she was too innocent for a guy like me.

Too pure.

But Sadie Sawyer is far from innocent. She might be dressed in the hue of purity, her virginity intact, but her kinky streak is as real as my love for her, and it's begging to come out to play.

I plan to bring her onto my playground with every orgasm and firm strike of my hand.

SADIE

Ashton's hands are magic, zapping my system like a live wire. As he trails his fingers over my shoulders and down my spine, I feel his touch at the core of my sex.

"Clasp your hands together." He draws them to the small of my back. "Don't move."

As I interlock my fingers, Ashton nudges my feet apart, and the space between them throbs, my pulse gallops, and a shiver travels down my backside. I'm exposed to his gaze, vulnerable to his whims, the thin piece of lace the only thing barring his access to my pussy.

His breathing is a soughing song, his warmth permeates the winter chill, and his presence...it's more overpowering than I remember.

The soft pad of feet hint at movement, and he settles between my spread legs, the crown of his erection a frustrating tease against my slit. He leans over me, skin hot against mine, and wraps my thick hair around his fist.

"Head up. Understand?"

"Mmm-hmm."

He gives my hair a gentle tug. "When I ask you a question, I expect an answer."

My breath hitches. "I understand."

"That's my girl." He loosens his fist, and my locks slip free. With each shift of his body, his jeans are a coarse sensation against my legs, arousing me further, eliciting sporadic whimpers.

"Best birthday present ever." He settles his palms on my ass. "You have no clue how gorgeous you are, do you?"

"Freckles and all?"

"Especially your freckles," he says, caressing the lone one on my left butt-cheek.

"Ash?" His name tumbles off my tongue with an unspoken question. An unspoken need tightening my core.

"What's on my girl's mind?"

"I need you to touch me."

He smacks my ass. "Ambiguity will get you in trouble, Sawyer. Tell me where you want me to touch you."

I groan, and if my cheeks weren't flushed before, they are now. "You know where. Between my legs."

He caresses my inner thigh. "I can touch you like this all night. Tell me *where*."

He's going to make me say it.

"My pussy."

He dips his fingers beneath the edge of lace, and as those digits spear into me, I lose control of my breathing. He works me into a lustful frenzy with the shallow thrusts of his fingers, and I need more. God, I need more.

I arch into his touch, my muscles tightening with the need to come, but he refuses to finger me deeper.

"Please, Ash."

That's when his palm connects with my flesh. I jump, the strength of that blow a sharp sting, and I cry out in a mixture of pleasure and pain. He spanks me again and again, alternating butt-cheeks as he sinks those fingers inside me a little deeper. Self-conscious of the noise I'm making with every strike of his hand, I muffle my next cry into the bedding.

He yanks me up by the hair until my throat is exposed, neck arched back, his grip a burning pull on my scalp. "I want the whole house to hear you come for me." He pushes his fingers to the knuckle, and I cry out.

"Christ, you're wet, and so damn tight." His touch plunders until I reach zenith, crying out "oh God" half a dozen times, each sinful prayer an octave higher than the last. I have yet to come down from the high when he pulls me to my feet. His mouth slams down on mine, and we go to war with our tongues.

I could lose hours kissing him. Spend days discovering the map of his body. Years upon years of loving him.

His hands land on my shoulders, and the kiss breaks as he pushes me to my knees. He shoves his pants down his muscular thighs, trembling with an air of desperation, and grabs the root of his shaft. I catch sight of the glistening head before it's pressed against my lips.

"Suck me."

This bossy side of him shouldn't turn me on so much, but I'm already building toward the next summit and eventual fall, my pussy tingling in anticipation of fulfillment as he demands the glove of my mouth. He palms my cheeks, thumbs brushing my temples as he pushes between my lips, working his way toward the back of my throat with each lazy thrust.

"I can't believe I get to call you mine," he says, almost reverently, eyes deepening to the hue of the ocean at twilight. "*Mine.*"

This is what it means to submit to Ashton Levine.

To put my trust in his hands.

Give my body over to his mastery.

Enclose my love in the shelter of his heart.

His lids are at half-mast, and I sense him striving for control, mouth pulled tight at the edges as he withdraws. He brings me to my feet, and our mouths mate in another wet kiss.

But I'm growing impatient.

"Make me yours."

I step out of my panties.

Unhook my bra.

Climb onto the mattress.

And lie before him, legs open in silent offering.

"Hell, Sawyer. I'll never forget the sight of you like this." A moment passes, and he exhales.

Sheds his jeans.

Kneels at the juncture of my thighs.

Blankets my body, weight braced on his forearms.

We're pressed together, chest to chest. Groin to groin. Heart to heart.

"Are you nervous?" he asks.

We've been this close before, but it feels different this time. It *is* different this time because he'll be inside me in every way that matters.

"No. Nothing's ever felt so right."

"I want to make this special for you."

"You are."

Tempting me into a slow kiss, he reaches between us and rubs the head of his cock along my slit, through the wetness. It's a tease I can't stand, and I buck against him, grasping for that high.

Aching for it.

"I'm so close."

"Not yet, sweetheart." He positions himself, on the cusp of entering me, and entwines our hands before shoving them to the mattress. His gaze pins me more effectively than the grip of his fingers, and I wish we'd turned off the lamp on his nightstand, because that stare of his is more intimate than the joining of bodies, the sharing of secrets.

I cast my attention over his shoulder and study the spackle on the ceiling.

"Look at me."

Of course he picked up on my sudden shyness. I drag my gaze back to his.

"Stay with me," he whispers, and then he's pressing into me, just past the tip, returning the tight grip of my hands as he works his girth in another inch, then another.

And that's where he stalls.

"Fucking hell." He buries his face in the curve of my shoulder, breaths shuddering against my skin, arms shaking under his weight as I stretch around his cock. I'm tingling and burning where we connect, and yearning for more.

"Please, Ash." I raise my hips to make my point.

"Give me a moment. I don't want to hurt you."

"You won't hurt me."

"I will if I fuck you the way I want to."

"I'm not breakable." I'm so worked up I'm about to rip apart at the seams.

He lifts his head, our eyes lock, and we're suspended in a defining moment. Then, with a final thrust, he's inside me, breaking past the last barrier.

"Aaah!" As I bow into the ache, he silences my sharp cry with his mouth. Sparks of pain and pleasure erupt behind my lids, and I whimper, letting him taste the surrender on my tongue.

"Sadie," he groans against my lips. He pulls out, pushes in again, and I experience every hard inch of him becoming one with me.

The pace he sets is slow, maddening. Wrenching my hands free, I clutch his shoulders and dig my heels into the mattress, arching into him, gritting my teeth through the stretching sensation as I bring him deeper.

Sweat breaks out on his back, dampens his hair, and he's shaking, struggling to hold back as he waits for me to catch up.

Every plunge feels better than the last, shooting me higher, cocooning me in another headspace entirely—one where I'm drifting, my awareness reduced to the sensation of him thrusting inside me.

And I'm aching.

Aching in a way I've never ached before.

It pulls at me, subtle at first, then with more strength until I have no choice but to let it haul me into explosive surrender. I don't recognize the sound of my voice as I whimper and cry out in rhythmic bursts, flooded with intense waves of pleasure spiraling through me.

"I love you," I gasp, sinking my hands into his dark hair.

And that's when he jerks to a stop, grunting curses under his breath as he reaches the tipping point. His forehead drops against mine, his muscles tense, and when he comes, spilling everything he is inside me, I feel it to my soul.

The following moments seem endless, but I'm content to lie here with him, foreheads pressed together as we regain our bearings. His eyes drift shut, and he slowly relaxes, limb by limb.

"Ash?"

"I didn't hurt you, did I?"

"No, but you're..."

"Spit it out, Sawyer. Now's not the time to get shy on me."

"You're still inside me."

His mouth lifts in a grin. "Am I turning you on?"

"Maybe."

How much time do guys need to recover? A few minutes? The time it takes to shit, shower, shave and... smoke a cigarette or something? God, I don't know how this works. I only know I'm aching to do it again.

Right this second.

He pushes to his knees, and I immediately miss the weight of his body, the heat of his skin...the full sensation of him in the one place no one else has ever been. I follow the trail of hair below his belly button and find his cock taunting me, not quite ready to give me what I want, but not disinterested either.

He grips me by the waist, and suddenly I'm dragged on top of him. Tucking one leg then the other on either side of him, he aligns our bodies, and his eyes are pure lust and mischief as he flicks his thumbs across my nipples.

"Ready for another lesson?"

"God, yes."

"Now it's your turn to call the shots." His hands fall to my hips, offering guidance.

With a shy grin, I rock into him and take the lead.

SADIE

Seven months later

The rush of waterfalls. The warmth of August sunshine on my skin. The aroma of coconut sunscreen in the air.

And Ashton half-naked at my side, the cut of his abs a temptation to my tongue as his swim trunks ride low enough to hint at...other things I'd like to lick.

Life doesn't get much better than this.

We hiked halfway up the mountainside so we'd have a modicum of privacy from the people scattered in the area. Like us, they're in search of a good swimming hole and some fun in the sun.

Only our idea of *fun in the sun* is a bit more...risqué.

Which is why it's a good thing most people don't venture up here, put off by the steep climb and small space.

But it's perfect for Ashton and me.

We're sprawled on a blanket to the side of the falls, and

hidden behind that cascading wall of water is a cozy swimming hole fed by the falls as they spill over the hillside.

"Move in with me," he says, pointer finger doodling sweet-nothings across my mid-drift. The thong of the bikini he bought me last week is riding up my ass—as I'm sure he intended. He removed the top with his teeth shortly after we got here.

"After I finish school." I've told him this a thousand times, but he brings it up at least once a week.

He nuzzles the valley between my bare breasts. "I want to wake up every morning next to you."

"Wouldn't it be nice to wake up next to a girl with a degree in criminal justice?"

He levels me with his ice-blue eyes. "Do you know of any? The left side of my bed is in the market for a sexy chick."

I smack him on the shoulder. "The left side of your bed better stay empty until I'm ready to fill it."

"So," he murmurs, pushing to his knees. He crouches over me, hands planted on either side of my head. "What should I do in the meantime?"

"Deal with it?" I raise my brows, but when his tongue darts out to wet his lower lip, my gaze is dragged to his mouth. Damn him. He's an expert at distraction.

He lowers his lips to mine and coaxes me into a long, deep kiss. I still can't believe I waited so long to taste his mouth in the first place, and even longer to learn what it means to be loved by him in every sense of the word.

"I've got something to ask you, Sawyer."

"My answer isn't going to change."

"That's okay. This is a different question."

"Oh, well in that case, fire away." My tone is light, but the seriousness of his gaze makes my heart skip a beat.

Or several.

"Marry me."

I gape at him, thought processes slamming into a wall. "That's...that doesn't sound like a question."

"It doesn't?"

"No," I breathe.

"Okay." He lowers his forehead to mine. "Then it's a plea. Marry me."

"But...I mean...but I'm not even ready to move in with you yet!" Shoving against his chest, I force him back until we're both sitting. "How the hell can you jump from moving in together to marriage?"

Mischief teases the edges of his mouth. "I figure if I go for the big guns, you'll change your mind about *other* things."

"So you're trying to manipulate me?"

"No, Sawyer. I'm trying to love you until the day I die. Is that so horrible?"

God, he knows how to turn me to mush.

"It's not horrible," I whisper. "It's sweet and sexy and completely unfair because you know I can't resist you when you say things like that."

"Then don't resist. Say you'll marry me so I can put this ring"—he rifles through the pack of supplies we brought with us and pulls out a jewelry box—"on your finger."

I'm gaping at him again. "Ashton..."

"I can't give you expensive houses or cars, or huge

diamonds, but I can give you everything that I am." His blue eyes darken with sly satisfaction. "And intense orgasms. I can give you those."

I burst out laughing. Only Ashton would include orgasms in a marriage proposal. "It's a big step."

"No bigger than the steps we've already taken. You can move in with me when you're ready. We'll get married when you're ready. But let's make it official. Say you'll be mine."

"I'm yours." I don't even have to think about it. The vow slips off my lips as if they were designed to say such an oath to him.

"Is that a yes?"

"It's a yes...someday."

"I'll take it." I've never seen his smile so bright as he slips a solitaire diamond ring onto my finger. It's not overwhelming in size, but it sparkles with more brilliance than any piece of jewelry I've laid eyes on.

It's perfect.

"But this doesn't mean I'm moving in with you yet."

"Of course not," he says with a smirk. "After all, you're the girl that brought me to my knees long before you'd let me kiss you."

"I believe I was the one on my knees."

He presses his mouth to mine, and I feel his lips curving into a smile. "You're damn good at it too."

"I had an excellent teacher."

"Did you, now?"

"Oh, yeah. Sexy, on the cocky side, loves to get good head. You might know him."

"I might. This teacher you speak of. Does he enjoy pushing past boundaries?"

Shit, I know that tone. "He likes to think he's in charge."

Ashton lifts a brow. "He *thinks* he's in charge?"

"I wouldn't want to deflate his ego, so it's our secret." Before he can issue payback, I scoot out of reach and slip into the pool of water behind the falls.

He's quick to follow, and I sense him at my back, heat wafting off his skin as he stalks me through the water. I reach the other side, the falls spilling over my right shoulder, and that's when he makes his move. He bends me over the smooth rocky ledge, adjusts his swim trunks, and plunges inside me.

One hand tangles in my wet locks, and he pulls until my scalp tingles, and I can't move my head. I'm completely at his mercy, clawing at the stone beneath me as I stand on tiptoes for leverage.

"Baby," he groans, yanking even harder on my hair. "Say it. I want to hear you say it."

"Say what?" I squeal the question.

He thrusts upward, plundering so deep that it ignites the best kind of ache low in my belly. I can't breathe. I can't do anything but let him fuck me from behind as I cry out with each forceful thrust of his cock.

It's primal and animalistic and enough to hurtle me into orgasmic heaven.

"Yes! Oh fuck yes! Yes!"

"That's the answer I want." He jerks to a stop with a shudder, and then he's biting into my shoulder to smother his moans as he empties himself into me. The roar of the falls lulls us into serenity, giving our breathing time to even out. Several minutes later, he whirls me to face him.

"So I guess this means we *are* moving in together."

My eyes go wide. "Getting ahead of yourself there, aren't you?"

"No take-backs. You just screamed 'yes' to high heaven. *More* than once."

"Clever, Ash. Real clever."

"I have a degree in clever. When should I move your things?"

"How about when you catch me?" I sink beneath the surface and kick off the rocks, shooting across the small swimming hole, but he's got his fist around my ankle before I reach the other side. I don't know why I'm surprised.

When it comes to getting what he wants, Ashton has had me in his clutches from the moment I met him on the playground when we were kids, and he turned those beautiful blue eyes on me.

There are far worse destinies than loving Ashton Levine.

about the author

Gemma James is a *USA Today* bestselling author of sexy contemporary and dark romance. She loves to explore the darker side of human nature in her fiction, and she's morbidly curious about anything dark and edgy, from deviant seduction to fascinating villains. Readers have described her stories as being "not for the faint of heart."

She warns you to heed their words! Her playground isn't full of rainbows and kittens, though she loves both. She lives in Florida with her husband, children, and a gaggle of animals.

———

Visit Gemma's website for more info on her books:
www.authorgemmajames.com

Made in United States
Orlando, FL
01 June 2024

47420281R00202